PRAISE FOR

A SONG FOR THE ROAD

"Fifteen-year-old Carter Danforth is loaded down with guilt, dreams, and his dad's old Martin guitar. Hitting the long highway between Tulsa and LA may be his best hope or worst decision ever. Author Rayne Lacko takes us on a powerful coming-of-age journey that gets under the skin, calluses the fingertips, and works its way into the heart. *A Song for the Road* is packed with gritty wisdom, succulent humor, and great music. I'll be rooting for Carter for a long time to come."

—CONRAD WESSELHOEFT,
author of *Dirt Bikes, Drones, and Other Ways to Fly*

"*A Song for the Road* is a brilliant metaphor for life. That Carter Danforth is one determined young man, and as memorable a hero as you'll ever find. Bravo, Rayne Lacko!"

—ANDRE HARDY, former NFL running back

"Rayne Lacko brings forth the power of music in her inspiring coming-of-age novel *A Song for the Road*. The protagonist, a teenaged boy, is 'reawakening all the feelings he was trying every day to hold down.' Torn between facing his suppressed feelings and pursuing his passion, Carter chooses making music on his own terms. His choice is rewarded with personal healing and new friendships. A wonderful read about the magic of music and creating your own path."

—HEIDI DANIELE, author of *The House Children*

"A boy, a guitar, and the open road. In *A Song for the Road*, Rayne Lacko brings this timeless archetype to full, vivid life as fifteen-year-old Carter embarks on a journey that will define him as an artist, a son, and a man. Beautiful music abounds in these pages—in the story, the language, and the hearts of these well-defined characters. Tune up your six-string, grab a mic, and join Carter as he takes his memorable song on the road."

—MARK SARVAS, award-winning author of *Memento Park*

"I really loved Carter's gentle sweet soul and the magic of his journey. Really lyrical and exquisite moments; I felt really drawn in by its tenderness and charm. Very nicely done!"

—NOELLE AUGUST, author of the Boomerang novels

"His father's old guitar leads fifteen-year-old 'Cotton' Danforth on an emotional journey to reconcile his past and find his future in this sweet story about the power of song to bridge what divides us. Musical teens will love this book. So will any adult who's been moved to strum a few chords. I only wish it came with a soundtrack."

—PAM MCGAFFIN, author of *The Leaving Year*

"A lyrical, absorbing coming-of-age tale, *A Song for the Road* delights, surprises, and tugs at the heartstrings in equal measure. I fell in love with Carter Danforth on his epic cross-country journey to reunite with his estranged father—and so will you. An uplifting story of friendship, family, and the healing power of music."

—ANJALI BANERJEE,
author of *Maya Running, Looking for Bapu,* and *Seaglass Summer*

"Carter Danforth, a gifted teen musician, tugs guitar strings and heartstrings in Rayne Lacko's entertaining new young adult novel, *A Song for the Road*. Readers will love this inspiring physical and metaphorical journey of growth and self-realization through the American Southwest."

—RON BAHAR, author of *The Frontman*

"Full of heart and soul, *A Song for the Road* is a beautiful road trip through friendship, self-discovery, and the kindness of strangers. Carter's story of searching for his father and finding his own musical identity will strum on your heartstrings and make you sing with joy."

—LISA MANTERFIELD,
author of *The Smallest Thing* and *A Strange Companion*

A Song
for the
Road

A Song
for the
Road

A NOVEL

by

RAYNE LACKO

spark press

Published by SparkPress, a BookSparks imprint,
A division of SparkPoint Studio, LLC
Phoenix, Arizona, USA, 85007
www.gosparkpress.com

Published 2019
Printed in the United States of America
ISBN: 978-1-68463-002-8 (pbk)
ISBN: 978-1-68463-003-5 (e-bk)

Library of Congress Control Number: 2019936458

Book design by Stacey Aaronson

For Joe & Noah. You will always find love at home.

Chapter One

April 1, 2006

CARTER DANFORTH PRESSED THE BLACK INK OF HIS PEN into the palm of his hand. Across the lines and grooves, he wrote a few lyrics of a song he'd call "Hour of Freedom." His mother was out on a delivery that afternoon, but he didn't mind taking the Tulsa city bus home from school. If he played it right, he could set his secret plan in motion and still be home by four.

Springtime in Tulsa was wet season, and Carter knew the weather was a gamble. The day before it was hot as a billy goat in a pepper patch. But that afternoon, blasts of cold air circled the heat. Another storm was rolling in.

Stepping off the bus, Carter walked over to Tommy's Pawn Shop, the second store down from his regular stop. His father's guitar, a left-handed Martin acoustic, used to sit in the front window display. There was no telling whether Tommy had held on to it or if it already had found a new home.

The pawn shop had one of those old-timey bells that jangled when you walked in the door.

On display cases were older-timey items: farmhouse pottery, record players, and creepy old dolls with cracked porcelain heads.

The man behind the counter picked at something between his lower teeth with a thick fingernail, appraising Carter. "You're Sandra Bermejo's kid, aren't you?"

"How's it going, Tommy?" Carter nodded toward him. He'd come for the guitar, but he wasn't about to up and admit it. Better to play it cool, pretend Eddie Danforth's old guitar was nothing more than a passing notion.

"Going to buy anything or you just staking the joint?" The man's solitary interest was cold hard cash, and Carter knew he had just enough to cover the seven hundred fifty dollars Tommy was asking for the guitar.

On a shelf behind the counter were stacked rows of dead cell phones. Carter was pretty sure he was the only kid in ninth grade without a phone. His best buddies Landon and Caleb had had phones since middle school. Carter had a burr under his saddle over not being included in their texts, especially when they spent the better part of a boring school day repeating the punchline of an inside joke he wasn't in on. Carter's mom said she'd buy him a phone, "on the very day you need one." He couldn't convince her that day had arrived ages ago.

Squinting at Carter, Tommy grabbed a phone from the top of the stack and placed it on the counter in front of him. The hair on his bare arms matched the hair on his head, dark and oily. "All you got to do is take it down to the phone store, kid. You sign a contract and they power it up for you."

"How do you know—" Carter began as the crack and shatter of a flash downfall of hailstones pelted the sidewalk out front. "How do you know if it still works?" The sudden noise didn't bother him. He was used to the random piercing cry of his mother's band saw firing up from her basement woodshop at all hours. She'd made a career out of refinishing vintage wood tables, chairs, and dressers.

"All my goods is hundred percent," Tommy replied. He scratched the back of his neck, grimacing at the storm outside. "Crazy ping-pong-size balls dropping out of the sky."

There was only one thing Carter felt one hundred percent about, and that was buying his dad's guitar. He'd come for the Martin and he wasn't leaving without it. A phone would have to wait.

A patchwork of TVs lined both sides of the store, most of them on but muted. Several were set to news channels reporting the hail falling right outside the shop. Supercell thunderstorm warnings sped across the bottoms of the screens in red text. Any Okie grade-schooler could tell you hailstorms didn't last long, and supercell storms only turned into tornadoes about twenty-five percent of the time. But the sky was brewing a dark greenish tint and the winds were howling. Carter figured he'd best get what he came for and head home.

"I'm thinking about upgrading my axe." Carter tried using the slang word some musicians used for guitar. Carter pretended his heart wasn't pounding with longing. Above the TVs, dozens of guitars lined the ceiling. Eddie's guitar had a special marking, an inscription. Not one of those lame, engraved labels some musicians had made up and stuck on. No, this inscription was stained into it, a few shades darker than the guitar's own mahogany body, like a tattoo or a birthmark. Eddie's guitar was the last piece of evidence the man had ever stepped foot in Tulsa, and Carter aimed to lay waste to it.

"You still have that Martin left-handed acoustic I saw in here a while back?" Carter tried to act casual.

"I think that old Martin is in storage. Put it away to make room for new inventory." Tommy checked the time on his wristwatch. "Look, I got way better ones. Just right for a beginner."

Tommy waddled over to the guitar display carrying a long metal post with a hook on the end. He used it to fish down a beat-up electric guitar with faded stickers of extinct rock bands. "Name's Cotton, right?"

His mom had dubbed him Cotton, short for cottontail rabbit. "Mostly ears and legs," she'd say, like it pained her to witness him sprout up the way he did. He wished her rabbit comparison ended there. "Big brown eyes and hair like cinnamon," she'd add, mussing up his hair with her work-worn hands. Carter tried to convince her the same description might fit a white-tailed buck and not the bottom of the food chain. Any folks who knew his mother liked to joke, "Cain't never could change Sandra's mind."

"It's Carter, sir. Nobody but my mom calls me Cotton."

"How old are you, kid?"

"Fifteen."

"Dang. Tall as you are skinny, and you still got growing ahead of you."

"Yeah." Carter folded his long, lanky arms across his chest, anxious to find the guitar and get out of there. "I passed six foot by my fourteenth birth—"

"Let me tell you something, Carter." Tommy put on his salesman's voice. "It's smarter to start on electric. The strings are thinner and closer to the neck. It's easier to play chords."

"I'm looking for an acoustic, the Martin in particular." Carter was getting impatient, and the howl of the storm outside wasn't making him feel any easier. He knew the guitar so well he could recite its catalog description. "Dark mahogany, satin lacquer finish, Martin brand. Looks like it came right out of the history books."

Tommy moved along the line, taking down a few acoustics, a Seagull, and then a Larrivee. Carter shifted on his feet, uncertain whether Tommy was messing with him. He shook his head when Tommy pulled out a Taylor Big Baby with a blonde Sitka spruce top.

"I just want the Martin 000-15M. Do you have it?"

"You know the model number?" Tommy sniffed, wiping his

nose with the back of his hand. "Someone's done his home-work."

In his pocket, Carter made a fist around his money. He'd heard enough of Tommy's deals to know he took in pawned items at ridiculously low rates, then sold them to others as though they were part of the national treasure. The more Carter showed he wanted that Martin, the more expensive it would become.

"You say you put it in storage?" Carter also had witnessed his mom bartering over broken antique furniture at weekend flea markets. He tried using her lingo. "Let me take it off your hands. It's just wasting space, I reckon."

"Everything I sell is hundred percent," Tommy repeated but reached for his keys to unlock the storage door in the hallway behind the sales counter. "Hold on, kid. I might have already moved it."

Tommy flicked a light switch inside the doorway and disap-peared. Carter went through the guitars hanging on the ceiling again, making sure his dad's Martin wasn't right in front of him. Various news shows flickering across the wall of TVs broadcast one shared and repeated message: warnings of supercell thun-derstorms, accompanied by footage of an F5 tornado in Moore back in May 1999, one of the worst tornado outbreaks in Okla-homa history. Eddie's guitar wasn't there. He was pretty sure he'd have felt its presence anyway.

Tommy returned shortly with a couple of Martins, old but still good-looking, and set them on the counter. Carter looked them over, then shook his head.

"Left-handed," he said, pulling his left hand from his pocket and holding it up, the money he'd brought still clenched in his fist. When he realized what he'd done, heat crept up his neck, reddening his face. Carter plunged his hand deep into his pocket.

It was too late, Tommy had seen the cash. Carter could tell by the way his eyes lit up.

"Burning a hole in your pocket, ain't it?" Tommy grinned, his teeth as yellow as his fingers. "How'd you come up with that kind of cash?"

Carter narrowed his gaze at the man. He didn't want Tommy to mention the money next time his mother came around to junk hunt. "I earned it helping out my mom in her woodshop." Carter told him a bit of the truth. Tommy looked doubtful, so Carter stretched the truth a little. "And from doing gigs," he added, tossing a loose wave of his hair carelessly to one side, "with my band."

Tommy squinted at Carter, unsure whether to believe him. "Well, you came to the right place. Waste of money shopping retail. Everything I got is one of a kind, you know what I'm saying?"

The wind outside pushed against the glass storefront, rattling the bell over the door. The lights flickered overhead. Carter swung around, wondering if the door was going to hold. The sky had grown darker, even though it was just past three. Angry hailstones battered the pavement. Tommy scratched at the roll of fat circling his middle section and surveyed the empty store.

"Shop's closing early," he said. "Why don't we make this quick? C'mon, pick one and get out of here, kid."

Carter was sick of people telling him what he couldn't have. His father sold off his Martin guitar along with Carter's future when he left Oklahoma. As long as Tommy was holding on to proof of that fact, Carter's past was in the pawn shop owner's greasy hands.

Tommy coughed. "What's that, sulfur?"

Carter realized he'd been holding his breath. He sniffed the air; it smelled bitter and smoky, like someone just lit a match the size of a bow rake handle. It was hard to breathe. With a flash and a roaring sound, they both dropped to the dirty tile floor. The thunder sounded like a freight train had barreled off track and was crashing through the heart of Tulsa. The shop lights went out and the TVs fell silent, and the glowing electric alarm clocks died on the shelves.

He had to get out there. Seemed like every time he thought his plans were coming together, something or someone got in his way. Even the weather had it out for him. His mother would be home soon, and there was no bringing Eddie's guitar back in that rain. Shouting to Tommy, "I got to go before the storm gets any worse," Carter rose to his knees, fixing to leave.

"Boy, you ain't going nowhere."

Lightning flashed, illuminating the faces of the creepy dolls on the shelves. The bell over the entryway rattled. The front doors blew wide open, blowing the aging pottery off the shelves. The rows of hanging guitars slammed together on their hooks, then tore clean off the wall when the display bracket collapsed. The guitars' hollow-wood bodies cracked and groaned, hitting the floor. Their heads poked in every direction from a crumpled heap. Chunks of ceiling tiles and roof shingles, and all the junk in between, dumped on the mess, crushing what was left of the guitars. A blast of rain and howling wind ransacked the pawn shop, sending pieces of smashed pottery skittering across the floor toward Carter. He covered his head as Tommy's lumpy body careened over the counter like a sack of wheat. Tommy grabbed Carter's arm and hustled him back toward the storage room.

"Tornado" was all he said, the word swollen and distorted, like it took up too much room in his head.

Chapter Two

CARTER HUSTLED TO FOLLOW THE MAN INTO A storage room with painted cinderblock walls. A small emergency light attached to the ceiling gave the tight space just enough light to make out shapes of old furniture, trunks, and boxes, but sucked the color of out of everything.

"Don't touch anything, kid. I'm warning you."

Tommy lit a shaky cigarette. When he exhaled, the smoke gathered and swirled in the grayish light. Rain beat against the cracked rectangular window with a view of the parking lot out back. Carter didn't care to spend any longer than necessary in the cramped storage space with him.

Adjusting to the dim light, he spotted his father's guitar immediately, hanging next to the door. Carter froze, trying to still his racing heart. Clearly, Tommy knew exactly which guitar he'd come looking for, and was only holding out to make Carter beg for it. A desperate customer meant bigger bucks in the bartering world.

Removing it carefully from its hook, Carter ran his hand over the smooth body, examining it. Not a spot of dust on it, like it'd been polished up for a big sale. The price tag was gone, but everything else was exactly the way he remembered it.

"That the one?" Tommy asked, flipping through a stack of vinyl records.

"Might be," he stammered, his gaze flashing to the storm outside the little window. The guitar's back, sides, and top were solid mahogany, the wood grain surfaces mirroring one another like an open book. The strings attached to the body with a traditional maple bridge plate and a thin saddle Carter knew was made from real bone. The fourteen-fret neck had matching mahogany. Carter's fingers nearly sensed the vibration of the guitar's history, songs plucked and strummed on those very strings.

He held it so Tommy wouldn't see the inscription of tiny dark brown serif letters just below the pickguard: "Creativity, Victory, Heart, and Discipline." Those four words had mattered to his father, enough to have them custom-stained into the guitar. The inscription was as valuable to Carter as the guitar itself, proof his father once had some good in him.

"It'll do," he said, trying to be casual, his back turned to Tommy. "I'll give you seven fifty for it, no more."

"It ain't for sale, kid." Tommy laughed a cold laugh. "Already have a buyer."

Carter couldn't be sure if Tommy was bluffing. "How much are they offering for it?"

"Nine fifty."

Carter swallowed hard, thinking about how long he'd hated knowing his dad's guitar was still in Tulsa, but he wasn't allowed to play it. He thought about how hard it had been to save. The old coffee can he used as a piggy bank had weighed as much as a sack of hammers, but when he'd counted all the loose coins and random bills from chores and a faraway aunt on birthdays, he'd only cleared three hundred dollars. On weekends, his mother taught him to fix everything from the torque converter to the flywheel on her truck, but she wouldn't pay him for it. She said if he hoped to drive the old beast one day, he'd best know his way around the engine. He watched where she kept her savings, though. He knew all about where she hid her money. It was cash she wasn't going to spend on him—and certainly not on his dad's old guitar. She probably wasn't even going to spend it on herself. His mom wore the same dusty work clothes day in and day out. Born and raised on a scratch of desert north of Reno, Nevada, she didn't fuss with getting her hair and nails done. Even when the roof leaked last winter, she'd refused to pay to hire anyone. She went up there and fixed it herself.

His mother's savings just sat there, doing nothing and helping no one. Carter wanted to put an end to the guitar that once promised him a future in music. If he was never going to play the Martin again, no one would.

So he took the money.

It was just enough, added to the savings in his coffee can, to buy the guitar for seven hundred fifty dollars. And now Tommy wanted an extra two hundred?

"I can give you seven fifty, right now." Carter was firm but his voice had lost color. It felt like there was a ball of something scratchy at the back of his mouth. Carter cleared his throat, but the ball grew scratchier.

His guilty fingers felt clammy around the damp bills, all his mom's savings, in his pocket. It wasn't enough to buy the guitar. Stealing it was plainly the dumbest, most selfish thing he'd ever done.

"Sorry, kid. Nine fifty's the best I can do."

Would destroying the guitar guarantee him sweet payback if he had to steal from his mother to do it? He pictured himself smashing it with a hammer, the way he'd wanted to a thousand times since his dad left. No, he couldn't go through with it. He'd put back all her money before she found out and—

He'd let go of his father. Let go of the guitar.

"I don't want it," Carter said, unable to tear his eyes away from the instrument.

Tommy placed the Martin in an old guitar case and leaned it

against the wall. Black and dusty, the case seemed like a coffin to Carter's only hope. But there was no way of getting any more money. He'd already taken what wasn't his.

Rain pummeled the parking lot, the sky swirling with blue-black clouds. The howling wind picked up and thunder broke high above them. Carter cowered, ducking against the cold cement wall. It sounded like the storm was directly overhead. "Most of the time thunder plays a trick," Tommy assured him, taking a drag of his cigarette. "It sounds close, but it's miles away."

Carter leaned into the wall to steady himself. He figured his mom must be back home by then and wondering why he wasn't. She was in the habit of pitching a duck fit when he wasn't back in time for dinner. It's not like he had many places to be on the best of days, but a tornado was a whole new level of worry. "Hey, Tommy? Would it be okay if I called my mom?" His heart was pounding something awful. "I don't want her to worry." He was plenty worried himself.

"Yeah. Make it quick." In the small room, the rectangular light of a cell phone's lit screen appeared before him, shaking in Tommy's fist. The screech of bending metal cut through the darkness. "Sometimes the bark is worse than the bite." Tommy tried to make sense of the noise. "You know, reverberation."

"Thanks." Tommy must be coming unhinged, Carter thought, as he dialed his mother's cell. That storm was just getting started.

"Hey, Carter." Tommy kept talking, too unnerved to button his lip. "Everything's going be okay, you hear?"

He pressed the phone against his ear, listening. His mother didn't pick up. Everything was far from okay, he reckoned.

Debris blew about the parking lot in the screaming wind. Carter held the phone closer to his ear and covered the other with his free hand. In the distance, he could hear the grainy scrape of breaking brick and a loud crunching whine of metal crushed against metal. This wasn't any seasonal rain shower. It was a full-on tornado. He just wanted to be home. He looked at the black case holding his father's guitar and cursed ever having held the thing, ever having loved it. It'd brought him nothing but bad luck. He wished he didn't care about music, wished his father leaving didn't matter.

Carter pressed his body against the cinder-block wall. The cool, solid concrete felt safer. And permanent, he hoped.

A deafening noise cracked overhead. Carter slid down to the floor, burying his head under his long arms. He held his breath and closed his eyes, afraid the ceiling might collapse, crushing him and Tommy like the heap of guitars.

There was no going out in that mess. Guitar or no guitar, he was stuck. Carter pictured his mother in her basement workshop, her hair tied in a bandanna, sawdust on her forearms above her work gloves. He redialed, entering her number slowly and deliberately. She made it home from her delivery, he repeated to himself. But she wasn't answering her phone. He dialed again, pressing the phone back to his ear and listened to it ring and ring until it went to voice mail.

"Mama, it's me, Cotton. Are you home? You okay?" He wished he could tell her where he was, but she'd freak if she found out he was in Tommy's pawn shop with all her savings. "Um, I'm fine. Really. I'll be home as soon as the storm passes. I love y—" The call dropped, cutting him off. "Why isn't she answering?" he asked, as though Tommy'd have any clue.

"You got to keep trying," he said. His voice seemed rougher in the darkness. "She'll answer, I know it."

Outside the window, Carter watched a garbage can in the parking lot stumble a few feet, then fly away. He handed the phone back to Tommy. "Right after you call your family."

Chapter Three

THE STORM BATTERED THE PAWN SHOP ALL NIGHT. With nothing but hope and worry duking it out in their heads, Carter and Tommy didn't catch a wink of sleep.

The next morning the sky was dirty and gray, blotting the sun. It was still raining, but the thunder had let up. Carter and Tommy stood on the sidewalk in front of the pawn shop, neither of them speaking. Ambulance and fire engine sirens whined in the distance. Car alarms droned from every direction.

Through the long hours trapped in the pawn shop, they hadn't talked much about anything aside from the weather, but the storm gave Tommy the presence of mind to sell the guitar to the closest buyer offering immediate cash, rather than waiting on a better deal. Carter had handed over all his money, stuffing it into Tommy's meaty palm in the darkness. Gripping his father's guitar in his arms at last, Carter had hoped the emptiness of losing his dad would be over. Smashing the Martin was supposed to help him move on, become whatever a boy became when "rock star" was no longer an option. Funny thing, though, Carter had wished he could play it that night, hear the strings quiver with life. But he hadn't dared to take it out of the case, not when the wind wouldn't let up. Carter knew an F5 tornado could pick up speeds as fast as three hundred miles per hour. He was afraid the ceiling might peel off and disappear into the eye of a passing funnel. He'd already lost his dad. He didn't want to lose the guitar. Again.

♪♪♪

CARTER was itching to get home. He was worried about his mom. She hadn't answered her phone all night. He stuffed the receipt for the guitar in his pocket.

Tommy stared across the street at a crumpled Toyota hatchback wedged in a tea shop's window frame as if it had been thrown like a Frisbee. They were lucky to be alive, not a scratch on either of them. Pulling his gaze from the wreck, Tommy shut the pawn shop's front doors, securing them with an old bike lock wrapped around the door handles, even though the shop had a gaping hole on one corner where the roof fell in the night before. Half of Tommy's merchandise was trashed.

"Get on home," Tommy said with a grunt, sending the boy on his way. "What do you take me for, a babysitter?"

Carter hesitated a moment, trying to meet Tommy's eye, but the hatchback had reclaimed his attention the way only a car wreck can. "Thank you, Tommy," Carter said. "Sorry about your store," he added, throwing his arms around the big man in a solid hug. Surprised, Tommy thumped Carter awkwardly on the back and released himself, folding his arms across the roll around his middle. "Go on, now. Your ma is probably fixing to wallop you for not getting home last night."

Gripping his fingers tightly around the guitar case's handle, Carter took off running from Tommy's pawn shop, north on the sidewalk to Ballata Avenue, his street. The guitar weighed him down, wobbling and thrashing like he was dragging it against its will. He tried tucking it under one arm and then the other. Finally, he grabbed the handle with one hand, and hugged it to his chest with the other. Dodging loose roof shingles, fence posts, twigs, and branches, Carter forked right into his neighborhood without slowing to catch his breath. His house was four blocks down.

Carter stopped short, coming to a hard halt, and stared. The homes he passed every day on his way to school, many a hundred years old or more, were nothing more than piles of rubble. The booming crashes of the night before, the sound he'd imagined was a freight train running off-track, wild and untamed through the middle of Tulsa, must have chosen his neighborhood as a crash pad.

The truth was plain: his neighborhood was demolished, flattened, wiped out. Carter stared, uncomprehending. Where houses once stood he could only imagine people, the neighbors who occupied them. They all got out, he told himself. Plenty of warning on the news, they had to have gotten out in time. He couldn't bear the idea he might be standing in a graveyard. But what about his house, he wondered. What about Mama?

Carter sprinted home, rain pelting his wet hair against his forehead. On some lots, a garage held its ground. As though nature had played some twisted lottery, a short row of four or five homes stood untouched, humbled witnesses to the carnage around them.

As he neared his house, Carter slowed, blinking away the rain from his eyes. It seemed all right. Only the front door hung open, held in place by just the bottom hinge.

"Mama!" Carter yelled, taking the front steps in twos. "I'm home."

Carter pulled the front door straight, leaning it against the jamb. He stepped inside, trying to make sense of what he saw. Half the house was gone. Rain fell on the living room carpet, soaking it. Rubble lay everywhere, as if a junkyard had exploded. The staircase, a wet, creaking heap, no longer led to the second floor but to the endless gray, crying sky.

"Mama, where are you?" he yelled again, his eyes scavenging the shards of bent drywall, broken picture frames, and filthy furniture, ripped and soaking wet. The steps to his mother's basement workshop were buried in rubble, maybe five feet deep or more. Carter squeezed his eyes shut, regret bitter in his mouth. It was a dumb mistake, praying all night that she was down there, he told himself. Now he was sure she got out. She had to be okay. He squeezed the handle of the guitar case in his palm, guilt stabbing him in the gut. He nearly doubled over from the pain. Trying to steady himself, he grabbed on to his mother's carved wooden headboard, jutting out over soggy cardboard boxes that had been in the attic. Where the dining table once sat, a mattress cowered on top of the neighbor's motorcycle, a Yamaha V Star, wrapping it like a tent. Carter had taken a handful of lessons on the bike after he'd earned his learner's permit. It was no good now. The front wheel bulged to one side, the fork tubes bent like broken limbs. Carter brushed away hot tears with his wet arm. The salty, bitter taste of his snot ran down his lip. Getting his bearings, he tore into the mess, calling out, "Mama! Mama!"

Carter found a strength he didn't know he had, hauling away rubble covering the stairs to the basement with his bare hands. With the back of his arm, Carter wiped at the sweat beading across his forehead and dug away the filthy remains. When he came across an old box of baby blankets and onesies his mom had kept, he used them to wrap his hands, scratched and bleeding from digging. The song he'd written on his palm the day before, "Hour of Freedom," was nothing more than a distorted smattering of black ink.

Half-afraid he would find her dead, half-afraid he wouldn't find her at all, he begged her to answer him. "Mama, I'm sorry I was late," he sobbed, grimacing at the gassy stink in the air.

The rain wouldn't stop. Carter had to find a place to hide the guitar. The stainless-steel kitchen sink and a good portion of the Formica countertop had survived the storm. Carter cleared out the pots and pans and cleaning supplies beneath and hid the guitar there to keep it dry while he continued his search. An over-sized flashlight, the old kind with a six-volt lantern battery, hung on what remained of the kitchen wall. Carter hoped the battery hadn't died. Pulling it from its magnet, he tried the switch. A bright light cut through the dust and rainfall.

When he finally got the basement door open, he nearly flung himself down the stairs, shining the light into the darkness.

She wasn't there.

He bounded back up the stairs. Carter stumbled out of his broken home into the street. With all his strength, he barreled his voice across the deserted plain of rubble and debris. "Mama? Sandra Bermejo! Mama!"

The wind blew hard across the open field of downed houses. The air felt loud in his ears as he strained to hear his mother's reply to his calls to her.

She didn't answer.

No one answered. There was no one around, in any direction as far as he could see. That was good, he decided. Everyone had been evacuated. She was somewhere safe, with the others. He just wished he could tell her he was okay, too.

She would come back, of course, to look for him. He remembered one time when he was just a knee-baby, wandering off at the shopping mall. Eventually, she found him pitching a duck fit, sticky with tears and hungry enough to eat the north end of a south-bound polecat. "Carter Danforth," she'd scolded him, dropping to her knees to scoop his whole body into her arms, "next time stay where I can find you."

Carter returned to his house to wait. He kept his ear tuned to any sound falling between the moans of the wind and the downpour of rain, watching the horizon for the telltale dark funnel of an oncoming tornado.

It'd been over a day since he last ate. All Carter had left of his kitchen was the sink and a vivid recollection of the meals his mom had fixed there: barbeque pork, biscuits, and corn, and sweet peach pie. At that point, a ninety-nine-cent burrito from a gas station sounded pretty good. Carter thought again about the money he'd stolen. And spent. He didn't have a dollar in his pocket.

Carter wondered whether any of the chemicals his mother used in her workshop were flammable. He couldn't leave the house in case she came looking, but he worried the whole pile might go up in flames. He paused to look to the sky. The rain continued to fall hard, the clouds a battalion of firefighters.

Maybe she was at a friend's, in a cellar hidey hole, or had stayed with a client after her delivery. Isn't that what had happened to him? He'd found a safe place where she couldn't even imagine. He had to keep searching.

Chapter Four

BY EVENING, THE NEIGHBORHOOD HAD GROWN DARK, darker than he'd ever seen. The streetlights could have blown to the next county over for all Carter knew. There were no porch lights on; there were no porches. No golden lights glowing from quiet houses, where families sat around tables eating dinner. No flicker from TV screens. Just darkness.

Carter grabbed the guitar from under the kitchen sink and sheltered himself in the basement. He wondered if his dad knew, if somehow he'd gotten word about the Oklahoma tornado from the news. He wondered if he ever thought of him and his mama.

His dad had a new life some fourteen hundred miles away in Santa Monica. Carter wondered if his new wife's daughters, Scarlett and Aurora, were better at being his kids than he was. He supposed if they weren't, his dad would've come back by now.

Rain fell down the hardwood stairs with a sharp splat, pooling under the door into the dank workshop. Bracing the lantern between his shoulder and chin, Carter balanced the guitar case over two sawhorses and slipped out the instrument and hugged it to him. It would have been smarter to leave the guitar in its case to protect it.

He stroked the length of the guitar's familiar shape, running his hands around the curved sides, to the heel of the body, then up the neck, bumping over each fret. At the headstock,

Carter traced his fingertips over the Martin & Company logo. *Established 1833*, it read. If the Martin company could weather nearly two centuries, maybe Carter could endure another night not knowing when he'd find his mother.

When he was little, his dad used to sit him on his knee and hold his hands to the strings. The 000-15M Martin was similar to smaller, 1940s-era mahogany guitars, his dad had told him. It had a balanced sound, and Carter found it comfortable to play, even though it was left-handed and he wasn't. Eddie believed playing left-handed had been integral to making Jimi Hendrix a star, and Carter's daddy used every notion, gimmick, and trick to make people sit up and take notice of his "boy wonder."

Carter wasn't the musician he once was, not by a long shot, but he'd retained a fair bit and could even read music. He tried a few chords. The mellow vibration in the tight space shook Carter with astonishment. He tried to lengthen the chords, draw out each note. He remembered his dad telling him, "There are about a million ways to play a quarter note." As though his daddy were there with him, as if no time had passed, he recalled his words. "You have to tease it out, sometimes thick, other times swinging soft and low. I like it with a quick grind at the tail." His dad had told him to repeat one ordinary word, over and over. Anything—*motorbike* or *chopper*, it didn't matter. Just repeat a word enough times and it starts to bend and warp, it loses meaning. Quarter notes can be handled the same way, he'd explained.

Rhythm and timing: those were his mom's secrets to sanding and polishing a piece of wood to perfection. After Dad sold the Martin and moved out west, she said, "You've got good eye-hand coordination. You were born to work with your hands." Then they got wind that Eddie had married another woman with not one but two potential "wonder kids," and it was clear that he was never coming back. Carter gave up believing he was born to make music.

An ache pounded in his stomach; longing raked at his ribs. *I'm just hungry*, he thought, but it hurt him enough to put the guitar away. Maybe it wasn't worth it. Stealing from his mama was plain stupid, and look where it got him. The best thing he could do was take the guitar back to Tommy in the morning and get his mother's money back. He'd pretend he never took it or spent it. They were going to need the money now anyway, to find another place to live.

♪♪♪

SOMEHOW sleep found him. He didn't know it until he was startled awake by the sound of sirens. He listened, his body sore and cramped. A voice called out to a more distant voice on megaphones. For a moment he was lost, wondering why he was sleeping in a damp, dark basement with baby blankets around his hands.

"Mama!" He sat up quickly. Squeezing out from his rubble heap, his guitar case in hand, Carter stepped carefully through the wreckage. A new sweat broke out on the back of his neck.

Out front, emergency service crews were scattered where houses once stood. A man in a reflective jacket with a Red Cross emblem and a megaphone spotted him immediately, Carter's movements visible in the bleak stillness.

"Hey, what are you doing here?" the man called out to him. "Are you hurt?"

"I'm fine," Carter replied, still disoriented from his fitful sleep. "I'm waiting for my mom, Sandra Bermejo. Have you seen her?"

Crewmembers glanced at one another with concern. The man quickly ushered Carter to an ambulance, draping a thermal blanket around his shoulders.

"I'm Will," the man introduced himself. "What's your name?"

"Carter Danforth. I live here." Carter turned and pointed at what was left of his house, then choked back a cough. No one in their right mind could live there anymore. "Do you know where my mom is?" he repeated.

"There was an outbreak of tornadoes, son. The governor of Oklahoma declared this county a state of emergency. We're here to help."

A rescue volunteer in the ambulance held out a cup of steaming chicken noodle soup, and Carter accepted it hungrily. "We'll find her," Will assured him, nodding with the solemnity one offers at a funeral. Carter didn't like the man's tone. Hope was all he had, and he needed everyone else to hold on to hope, too. "Jamison! Let's put some calls in to the temp shelters and hospitals. What'd you say your mother's name was?"

"Her name is Sandra Bermejo, sir," Carter politely corrected Will's use of *was*.

Carter waited on a gurney in the ambulance for nearly three hours before anyone gave him information. At last, Will appeared at his side. They'd located a woman by the name of Bermejo at Felicitas Hospital, being treated for multiple fractures and cerebral contusions. "Come on, Carter." He motioned him up off the gurney. "Let's go see your mother."

Carter grabbed his guitar and followed. Worry and relief circled him like two white-tailed bucks with their antlers in a tangle. There was no reason to lock up. He reckoned his house was empty of everything that ever mattered.

Chapter Five

CARTER HESITATED BEFORE ENTERING HIS MOTHER'S room at the hospital. What were contusions anyway? How badly was she injured? He asked if he might tuck his guitar behind the counter at the nurses' station while he visited with his mom, and the on-duty nurse took pity on him.

When he found the courage to walk through the door, his heart ached. It felt as cramped in the confines of his chest as he'd been in the soggy basement. His mother looked different, weak and small. Her hair, the same dark chestnut as his, was loose, not tied back with one of her bandannas. Her chin, usually held resolute, strong-willed like his, fell slack. The only sound in the room was her shallow breath, assisted by tubes.

When her puffed and swollen eyes fixed on him, they sparked to life.

Rushing to his mom's side, Carter dropped against her, wrapping his arms around her motionless body buried under crisp white hospital sheets and a scratchy blanket. For several minutes, neither mother nor son spoke. Blinking at her through the blur of his wet lashes, he searched her face and the outline of her body on the hospital bed. It was really her, not some fevered wishful dream. She was alive.

"Mind the patient's neck brace," the attending nurse scolded him. Without the need of a word, Sandra shot the woman a look that could've hushed a town gossip. She receded to the door and disappeared.

Carter's relief at finding his mother darkened his feelings of guilt into a raw, agonizing mass. Guilt for not being home when he said he would. Guilt for not telling her he was going to stop at the pawn shop after school. Guilt, for stealing her money.

Carter heaved his body against her, and she held him close with a broken arm clad in a fiberglass cast. She stroked his hair, an IV attached to the back of her hand.

"I thought I lost you," she said, smiling as much as her bruised face would allow. Her cheeks were wet with her tears. "I prayed you were safe, and I could feel it, Cotton. The tie between us never broke."

"I felt it, too, Mama," Carter sniffed, looking into her reddened eyes. "I knew you were alive. I knew it."

♪♪♪

CARTER slept next to his mother at the hospital for the next few days, finishing the meals she couldn't and reading to her. Her head injury brought on nausea and vomiting. He couldn't stand seeing her this way, and kept wishing she'd wake up back to her old self.

The hospital staff insisted Carter be referred to a temporary shelter. Felicitas Hospital wasn't a motel, after all. The doctors said Sandra's vision and speech were stable, but she couldn't seem to coordinate her movements. The patient needed treatment and rest.

Sandra remembered what happened to her like she'd woken up from a bad dream. She'd been delivering a dining room sideboard to a client when the rainstorm escalated from a relentless downpour to a blinding wall of water.

Her clients, the Liu family, had insisted Carter's mother stay, but she was determined to get home to him. She'd pulled on her rain boots at the doormat and tugged the hood of her raincoat overhead. The last thing she remembered was the branches of a tree crashing clear through the front door.

"What day is it?" she asked. Carter scratched his head. He couldn't say he knew. They were between times, the normal life they'd had only days before, and the great, empty unknown ahead of them. He'd slipped his daddy's guitar into a supply closet in her room, the receipt tucked in the case. Picturing it in his mind, he recalled it was April 1 when he bought it. Carter clicked on the small TV in his mother's room, flipping channels until he found a news station. No surprise, a news anchor was covering the damages from the storm. "April fourth, Mama," Carter read the screen.

He'd been so preoccupied with getting enough money to buy the stupid thing and put an end to the past, and now all he could think about was what they'd do when she got better. The power in her carpenter's arms had drained. Time in the hospital bed left her delicate and weak. Except for her spirit. Sandra Bermejo thought she knew best on every topic, and by and large, folks listened to what she had to say.

Carter couldn't stay at the hospital much longer, but Sandra refused to send her son to any victim shelter alone, even the ones offering assistance to unaccompanied minors. They needed to find help. He pulled the hospital room's phone over to the bed and his mom told Carter to call her friend Lola May Leggitt first.

It made sense; Carter figured Lola May owed his mother a favor. She'd helped Lola break free from her husband, Wayne Leggitt, a no-good troublemaker who'd brought her enough heartache to fill a country song, not to mention dislocating her shoulder once. Lola May was a local celebrity, host of the cable-access home-renovation show *Farmhouse Fancy.* Lola was no bigger than a bar of soap after a good day's washing, but Carter reckoned the woman sure could swing a hammer. After what they called the "Wayne ordeal," Lola May started hanging around all the time, even though her own place was only a couple of miles away, and pretty as any she featured on TV.

Carter dialed her number. "Hey, Lola. It's me, Carter," he said, setting the phone on speaker.

"I been worried sick about you," she squealed. Carter moved the phone away to arm's length. Lola May's force of presence took up nearly a square acre. "Is your mama okay? Is she mad at me? She hasn't returned any of my calls."

Carter yawned. "Her phone is broken, Lola May. Nobody's mad at you." It was always about Lola May. "Mama got hurt real bad in the storm. Our house is totaled."

"Oh no, Cotton. You too?" Carter hated that she talked to him like kin. "The roof blew clear off my house with me in it, hunkered down in the cellar," she continued. "Scariest thing ever."

"No way, you were in your house?"

Sandra took hold of her son's hand. They weren't the only ones with problems, and it hit Carter that they came close to losing a lot more than one another.

"What do you mean, 'hurt real bad'? Y'all in hospital?" Lola May asked.

Carter brought the phone under his mother's chin so she could talk. "Felicitas, but I'm on the mend, Lola May," Sandra said, doing her best to act normal. "Are you hurt, darlin'?"

"Don't have a scratch on me, thank the Lord for my husband—"

"Ex-husband," his mother was quick to correct her.

"—who swooped in out of nowhere and rescued me from a twister like a dern knight in shining armor," Lola May said.

Sandra rolled her eyes. It was just like Wayne to show up at the last minute and reap all the glory. He was the same useless butt who raised his hand to her, she reminded Lola May. With what little breath she could muster, she begged Lola May to move into the temporary shelter at Bob Bogle High School and keep an eye on Carter.

"You know I love Cotton like my own," Lola May said. Carter tossed his hair out of eyes and curled his lip at his mom. Lola May was always acting too familiar. "He can stay at Wayne's place with me until you get sorted, Sandy."

"Sorry. I'm looking for a safe place for my son," his mother replied, emphasizing the word "safe."

Carter could hear Lola May fussing and squabbling on the other end. He pictured her adjusting her bleached-blond updo with those biggity fake nails she always wore, even while turning banister spindles on a wood lathe.

"Lola," Sandra said, trying to get a word in, "you said you were done with Wayne for good."

"He's a changed man."

"I daresay you're the one who's changed," Sandra said in place of a good-bye, and set her jaw hard. His mother didn't have the muscle strength to hold a phone to her ear, but she could end a conversation by cutting to the finish line with nothing but the tone of her voice.

Carter tried to hide his relief. Bunking in at the high school gymnasium would be bad enough, but knowing Lola May Leggitt, she'd put a fire under the principal to let her add a screened porch. Wayne was no prize pig; Carter knew he'd made mistakes. But if his father had half a mind to *swoop in* and help them, he hoped his mom would give him a second chance at their future. Ever since his daddy left, Carter had lost any and all hope of what was supposed to become of him.

♪♪♪

CARTER suggested they call the few kids at school he considered friends. Turned out, things were tough all over. Caleb's family was holed up at their neighbor's farm, having lost their own home, and Landon's had high-tailed it to his cousin's condo in Florida. Sandra and Carter had some family friends a few counties over, but they'd already taken in relatives affected by the tornadoes. Their options dwindling, Carter's mother held firm.

It was bad enough Carter had neither a bed to sleep in nor a roof over his head. Just when things couldn't get any worse, he found out he had homework to do, and plenty of it. Because the schools were closed, everyone in ninth grade was expected to hand in an independent research project by April 30th to complete their grade level. Carter's grades were none too pretty as it was. When a boy didn't know where he's headed, he didn't pay much mind to his studies.

"I have money hidden," Sandra told him, her breath coming at short intervals. "It's not much, and I was hoping to save it for something real important, but it's enough for you to fly out to your aunt's in Nevada." Carter adjusted the tubes going into her nostrils the way he saw the nurses do it. She pressed on, explaining she had cash—tens, twenties, and fifties, dozens of them—inside the rattling door panel of her old pickup truck. Carter's skin prickled. He knew exactly what money she was talking about and where she'd hid it. It was the savings he'd taken to buy the cursed Martin. Only one thing that guitar was good for, he reckoned, bad luck.

Sandra labored with her breath, gathering the strength to say, "I want you to call your Aunt Sylvia in Nevada."

Carter had every intention of confessing the dumb fool thing he'd done, but just then he decided telling the truth might hurt her more than any good that might come of it. Instead, he stalled, trying to buy some time until they could figure out a plan that didn't involve buying a plane ticket. "Didn't you say, 'If brains were leather, Sylvia wouldn't have enough to saddle a june bug'?"

His mom's brow twitched like she was fixing to set him straight. He didn't want to get in trouble, but somehow it pained him to see her unable to give him what he had coming.

"Sylvia is family after all," she managed to get out, "and we don't have much of that to count on. It'll only be a few weeks, just until I'm out of the hospital," she assured him. "Then we'll find ourselves a new house. Maybe a piece of property with a real workshop out back; wouldn't that be something?"

Carter pulled away from his mother, telling her he'd round up some cold drinks. He was afraid if he stayed any longer he might go haywire and admit he'd taken her money and spent it. He was smart enough to figure there'd be medical bills on top of taking out a new mortgage. His mother's income barely covered the tiny house they'd lost. Carter heard something about insurance, but he knew well enough they don't move you from a pigeonhole to a palace on account of some bad weather.

Hesitating a moment, Carter strummed a few beats against the hollow metal doorframe with his fingertips. "I hope you get that workshop, Mama."

"We'll start fresh, Cotton," she whispered back. "Just you and me."

Chapter Six

CARTER WAS IN A BIND. HE COULDN'T FLY TO SYLVIA'S because he didn't have the money to buy a plane ticket. He couldn't take the guitar back to Tommy's because he'd be right back where he started before the storm. Buying that thing, in truth, had saved his life, and he still hadn't fessed up about it.

Carter couldn't help thinking that Eddie ought to help. Where'd he been all these years, anyway? He never called on Carter's birthday, never sent a present. Not even a card. And now his mother was laid up in the hospital and they had no place to go once she got out. He'd promised Carter a life of music, but before he had a chance to really come into his own, Eddie split. He sold Carter's guitar and never looked back. Just looking at his mother laying in her hospital bed all weak and bruised made him angry. Somehow, this was Eddie Danforth's responsibility, and Carter was going to see to it that Eddie helped them out.

"Mama, we need to talk," he began, leveling his best *y'all-listen-up* looks on her when they had a moment alone. "We're going call my father. We haven't got much in the way of family, like you said. He's got the means to help us, and far as I'm concerned he owes us both."

Sandra frowned. She didn't like the tone he was using with her, or the idea. "Why on earth would you want to stay with—" She winced, the pain in her neck seeming sharp as she leaned toward him. "—Eddie?"

Carter glanced up at her in surprise. He hadn't heard her speak his name in six years.

"I figure it's high time I gave the old man a piece of my mind," Carter told her, squaring his shoulders and standing a bit taller. "Got a few things I'd like to say about the way he left."

His mother managed half a smile, the dry scab of a cut across her chin pulling.

Carter swallowed hard, clearing his throat, his gaze landing on the supply closet hiding his guitar. The truth was he didn't have one solitary word for Eddie. Carter wanted to forget his dad was ever there, because then he wouldn't have to wonder what he might have become with his famous father's guidance.

Eddie hadn't given him a passing notion in six years. But Carter'd never asked him for anything. He hoped his father would help him when he needed it the most. "What if Dad doesn't—" he coughed, his throat scratchy. "What if he doesn't want me?"

"Let's just hope your father is reasonable," his mother said. A flicker of her eyelashes batted away the doubt whether they could trust him.

♪♪♪

CARTER sat at the foot of the hospital bed, tapping his foot on the linoleum tile. He didn't know what to make of his mom dialing Eddie's phone number from memory. Had she been keeping it secret all these years? Or had the long-forgotten digits busted loose as a side effect of head trauma? Carter was about to hear his father's voice for the first time in far too long. He found himself leaning in closer to the phone.

Eddie's new wife, Camellia, answered. Carter noticed his mother stiffen, but she didn't miss a beat, reciting the facts, cool and efficient. Mama wasn't the type to get sentimental or whiny or anything. It was only reasonable that his father take him under the circumstances. Temporarily, of course. Carter hoped his dad would cough up his plane fare so he wouldn't have to tell his mom her money was gone.

Camellia refused Sandra with a polite apology. She said Eddie was far too busy with work to be able to babysit. Sandra stared at the phone, her tongue stone still. At fifteen, Carter was no baby. Just the man's own flesh and blood, Carter wished she would tell her.

"Get well soon," Camellia said at last, then ended the call. The phone screen lingered with the broken call a second longer before it went dark. Neither mother nor son spoke. Carter wasn't sure what he'd do if his dad turned him away again. But his new wife speaking for him? Worse than six years of his father's silence.

Arrangements were made for Aunt Sylvia to take him instead. Aunt Syl pitched a fit when she heard about Sandra's bad luck and offered a helping hand straight up. "I'm in a stitch of trouble myself," Sylvia said. "I could use your boy's help with the shovel." Aunt Sylvia had a double-wide trailer in the flea-bitten town in Washoe County where Carter's mother and her sister grew up. The trailer was having septic issues, something about the soakaways failing, and "wet waste" creeping up around her porch. Carter made a gagging noise. He hadn't seen his aunt since he was a toddler. Carter was raised to put family first, but the last thing he wanted was to get up close and personal with Aunt Syl's toilet problems. His mom hushed him. "Happens all the time, totally fixable," Sandra said.

"But you call everything 'totally fixable,'" Carter argued when she hung up. "I don't want to go."

"The safest place for you is with family, honey. Who knows

what kind of shady characters are at those shelters? You're better off with my sister in Nevada, and I won't hear another word about it."

She instructed him to collect the hidden money from her pickup. It would have been enough to purchase a plane ticket to Reno, the closest airport to Aunt Syl's. He had no choice but to get his mother's money back from Tommy.

Chapter Seven

THE HOLE WHERE THE PAWN SHOP'S ROOF HAD
caved was covered with a checkerboard of tarps and duct tape.
Carter set the guitar case on the glass counter housing vintage
belt buckles big enough to block a bronco's lethal buck. "I'm going to my aunt's in Nevada," he told Tommy. "I need my money
back."

The rolling office chair Tommy was sitting in squeaked its
relief when he heaved himself out of it to have a closer look.
"There's water damage on the case," he pointed out, tapping the
burning orange embers of the last inch of his cigarette into an
ashtray. "You mess up the guitar, too?"

Carter opened the case, revealing the Martin guitar nestled
in burgundy satin. He ran his hand across it, game-show-host
style. Carter remembered the way the guitar felt against his body
in the damp basement of his childhood home. It had kept him
company through the night, awakening memories of his father.
The guitar had held him to this world, saved him from blowing
away with the storm.

Tommy stood back to consider the instrument, his arms
crossed over his chest. "I cut you a decent deal on it; I felt sorry
for you. Do you know how much I lost on that piece of junk?"
He sniffed with annoyance.

Carter wanted to argue the Martin was anything but junk,
but he was worried Tommy might ask him for the extra two
hundred dollars again. He was deep in the hole as it was. "It's like

you always say, you stand by your merchandise one hundred percent." Carter tried his best to keep the negotiation light and easy, but his heart wasn't in it. "I need the money I gave you. Tommy, please."

Carter's mom didn't want a guitar in the house anyway. It wasn't that she didn't like music. She just had higher aspirations for him, she said. But his father, Eddie Danforth, did fine for himself as a Top 40 pop singer. He even had a song that got played in soda pop commercials. Hitting it big as a performer was the reason he'd left Oklahoma for California. It must have made him happy because he never came back.

"I pulled the paperwork on it." Tommy smacked a wrinkled invoice on the glass counter. "Pawned by one Sandra Bermejo. The name ring a bell?" A chill stiffened Carter's spine, the kind you get when your mama opens your report card before you have a chance to come up with a good alibi. His father must have been a bigger coward than he reckoned, pawning it under his mother's name.

Tommy scratched at an armpit, his loose tank top exposing dark hairs. "I got to pondering, what's the connection between your ma and Eddie Danforth's guitar, you know what I'm saying? Then I noticed you signed the receipt, 'Carter Danforth.'"

Shaking, Carter closed the lid on the guitar case and pulled it off the counter.

"Why didn't you tell me it belonged to your pa?" Before Carter had a chance to reply, Tommy's voice grew louder. "We sat in my storage room from dusk 'til dawn and you never thought to bring that up?"

Carter's mouth went dry, words caught in his throat before he could offer any explanation. He couldn't make sense of it himself. He shook his head, unable to calculate how much the guitar had really cost him. Every last dollar of his mom's savings.

Six years of wishing he never even learned to play it, and the same six years longing to hold it in his arms again.

"Get out of here, kid." Tommy waved the boy away. "I don't do business with liars and cheats."

"But I need the money." Carter wasn't sure he could show his face back at the hospital without it. "My mama, she's in the hospital. I have to buy a plane ticket, and I spent—" Tommy already had called him a liar and a cheat. Could he really admit the money he used to buy the guitar was stolen?

Tommy didn't seem too interested in hearing what Carter had to say anyway. "A real axman," he said, pointing to the meager guitar display left after the storm, "would throw down and feel it out. A real guitarist would try dang near everything I got in stock, searching for a certain sound. But you didn't pluck a single string. I figured you was some spoiled brat with air-guitar dreams looking for a fancy play toy. I shoulda known it was sentimental value."

He was wrong about Carter. Eddie Danforth had left Carter with nothing but a hankering to pluck strings, but with every passing year his destiny as a musician dwindled away. When he was little more than a knee baby, his daddy dragged him round to every tavern, gin joint, and road house, and stood him on a milk crate to perform. Eddie was going to strike it rich when little Carter grew up to be a big rock star one day. Carter never minded the late nights and shady places, he just loved playing his daddy's guitar. Music was his connection with his father. Music was all he understood, or wanted. A future built on the foundation of music was all he knew, and all he wanted. That is, until Eddie up and left with his dream and never came back.

"Sentimental value," Tommy went on, rubbing his thumb against his fingers like he was caressing a fat wad of bills, "comes at a premium."

"I paid a fair price," Carter tried to point out, but he was losing steam.

Tommy took a long drag on his cigarette and considered the boy. "I hear your pa is releasing a new album this summer."

Shaking, Carter gripped the handle of his father's guitar. "Yeah, I'm real proud of him," he said, bluffing. "He's giving me a way better guitar for my birthday, so I figure I'd best sell this one back to you so I can help out my mama." His chest grew tighter with every untrue word. Worse, he wished what he was saying was fact. "C'mon Tommy, help me out." He managed a grin. "Remember? We survived a tornado together?"

Tommy scoffed and stamped out his cigarette. "Because you're a good kid and I like you, I'll let you keep it."

"No, you don't have to, sir," Carter replied too fast. He wasn't sure anymore if he wanted to keep it, or get rid of it. The dang thing got him all mixed up.

Tommy leaned his sweaty forearms on the counter and motioned Carter closer. "I tell you what you're gonna do, boy," he said, his smoker's breath moist on Carter's cheek. "This old left-handed guitar is worth ten-fold with your pa's signature. Get him to autograph it, and bring it back to me. We'll find a buyer for top dollar and split the difference."

Carter hugged the guitar case to him. The Martin was all he had left of his past or his future, and only days before he'd wanted nothing more than to destroy it. Camellia had said he wasn't welcome at his father's, and frankly there were plenty of sleepless nights he'd sworn he never wanted to see the man again.

"No problem, Tommy." Carter breathed hard, backing away from the counter. "I'll get my dad to sign it."

Chapter Eight

CARTER BOARDED THE CITY BUS BACK TO THE HOSPITAL. Out the window, loose pieces of grocery ads and fast-food wrappers flitted about in the wind like toddlers playing musical chairs, waiting for the song to stop before touching down on the sidewalk. He'd have to tell his mother about the guitar. About everything. There was no way to pay for a plane ticket now. But what he wished for more than anything was to repay what he'd stolen.

♪♪♪

SANDRA Bermejo had visitors. Carter was glad he'd taken the time to run a brush through her uncooperative hair that morning, coaxing it away from her neck and piling it all on one shoulder. He had to help her; she couldn't reach her own head, let alone hold the brush. Sandra wasn't fussy about her looks, but she had her dignity.

A dark-haired man wearing a shirt the color of Key lime pie stood frowning at the end of Sandra's bed. The bright color he wore did nothing to lighten the serious-as-a-cocked-rifle look on his face. He was nearly a full foot shorter than Carter, and the man's slender arm encircled the shoulders of an even smaller woman holding some kind of complicated-looking flower, a bow around its pot. In a straight-back chair next to the window, Carter recognized a girl from his class, Kaia Liu. Less than a month after she'd transferred to Tulsa from New Jersey, Kaia had stolen a two-hundred-dollar pocketbook from the outlet shops off the highway and given it to their homeroom teacher. Ms. Coyne fancied that purse was the next best thing to sausage gravy and carried it everywhere, like a fool. Smug Kaia ruled as prettiest bully at Bob Bogle High School.

Carter left his guitar with one of the nurses who didn't treat him like he was in her way. He wasn't interested in any public confessional.

"Hey." Carter gave Kaia a half-wave, then tucked his hand in his pocket. He wasn't in the habit of talking to her and she wasn't in the habit of paying him any mind. Besides, he'd never seen her cry before.

"You must be Carter. I'm Tom Liu. This is my wife, Jiao."

Carter glanced past Tom and Jiao to his mother. She was awake and seemed comfortable enough in their company. When Carter shook the man's hand and said, "Nice to meet you, sir," Kaia stopped sobbing just long enough to roll her eyes. She'd made it crystal clear to everyone at school that Jersey was far superior to living in Oklahoma. Carter reckoned good manners plain offended her.

"A tree came clear through our front door," Mr. Liu told him, his words spongy and not fully formed, as though he still didn't believe they were true.

"My mom told me," Carter replied, dropping his gaze to the linoleum tile. She was injured at their home, but it wasn't their fault. Bad timing was all.

"We're so sorry about what happened," Mrs. Liu said, her eyelashes glistening with tears. Carter sank into the empty chair next to his mother's bed. His mom was going to be okay; the doctors had promised him. Why were the Lius acting this way?

Sweeping dark curtains of hair behind her ears, Mrs. Liu

forced herself to face Carter. "I understand you lost your home?" she asked, her voice barely a squeak.

"Yes, ma'am." Carter kicked the linoleum with the toe of his Converse. "But it's okay. My mom and I, we'll—" Carter's voice trailed off. He didn't have a clue what they'd do. He looked at his mother, broken and bandaged under the starched hospital sheets. Her warm gaze, the only part of her still shining with life and hope, met her son's. Carter straightened himself, brushing a loose curl of hair from his eyes. "My mom's made a career out of turning the bad into good. 'Garbage into glory,' that's what she calls it."

"Your mother tells us you'll be staying with your aunt in Nevada," Mrs. Liu said, trying to sound cheerful.

"Looks like it." He nodded.

Sandra's gaze shifted to the backpack in his lap. "Were you able to take care of everything, Cotton?" she asked. Carter pulled the pack closer to him. All he had was a notebook from school and his Windbreaker. He wasn't about to tell her he didn't have the money, not in front of Kaia and her parents. But he didn't want to lie to her again either. It seemed he was heaping one lie on top of the other, and it was starting to stink something awful. Avoiding her question, he reached for the limp hand at her side and squeezed it.

"I'll be back on my feet before long, honey," his mother said, like she already had her walking papers. "Don't bother acquainting yourself with the desert. Nothing there but dust."

He wasn't sure which was worse, not having the money to buy a plane ticket, or going to Aunt Syl's if he did.

"How will you get out to Reno?" Mr. Liu asked, his frown deepening. "We were going to fly to Jiao's parents in Albuquerque while the insurance company fixes our house, but the airport was evacuated. All flights are cancelled for the week."

Carter glanced at his mom. Maybe he was stuck in Tulsa, and he wouldn't have to tell her about the money until he had enough to pay her back. Mr. Liu's brows met in the middle, where heartache introduced them. "The last thing I want to do is drive. Worst place you can be in a storm is a car."

Carter nodded but said nothing. Okie intuition told him the worst was over, but no one knew for sure which way the wind might blow.

"But you have to go to Sylvia's." Sandra tried to sit up. Pain seized her and she stiffened to a statue. Carter placed his hand behind her back and lowered her gently to her pillow.

Mr. Liu stroked his hand over his pinched forehead. The ashen rings under his eyes reached halfway down his cheeks. "It'd be easier to fly out of Albuquerque International Sunport," he said. "Sandra, we want to help however we can. If you'd like, we'd be glad to see your son to ABQ airport."

"Daddy, no!" Kaia sat up suddenly. "We don't even know him. You can't expect me to sit next to some random boy through two states."

"I go to Bob Bogle with Kaia," Carter stammered. It was bad enough she acted like half the kids at Bogle were invisible. If she were any more stuck up she'd drown in a rainstorm. Carter reckoned Kaia ought to write her ninth-grade independent research project on the fine art of making other people feel lower than a crawfish frog in a dry well.

"Would you, Tom? It would give me peace to know my son was safe," his mother said. "What do you think, Cotton?"

It was a ten-hour drive to Albuquerque, Carter knew. That was ten hours to figure out a plan for getting the rest of the way to Nevada. Not that he even wanted to go to Aunt Sylvia's. Her nasty septic problem was bad enough, but his mom never showed the tiniest yearning to revisit her hometown. Just how bad was the desert? What Carter needed, what Carter was convinced his mom needed, was to get her savings back, and then some. If he could figure some way to convince his dad to sign the Martin, he'd see to it that Tommy made good on his promise to sell it and share the money.

He needed to talk to his father. Compared to them, his dad was rolling in cash. Maybe if he knew Carter had his old guitar, he'd remember how they used to play together. His dad might be willing to send him money for a plane ticket to LA, and he wouldn't have to go to crazy Aunt Sylvia's. Maybe his dad would let him do some odd jobs around his house, like mowing the lawn, washing dishes, or babysitting his wife's daughters. Then he could repay his mama, and clear away the bad taste lying had left in his mouth.

"That'd be kind of you, sir." Carter nodded his thanks and glanced westward out the window, like he could see Albuquerque from where he stood. Kaia got up from the chair, whining to anyone with an ear, but Carter paid her no mind. If he could get as far as the airport, he hoped his father could help him the rest of the way.

Chapter Nine

THE LIUS' SUV WAS BRAND NEW. IT HAD A SMELL, a curious blend of leather and cash in the bank. The quiet interior was unfamiliar to Carter, who was used to the clanging rattle of Sandra's old Chevy pickup. Not *old*, his mother would say, but *vintage*.

It was good to be on the road. It meant he was done with lying and on his way to making things right. He promised his mother he'd call the minute he got to Aunt Syl's, but he reckoned that was his last lie because he was still going to call her. It'd just be from Eddie's house instead.

Kaia pulled the tissue box from the console and held it in her lap. She had no intention of sharing. As far as Carter was concerned, Kaia could cry her sorry face off. If she thought he'd be dealing with his own waterworks, she was sorely mistaken. The Liu family had moved to the area the year before, from tornado-free New Jersey. Carter was a true Okie, born and raised. He'd seen folks pull out lawn chairs to watch funnels touch down in farmers' fields. Nothing to cry about.

They drove in silence for the first half-hour. Carter held his guitar propped between his legs and licked his lips. The cool, dry air fanning from the air conditioner was the only sound in the SUV, other than Kaia's steady sobbing. "Poor darling." Mrs. Liu nodded to Kaia. "She's had some nasty nightmares ever since the storm. It'll be good for us to get away for a while."

Kaia stopped blubbering long enough to correct her. "Oklahoma is my nightmare, Mother."

Carter shifted in his seat, placing one ankle over the other, then trading them. He couldn't very well drum up a conversation about school. It was closed down temporarily, with so many families displaced. He didn't want to ask about the damage to the Lius' house because he didn't want to talk about his own.

The guitar propped between his legs felt conspicuous, like he was smuggling contraband in plain sight. He wondered if they could tell it was special, if they could feel its presence the way he could. Carter had worked very hard to keep the secret that his daddy was famous. It was bad enough the man left and never looked back, but what did it say about him? It was better to let kids think he never had a dad to begin with, than one who didn't pay him any mind. But all that was going to change once he made it California. For once, his father's good fortune was going to be a help to his mom and him, and not a sore spot.

To direct attention away from the guitar, Carter reckoned a little charm might fix Kaia's bellyaching. "Do you know what we use for a wind sock in Oklahoma?"

Kaia sniffed and wiped her nose, looking blankly at him. "What?"

"A brick on the end of a chain." Carter tried a smile, watching her face for any break in her sorrow.

In the front seat, Mrs. Liu made a choking sound in no way resembling a laugh.

"It's a little early for jokes, wouldn't you say, son?" Mr. Liu asked, his voice as rough as his stubble. To Carter's relief, he reached forward and turned on the radio, breaking the silence.

Carter cleared his throat and stared out the window. He watched the mile markers go by, gazing out over farmland, surveying the storm damage to farmhouses, outbuildings, and barns. Doubt stuck in the back of his throat like a hair in a biscuit. Getting in the Lius' car was a dumb idea. It seemed Carter had been acting on a whole mess of dumb ideas from the minute he stole his mother's money. Now he was watching the only home he'd ever known fly by, without a plan or a dollar to his name. Leaning his chin on his hand, Carter tried to focus on the few things he had some control over.

He tossed around ideas for what he'd write about for his independent research project. Maybe Carter could write about surviving an F5 tornado? No, he'd had his fill of the weather. He needed something original. It wouldn't be half-bad to pass the time researching his favorite motorcycle brand, Harley-Davidson. He might pay his respects to his neighbor's wrecked Yamaha V Star while he was at it.

Another thirty minutes went by, and Carter was losing the patience to bear another snotty sob from Kaia. When Mr. Liu pulled into a gas station to fill up, Carter was glad to have a break. It felt like a funeral home in that car. He stretched his legs, walking across the parking lot to a field of Indian grass, swallowing deep breaths of fresh air. He hoped his mother was all right. It crossed his mind that she should have given him a cell phone when he asked for one.

Carter spotted a collared lizard sunning himself on a rock without a care in the world. He bent down and stared at the blue-throated feller, feeling just a little jealous.

When Kaia's dad called everyone back to the car, Mrs. Liu held a large paper bag. The smell of it stabbed Carter's gut. What nature had given him in height, he got twice in appetite. He was hungry from sun up to starlight. She handed a napkin to everyone, telling the kids to spread it on their laps, then doled out fresh-baked cornbread muffins, as big as melons. Kaia shook her head, refusing hers. Carter ate his muffin as slowly as possible, savoring it.

He stole a glance at Kaia, clutching a ratty old stuffed koala bear in her arms. What her long dark hair didn't hide of her tearstained face, a crumpled and wet tissue finished the job. This wasn't the Kaia he knew at school. That Kaia had a cutting, razor-sharp beauty and a cold, raw confidence. Carter's buddy Landon said, "Kaia's meaner than a wet panther." But from where Carter stood, it seemed like moving to Oklahoma had been a demerit, a hit to her pedestal. Still, the girls in their grade worshipped her, backing up her reign of resentment whether from fear or awe.

But there she sat, reduced to this helpless thing. Carter was nearly elbow-to-elbow with her, but he didn't have a clue how he might reach out to help. Or stop her fool tears. Even if he had a half-decent idea, chances were good she'd reject him. This thought brought him back around to his plan of seeing his dad, the king of rejection. Carter had long suspected he was to blame for his dad leaving. But if Carter was a breaker, maybe he could learn to be a fixer.

The guitar held between his knees in the cramped space was all he had. Once, it was going to be his future. Now, it held the promise of turning all his wrongs into rights. Since he couldn't very well tuck it in his pocket and pretend it wasn't there, Carter wagered that he ought to make the Martin seem commonplace, something he would be carrying around because it was only natural. People only remembered the remarkable. Placing his napkin in the trash bag Mrs. Liu offered him, Carter hoisted the case up onto his lap. Kaia curled her lip at him when it bumped her shoulder. "Pardon," he said without looking her way.

He took out his guitar and leaned forward to place the strap over his shoulder, his first time holding the instrument properly in nearly a decade. Laying his fingers across the familiar strings, he sat in silence, watching farmland off the I-40 roll on for miles to a cloudless horizon and trying to decide if he could really play it.

The collection of strings under his fingertips hurtled him back through time, bumping over the Muskogee plains and shooting down crop rows to when he was just a little kid, sitting on his back porch for a guitar lesson. Eddie taught him a twenty-minute set of songs, kid stuff like Dylan's "Blowin' in the Wind" and Simon & Garfunkel's "Bridge Over Troubled Water," to play on amateur and open-mic nights. Carter reckoned any mention of wind or water was sure to catch him some trouble. There was one other he remembered, though. How did it go?

Carter tried to find the beginning chords on the strings. Mrs. Liu glanced back at the guitar with an anxious smile, her lips a tight, bleak line. Mr. Liu stared at the road ahead of him. The corn bread and a full tank of gas must have refreshed some hope in him because every now and again he'd turn to his wife and say something on the bright side, like, "Glad we sprang for the low deductible, Jiao. Insurance will pay for those smart-glass windows, the kind that block heat and UV rays."

Kaia stared out her window, her back to Carter. *Try or die trying*, he told himself. Clearing his throat, he lifted his hand and strummed the first chord. The song was corny, he knew it as well as anyone, but if he was lucky, they might sing along with him. An entertained audience, Eddie used to say, will forgive you all your sins.

This land is your land
This land is my land
From California to the New York island;
From the Redwood Forest to the Gulf Stream waters
This land was made for you and me.

Kaia shifted abruptly in her seat and stared at him like he was laughing over an open casket. "It was written by Woody Guthrie," Carter explained, "a Sooner state legend."

Mrs. Liu's grimace softened. "I remember that song. I learned it when we immigrated from China to the United States when I was seven." She turned a gentle gaze on her daughter. "You think moving to Tulsa was tough? Try starting a new school in a new country." Kaia responded with a roll of her eyes.

"But on the first day," Mrs. Liu went on, considering the farmland blurring past, "my teacher taught the class 'This Land Is Your Land,' a song to welcome new citizens to America."

Carter decided it was best not to tell her Guthrie originally had written the ditty as a protest song. If what Kaia's mother heard made moving across the world a little less lonely, he wouldn't quarrel over it. Songs meant different things to different people.

"Do you know the rest?" she asked.

Picking up his hand again, he continued playing, shaking as the song was reborn to him. Every vibration of the strings brought him back to his mother's kitchen, his daddy's hand over his, showing the placement for each chord, and the seesaw sound of his mother's sandpaper wiping back and forth over the legs of an antique end table she was refinishing.

As I was walking that ribbon of highway,
I saw above me that endless skyway;
I saw below me that golden valley;
This land was made for you and me.

Kaia's crying stopped. She clutched her koala bear closer to her chest and looked to him every bit a little kid awoken by a nasty nightmare in the middle of the night. Carter's hand sought the chord pattern change and found it. He met Kaia's eye and nodded to her to join him, urging her to remember the words she'd probably learned when that koala was new.

I've roamed and rambled and I followed my footsteps
To the sparkling sands of her diamond deserts;
And all around me a voice was sounding:
This land was made for you and me.

She didn't sing, but she stopped blubbering. Mrs. Liu, bless her heart, harmonized with Carter. The familiarity of the song bounced and reverberated inside each one of them, filling the empty spaces still sore from having the things they'd held unchangeable torn out and changed.

When the sun came shining, and I was strolling,
And the wheat fields waving and the dust clouds rolling,
As the fog was lifting a voice was chanting:
This land was made for you and me.

The SUV passed out of Oklahoma into Texas. They were on their way, moving forward.

"Again," Mrs. Liu said, when Carter's song drew to a close. Carter turned in his seat and looked back down the highway. Oklahoma was a distant speck behind them on the dark line of the horizon. The guitar was home to Carter and he was glad he still had it.

Quietly to himself, he dedicated the next round to Tommy and strummed it out from the top.

Chapter Ten

AMARILLO, TEXAS, MARKED THE HALFWAY POINT between Tulsa and Albuquerque. Mr. Liu pulled into a Ma Joad's, one of a chain of twenty-four-hour pancake houses. No sooner had he put the car in park when Kaia said, "I'm going to splash some water on my face," and sprinted from the car through the balmy Texas sunshine to the restaurant. She left her koala behind. Just inside the entryway, Mrs. Liu put an arm around Carter while her husband made arrangements for a table. Her touch surprised him. He wasn't sure if she was comforting him or leaning on him for support, but the gesture made him feel a little less alone.

Directed to a booth with a view of the freeway, Mrs. Liu pulled her cell from her purse. "Let's put a call in to your mother, hmm? I'll look up the hospital's number." She smiled the kind of smile a person gives the last kid left after preschool.

Mrs. Liu and Sandra exchanged a few words, a generic report on their travel progress. Then she said, "You must be so proud of your son, Sandra. His talent with—"

Carter's eyes flew wide open. *Don't say it*, he begged her in silence. *Don't tell her about the guitar.*

Mrs. Liu didn't finish her sentence. Carter's mother talked over Mrs. Liu, like time wouldn't oblige any small talk. She passed her cell to Carter without a word.

Carter took the phone. "Mama?"

"What talent?" Sandra asked, her voice weak. "Did they need your help with some engine trouble?"

"Something like that," he said, then changed the subject. "Mama, how are you doing?" He'd only just seen her that morning, but she didn't sound like herself.

"I'm going into surgery this evening, Cotton. Turns out they're worried about edema, which means swelling or some such." Sandra drew in a breath, then added, "Nothing complicated."

"I should be there with you. I should come back." Carter looked at the traffic speeding by on the freeway. He could hitch a ride, he reckoned, with one of the commercial trucks roaring eastbound to Oklahoma.

"Son, I'm fine. The important thing is that you're safe."

"You shouldn't be alone."

"Let's make a deal, sweetheart. I'll handle this surgery tonight, if you'll handle Aunt Syl's septic issues." She laughed at her lame joke. Carter's mom was stronger than anyone, he was sure of it. Before he could argue that if it were him going under the knife, he'd want her there, she said, "I expect you to get on that plane," without letting him get a word in, "Deal?"

There was no turning back. "Deal," he mumbled. Carter could feel the sting of tears in his eyes as he handed back the phone. Not once did he cry after finding his mama; he sure wasn't going to be the crybaby now. He glanced at Kaia, hoping she hadn't noticed. Across the freeway, a sunburned billboard for a local water park held her gaze. "'An all-day unstoppable torrent of water'?" she said to no one in particular. "Yeah, no thanks. Been there, was almost killed by a flying tree."

Carter couldn't help but agree, but he picked up the salt shaker, examining it to avoid having to say anything. He wondered what else they'd outgrown and didn't know it yet.

A single tear streamed down Kaia's cheek. That first tear invited others, and soon she was crying again. She pushed the silverware off a folded napkin and used it to wipe her face.

Carter'd had enough. "Why are you bawling all the time? It isn't normal."

"Shut up," she cried and bolted for the front entrance. Mr. and Mrs. Liu glanced up at Carter. They looked exhausted. Carter had only been listening to her sniveling for five hours. They'd put up with it for days.

"I'm sorry. I'll go talk to her." Carter followed Kaia out to the parking lot, where she stood in a patch of shade under an ash tree. The Texas midday sun made the asphalt in the parking lot soft as charred marshmallows under his Converse.

Out of earshot of her parents, Carter let Kaia have it. "What do you have to cry about?" he asked, handing her another napkin. "You have both your parents right there." He gestured to the table inside the restaurant, where Mr. and Mrs. Liu sat sipping iced drinks under a window-mounted air conditioner. "And by the end of today, you'll be snug as a bug at your grandparents' house." Carter cleared his throat; there was dust in the air. And worse, a lump in the back of his throat threatened to bring his own flood of tears, enough to fill Amarillo's water park. "Your grandma will probably fix a nice supper, too. Maybe sausage and gravy and pecan pie." Carter wiped at his eyes with the back of his arm. "Dusty plains," he cursed.

Kaia slumped to the ground, gathering her knees to her chest and wrapping her arms around them. The only way Carter was going to hold back his worry for his mother was to keep talking. He wasn't going to let himself think about being scared. "And when your house is all fixed up, you'll go back to the life you knew. As far as I can see, you're sitting pretty."

She spoke up at last. "I don't want to go back. I wish we

never left New Jersey. My brother Ethan didn't have to move; he stayed to go to university."

Carter didn't know New Jersey from old, but he remembered the first storm he'd ever weathered. "It's hard to trust the wind again once you've seen it blow," he admitted.

She wiped a tear from her face and squinted at Carter, sizing him up. "Ethan and I were seriously into cooking shows, you know, chef contests and all that."

Carter didn't say a word, so Kaia went on the defense. "I don't care what you think, Sausage Gravy. We made all kinds of fancy dishes, really upscale," she continued, tossing her hair over her shoulder. "I bet you aren't aware that cooking is science."

Whatever patience he had left for her was sorely slipping. "Look, if you're into cooking, you should cook. Easy." She didn't seem to need anyone at Bogle; she could make food without her brother.

Kaia turned and stared out at the endless stream of traffic, heading in both directions. "It's no fun cooking by myself, no matter how good I get at it," she said, quieter. "I mean, when Ethan and I are in the kitchen together, it's the best."

Carter thought about what it was like jamming on the guitar with his daddy. He loved music when he was little, no doubt. But how much of his good feelings had come from playing with him? Must have been bushels because Carter never wanted to play again once he left.

"It's the same with music," he mumbled. It was all he was able to tell her. He glanced over to her parents again and then approached Kaia carefully, kneeling. That tree ploughing through her front door didn't break his mother's resolve. It broke the vat of tears Kaia had stored up. Everything had changed and there was nothing either of them could do about it.

Her long dark hair shone in the sun, shiny as a raven's wing. He dared to place his hand on her shoulder. Her hair was softer than he could have imagined, and she didn't brush his hand away when he stroked it.

"Ethan used to watch out for me." She sniffed. "He said he'd always be there, whenever I needed him. But he wasn't there when I was the new kid at Bob Bogle. And he wasn't there when a flying tree smashed right through the front of our house."

Carter nodded without replying. His dad had said he'd be there, too.

"I don't understand why we had to move," she sobbed, burying her face in her arms. "I wish we were still a family."

"I'd give anything to go back to the way things were." He didn't know why he said that, not when he'd been telling himself the opposite for the last six years. But he felt a whole bunch lighter for having said it. "If my dad was still around, I'd know how to play a whole lot more than 'This Land Is Your Land.'" It was the first time he'd ever admitted to anyone that he'd known his father, and he was surprised he was telling it to a girl he'd never spoken two words to before that day.

Kaia managed the shadow of a smile. "I like that song." Her eyes were as dark as the wings of a black swallowtail butterfly. Carter hadn't noticed that before.

"Playing old songs is like holding on to the past but living well in the present," he told her. "We need to take care of what we have. My mom says, 'If the leg of a chair gives out, or a scrape across a tabletop runs deep, we don't give up. We can look at it in a new way.'"

"Is your aunt as cool as your mother?" Kaia asked.

No one had ever used the word *cool* to describe his mom, but Carter appreciated it. "I'm not going to my aunt's." He figured he ought to tell someone. "I'm going to my dad's house in

Los Angeles. Well, Santa Monica to be exact. But he doesn't know I'm coming."

Carter took his hand from Kaia's shoulder and stood up, looking into the restaurant's wraparound windows to where his guitar leaned against their table. "I haven't told him because he might not—" Carter swallowed hard when Kaia picked her head up and looked him straight in the eye. "He left when I was nine and he never looked back." That was enough, he warned himself. He wasn't about to go and admit his daddy was none other than Eddie Danforth.

"You're flying to LA without telling him? If your aunt's expecting you, don't you think she's going to call your mother when you don't show?"

Carter didn't want to consider the answers to any of Kaia's questions. They were too painful to consider and besides, they weren't his biggest trouble.

"I can't buy a plane ticket."

Carter picked up a stick and scratched at the dry earth. Kaia stared at him, mouth hanging open but no words coming out.

"I spent all the money on my guitar." Carter didn't bother to mention that he'd stolen it. He could barely admit as much to himself.

"How are you going to get there?" Kaia asked, shielding the sun's glare with a hand covering her brow. "Santa Monica is a long way from Albuquerque." She didn't have to tell him that; he wasn't failing geography.

"Just like I am now, hitching rides." Carter squared his shoulders, firm in his decision. Why risk asking his father for money when he could just get there himself?

"Kids! Come inside, your pancakes are ready," Mrs. Liu called from the doorway of the restaurant. He watched Kaia walk ahead to the table, wishing he'd made her promise not to tell.

Chapter Eleven

AFTER THEY FINISHED EATING, KAIA AND HER MOTHER climbed into the SUV. Carter hung back while Mr. Liu settled the bill. "I just want to thank you, sir," Carter said. "For everything."

"Son, it's nothing. You've been through a lot. Jiao and I both feel terrible about what happened with your mother."

"She's going to be okay." Carter heard himself reassuring an adult, when he himself couldn't be sure at all. "She can handle anything." That much was true, so he decided to hold to that thought.

When Carter returned to the car, Kaia was holding her violin case in her lap and shuffling through pages in her schoolbag. "Here, I think you should try these," she said, shoving sheet music at him and nodding to Carter's guitar. He looked at the papers she'd handed him. Classical music, of all things. Rachmaninoff, Tchaikovsky, Mozart.

He cocked a brow at her. "You realize all this time we've been driving historic Route 66?" Carter bet that was a bit of geography she didn't know. He shook his head with a grin. "I think there's a law around these parts prohibiting European composers." Carter unlatched his guitar case and pulled out the Martin. "There used to be famous music halls right here in Amarillo, the Nat Ballroom and the Aviatrix. My dad told me all about them. Louis Armstrong played there, and Jimmy Dorsey, Duke Ellington, and lots of others. How about we try a few of the old—"

The quiver of Kaia's bow on her strings stopped him short. With her sheet music propped on her knees, Kaia played a minuet. Her bow rocked back and forth over the violin's delicate arc of strings.

Carter had heard the violin plenty of times, and fiddlers were popular at street festivals and county fairs around Tulsa. But her music sounded different, richer, in the soft, upholstered interior of the Lius' SUV.

Carter held his breath and listened. He sank back in his seat and closed his eyes, focusing his attention on the tiny space between the strings and her bow, their meeting and sliding apart. Without opening his eyes, he wrapped one hand around the neck of his guitar and laid his other over the strings. He tried to follow her lead with his ears. It would be easier, he supposed, to just look at the sheet music. He wouldn't make so many mistakes. But every time he opened his eyes, each note became too real, chained to the material world, the place where he made one dumb mistake after another. Besides, Kaia said nothing. She just played on.

He did his best to keep up, listening with more than his ears, anticipating the rise and fall of the music. When Kaia repeated the music a second and then a third time, he caught it. Holding it like a butterfly in his cupped hands, Carter played along with her. When she finally laid her bow to rest, he opened his eyes and looked at her. It was the first time that day he'd seen her smile.

Shuffling through her sheet music, she chose another song. This time, he read it through with her first, learning the melody before closing his eyes. On the third piece of music, they traded. He held it in his lap and she checked out, closing her eyes and following his lead.

"You've got some talent, son," Mr. Liu remarked. "Have you been playing long?"

"My dad taught me when I was little," Carter responded. He didn't bother to mention that music was his past, not his present. The truth was, right then, Kaia was as much his teacher as his father had been.

There were only a few hours left until they made it to Albuquerque. In the backseat, Kaia pulled her notebook from her schoolbag.

What are you doing for your independent research project? she wrote on an empty page and passed it to Carter, offering him her favorite scented sparkle pen. He read her note and ignored her offer of the pen, turning to look out the window. Carter worried he'd already told her too much back at Ma Joad's. Telling Kaia his secrets came too easy. There were certain things he knew best to keep to himself.

She dropped the notebook to her lap and clicked the pen shut. They rode on in silence, long enough that Mr. Liu began to fiddle with the radio again. At last, Kaia sighed and leaned forward to return the notebook to her bag.

Carter shook his head, thinking he ought to know better, and reached over and took the notebook and pen from her hands. He appraised her pen's scented sparkles with an eye roll, then clicked it open and wrote: *No clue. Guess I'll figure that out when I get to my dad's. You going to write about fancy food?*

She smiled, looking thankful to have him "talking."

Historic Route 66, she wrote in large bubble letters, drawing hearts for the two *i*'s in *historic* and a huge heart around all of it. She held it up to show him with a smirk, then lowered it to her lap. *JK,* she wrote across the bottom: just kidding. Then she struck that out and wrote, *But seriously, Route 66. For sure. I'm not cooking without Ethan.*

He laughed and motioned for her to give him the notebook. *Then I guess I have to write about Rachmaninoff?*

He handed it back to her and they both broke out in giggles. In the front seat, Mr. and Mrs. Liu talked quietly about paint colors for their new front entrance. A crescent moon rose over the city line as they approached Albuquerque.

The notebook passed back and forth between Kaia and Carter faster now. As their trip came to an end, it seemed there was still so much they needed to say.

You're really going to do this, huh?

What? Carter replied, sketching a winky face.

Hitchhike to California, stupid. You're fifteen, last I heard, she wrote back.

Not much choice. Hey, I'm already ten hours closer than I was this morning. Day One of my trip was a winner.

Kaia drew a smiley face, then stopped. She hugged the book to her. Clicking the pen shut, she covered her heart with her hand. Carter held her gaze across the backseat. He would never forget this ride. Kaia turned the notebook back to her lap and scribbled her cell phone number. *Text me,* she wrote, pushing the pen tip harder, like it was an order.

I don't have a phone.

Kaia crinkled her nose, shooting him a look that said she didn't entirely believe that. Sighing, she scribbled her grandmother's address in Albuquerque. Below it, she wrote, *This is crazy. Write me every day to prove you're alive. If you know about Paleozoic music halls, you can stick a stamp on a letter, right?*

Carter took the book and tore the page out. He folded it neatly and tucked it into his backpack. On a fresh page, he wrote, *It's crazy, but I can do it,* and passed the book back.

The day I don't get a letter, I'm sending the cops with a canine unit to your last location so they can sniff out your dead body, she wrote, and stuck out her tongue at him. She passed the book and pen to him, but he set them on his lap without responding. The SUV passed under a sign directing them to the airport. Kaia smiled a hopeful smile, but worry dented her brow. The last rays of sunlight hung like loose threads in the dark sky.

A greenish glow from the dashboard illuminated Carter's hand when he reached across the backseat to offer it to Kaia. She took it in hers and they held on until her father pulled into Departures.

"There's the ticketing counter." Mr. Liu left the engine running but got out to open Carter's door for him. "You need a hand?"

"Don't be silly, Daddy," Kaia interrupted before Carter could respond. "He flies to his Aunt Sylvia's by himself every summer."

Mr. Liu patted Carter on the back. "You'll be safe at your aunt's before you know it," he said, slipping him a twenty-dollar bill. "Get yourself some dinner."

"Thank you, sir," Carter said.

From the backseat, Kaia scribbled invisible words in the air with an invisible pen, mouthing their meaning: *Write every day.* When he lifted his hand to wave good-bye, Carter was still holding her pen.

Chapter Twelve

THE EVENING WAS WARM AND DRY. CARTER
sauntered through the automatic sliding doors toward the ticket
counter like a seasoned jet setter, throwing his jacket over his
shoulder. When he was sure the Lius were gone, he circled
around a bank of pay phones and tried to blend into the passing
herd of travelers with cell phones pressed to their ears.

They know full well where they're headed, Carter thought, *and
probably when they'll return. Unlike me, hanging in the gap between
hasta and luego.*

The reality of what Carter was doing started to fall on him,
one drop at a time, thudding with a hard splatter like rain into
the bottom of a bone-dry rain barrel. It'd been easy to brag to
Kaia about hitchhiking across the country. It was something else
entirely to find himself alone in an airport in Albuquerque.

He'd scratched his dad's home number across the backside of
a losing lottery ticket at the hospital. It would be stupid not to
try calling one more time before getting in a car with some
stranger. Camellia had no business deciding whether his dad
should take him in. It would only be temporary, after all, and the
man was his own blood.

For a kid who'd wanted to destroy all evidence his father
was ever in his life, he was now about to ask the very same man
for a plane ticket, a place to stay until his mother was better, oh,
and would he mind autographing the guitar he pawned when he
left his boy and skipped town?

Carter picked up the receiver of a pay phone. When his

father used to nudge him out of the shadows and into the spotlight as a little boy, he'd tell him: just put it out there. Holding his breath, Carter dialed the number. He hated to admit he'd forgotten the sound of his own daddy's voice.

"Hello?" The voice on the other end was just a kid. A girl.

"Uh, hi, hope you don't mind my calling so late. Is your," Carter began, caught off guard, "dad at home?"

"You talk funny."

"I reckon I talk like anyone from Tulsa." Carter wished he hadn't taken a tone with . . . what should he call her? His sister? "Would you kindly put him on the phone, Miss?"

"Who are you?"

He let out one long audible breath. "I'm Eddie's son, Carter Danforth."

"His son?" She sounded about as sweet as dill pickle pie. "Oh yeah, Daddy had a starter wife. He never said anything about having a kid with her."

"Starter what now?" Carter didn't like that crack one bit. But his daddy never spoke one word about him? Couldn't be true. She must be messing with him. Wasn't Camellia's oldest girl Aurora only thirteen or some such? A Southern mother would smack that kind of sass faster than green grass through a goose. Worse, she'd called his father "Daddy." He couldn't ignore the stab of jealousy he felt when he did the math: Eddie had raised her from about age seven. He was more her father than his.

He tried to get on the girl's good side. "Looks like we might be family of sorts. Hope to make your proper acquaintance one day."

"Hoo-wee." Aurora affected a cartoonish twang. "Y'all country up in here, ain't ya now?"

Why was she making fun of his accent? His father was Okie, born and bred. She ought to be used to it.

"May I speak with Eddie, please?" Carter chose his words carefully.

"He's out of town. Seattle, I guess. Maybe Austin; can't remember. Should be back Saturday."

Carter checked the Departures board for the date and counted two forward. "April eighth; got it."

"Yee-haw. Can't wait to tell Mom we've got a hillbilly half-brother." Clearly, she didn't know the difference between a half-brother and a step-sibling. Carter figured she probably couldn't tell a crawdad from a Cadillac either.

"May I, uh, does he have a number where I can reach him directly?"

"Yeah right. Do you know how many *randos* ask for his private cell? He'd kill me if I told one more person. If he wants you to have it, he'll give it to you himself."

Carter had been telling himself the same thing about the Martin for six years.

♪♪♪

WANDERING aimlessly through the airport would sure enough draw the wrong kind of attention. The last thing Carter needed was some security officer to notice him, so he found a bench in Arrivals and pretended to wait for someone to pick him up. For a while he watched cars and trucks pull up to the sidewalk. Suitcases wheeling past him were loaded into trunks. The hugs were the hardest.

A flickering clock over the baggage claim carousel caught his eye. Back in Oklahoma his mother was about to go into surgery. Unconscious, going under the knife. Alone.

Reaching into his backpack, he pulled out his notebook and wrote a quick letter to his mother, confessing everything he'd done. The stolen money, the night he'd spent in the pawn shop, and the truth that he was fixing to get to Eddie's house in Santa Monica whether he was wanted there or not. He had to make that unlucky guitar lucky again, and the only way to do that was to sell it for as much money as they could get. He wanted to do right by her.

Carter looked away from the page, away from his fool feelings, and tried to get a grip on reality. He was as invisible to the world as the words Kaia had written in the air as her dad's SUV pulled away. Carter ripped the page from his notebook and crushed it into a ball between his palms.

He needed his father's help. It was bad enough they'd lost the house they'd lived in together as a family. But he was fifteen, soon enough a man. It was high time he and his dad had a few words.

Carter found another pay phone and dialed. When Aunt Sylvia's voice mail came on, he almost hung up. At the last second, he blurted out, "Hi, Aunt Syl; it's me, Carter. I, uh, can't get a flight for a few days. I'm staying with our neighbors, the Lius," he said in one rushed breath. "In Albuquerque?" he added, his voice rounding up at the end like a question. Awkward. "I'll call you when I get a flight out." He didn't like lying. "So, thanks. Bye."

Hanging around Arrivals wasn't doing him any good. There wasn't much to see this side of the security gates, so Carter slipped through the automatic doors to the sidewalk. The stars seemed sharp points puncturing a thin-skinned sky. He put his jacket on and walked, leaving the airport behind.

In less than ten minutes, he found himself on the corner of Sunport and Yale by the Shoretown Inn, a chain hotel with an airport commuter van parked out front. The deep fabric sofas in the lobby looked mighty cozy. He remembered staying at a

Shoretown once that offered free hot chocolate and a snack buffet in the breakfast room.

It was late, past midnight. Carter was fairly certain his friends, Landon, Caleb, and Kaia—he reckoned he could count her among his friends—were warm between soft, clean sheets somewhere, fast asleep. Carter was tired by the weight of a day that'd held both its hours and the miles between him and his hometown. He'd played his father's guitar again, to an audience no less. That was heavy, too.

Sure enough, the Shoretown had a breakfast room. The place was deserted and the only sustenance was a tray of cookies and a bowl of apples and bananas. Carter descended on it, gorging himself. Before long, he had company.

Chapter Thirteen

A GROUP OF FOUR GUYS PILED INTO THE ROOM, loud and wide awake. Three of them carried guitar cases. Carter stopped chewing and listened in on their conversation. He overheard them discussing their gig that evening at the Piñon Music and Art Festival.

"Where y'all from?" Carter tried to be polite, sitting up in his chair in hopes of looking older.

The one wearing a ripped black tee with a psychedelic bottle rocket graphic on the front shoved a whole cookie in his mouth. His words muffled by chocolate, he said, "We *all* are from Boulder," poking fun at Carter's *y'all*.

Carter reckoned he could spot a rock band's front man in any crowd, be it a coffee bar or a criminal lineup. He ought to write his independent research project on it, he thought. The guy buzzed with energy and an easy swagger.

Carter pulled his own guitar into view, brushing his hair from his eyes. "What kinda music you play?" he asked, careful not to say *y'all* again. He hoped not everyone west of Oklahoma was as harsh as Camellia's kid.

"Experimental hardcore," the one with two-toned hair—dark roots and faintly lime-green tips—piped up. "Maybe *y'all* heard of us?" he said, not willing to let Carter live it down just yet. "We're Poly Virus. We get a lot of play on indie radio."

Carter listened to tons of college radio back in Tulsa and he tried to recall the name. "Yeah, sure," he nodded, a twinge of excitement lighting him up. He knew these guys. "I really like the direction of your new album, especially that one song, Candle something." Carter knew well enough to compliment a musician's latest recording. No artist wanted their best work to be behind them, like Carter's was. In truth, Carter thought Poly Virus kept getting better.

"'Shotgun Candle,'" the one without a guitar corrected him. Must be the drummer. His forearms were tattooed with two halves of the same scene. Carter wondered if the image blended into one when he played. "Cookies aren't gonna cut it," he said to the others, pulling his cell from his pocket. "I'm starving. Let's order pizza."

As the drummer put in a call, Carter felt drawn in by the energy that connects one musician to another, the invisible tie between performers when they play the same song but on different instruments. Like he had with Kaia in the SUV. "I'll tell you the truth, I can't reckon what 'Shotgun Candle' is all about," Carter began. He was also curious to find out what they meant by experimental hardcore.

"Garrett," the drummer yawned, "you wrote it." The guy Carter pegged as the front man grabbed a chair and pulled it over to Carter's table. "That's just it, bro. It's a hidden message, a cry for help. 'Shotgun Candle' is like when you're trapped, held against your will, and you fire out some sort of SOS—a candle, a light in the window—that only the one person who can rescue you understands."

Carter leaned forward, taking it all in. He liked it. The letters Kaia asked him to write were a kind of shotgun candle. "How's it go again?"

Garrett pulled out his guitar and strummed the intro. He paused to sweep back the choppy locks dripping over his forehead and introduce the band, as if the opening bars had triggered his showmanship. "I'm Garrett, and this is Dex on bass," he nodded to the lime-tinted tips, "Austin on drums, and Nate, electric guitar." Nate stood silent, stoic as the mammoth beard on his face. It didn't take much to talk the other guys into joining him. Around the small table, they played an informal, acoustic version.

"How'd you do that transition, from the bridge?" Carter asked, watching each chord as it was strummed, their hands flying up and down the necks of their guitars. Garrett showed Carter how to play the sequence of chord changes on his dad's guitar. "Bro, pull up," Garrett told Carter. "You're holding it too far from your body." Carter nodded, pretending to hug the Martin to him the way Garrett held his electric guitar. Holding it against him felt too close, too personal. The strings under his fingertips were good enough.

Poly Virus's sound was modern and energetic, like the whole world was within reach and they only had to open their arms to grab onto it. He about had the melody down when the pizzas arrived. Without missing a beat, the band invited him to grab a slice.

He was more thankful than they could reckon. "Mighty kind of y'all."

Smirks and chuckles dominoed around the table, but he paid no mind. He was a Southern boy and *y'all* came natural. Truth be told, the whole episode reminded him of when Kaia had read that Blanche DuBois passage from *A Streetcar Named Desire* in English class. She'd put on an exaggerated drawl when she recited the famous line, "I have always depended on the kindness of strangers."

The Lius had been kind, and now Poly Virus was seeing him through the night, much as Tommy'd done back at the pawn shop. Tommy wasn't exactly Mr. Nice Guy, but he'd been kind enough when it counted most.

The kindness of strangers: that's how he'd get to LA.

Around three in the morning, the pizza was gone, the cookies long gone. Before calling it a night, Garrett grabbed a Poly Virus tour T-shirt from a gym bag and tossed it to Carter as a souvenir. Carter gave them a bushel of thanks, pulling it over his head. When they disappeared into the elevator, he slipped out and curled up on a chaise longue in a shadowy corner next to the deserted hotel swimming pool, where he hoped he wouldn't be caught by security. A song rattled around in his head, a melody somehow familiar to him, but he didn't know where he'd heard it.

At sunrise, Carter sat up on his lounge and looked out over the Sandia Mountains. The early morning light crept across the mountain range's long greenish ridges, the zigzagging pattern of a watermelon rind. Painted clouds feathered across the sky, the same colors as the sandhill plums, Indian blanket, and butterfly milkweed growing wild in his old backyard.

Was his mom awake yet? He tried to picture her, righted by the doctor's careful hand. *They're bringing breakfast to her room,* he comforted himself. *They're saying everything is going to be just fine.*

Holding his notebook open in his lap, it was like the written conversation with Kaia in the backseat of her parents' SUV had never ended. Carter didn't even mind using her sparkly pen. He breathed its scent deeply. It smelled good.

He told her all about Poly Virus and the chord changes he'd learned and how cool it was to learn a new song. He wrote a few lines about the mountains, asking if she could see them from her grandparents' place. *If you can, I hope you might get up before daybreak one morning and watch the sunrise sometime.* He asked her to tell him what she saw, so he wouldn't have to get all poetic or whatever. Carter turned the page and, at a loss for what else to tell her, made a rough line drawing of the Martin guitar. As he tried to recreate the pickguard, he debated whether to add the inscription. He left it off.

At a little convenience shop next to the inn lobby, Carter used the twenty bucks Mr. Liu had given him to score a travel toothbrush, a box of envelopes, and some stamps, like it was the 1880s and he was writing home from his Frisco job, laying the St. Louis–San Francisco railway between Tulsa and Texas. He stood in line at the checkout, waiting behind a gray-haired man with deep ridges in the loose skin at the back of his neck, who bought a car charger for his cell phone. Just before mailing his letter to Kaia, he unfolded it one last time and sketched the serif letters of his father's inscription: *Creativity, Victory, Heart, and Discipline.*

Chapter Fourteen

THE SMELL OF FRESH EGGS AND TOAST LURED Carter back to the breakfast room. He helped himself to the buffet and sat down at a table next to the window overlooking the parking lot. He read license plates while he ate. Most of the vehicles were local, but some were from Texas or Arizona. A family, sunburned and loaded down with shopping bags and luggage, approached a station wagon with Kansas plates. He spotted a cube van from Colorado. He figured it must have brought Poly Virus to town. He didn't expect the band would be awake anytime soon.

After breakfast, Carter left the hotel and looked up the road, considering his next move. He was fresh out of bright ideas.

Next to the curb sat a work truck with Arizona plates. Much like his mother's, it had tool boxes welded into the bed and was battered in several places. Route 66 ran straight through Arizona and ended in LA. If this pickup was headed to Arizona, maybe he could stow away in the truck bed. He'd get that much closer to his dad's house. Carter figured if he showed up on his father's doorstep he wouldn't—no, he couldn't—turn him away.

"What in blazes do you think you're doing?" A guy, maybe twenty-five or so, hollered at him. Carter turned to find the man standing so close he could count the freckles on his ruddy cheeks, whiskers and all.

"Nothing. Sorry," Carter said, backing away, his grip tight around his guitar case's handle.

"Step off, little man. Ain't nothing here to look at." The man adjusted his ball cap, his work boots and jeans marked with stains of a good day's work.

"Where you headed?" Carter dared to ask, nodding toward the keys the man pulled from his jeans pocket.

"Back home to Tucson. Just finished a job, repairs on a—" he paused long enough to pull out a cigarette and light it, "—ain't none of your business."

Carter set his guitar at his feet, and took a long look at the man. He was none too neighborly, but it was hard for Carter to dislike him. His toughness matched his work boots, and the Southern flavor of his griping made Carter feel he'd fit right in with Lola May's off-screen work crew on *Farmhouse Fancy.* "I'm Carter Danforth," he offered at last. "I didn't catch your name?"

"Bartles." The man steadied the cigarette between his lips. "Darren Bartles."

"What if I told you I happen to be looking for a ride into Tucson, Mr. Bartles?" Carter fought the urge to clear his throat, a nervous tic he'd sooner be rid of. He didn't expect the man to offer him a lift. This was just a practice run until he could put a plan together.

"It's a mighty long drive, six hours or thereabouts," Darren Bartles said, squinting in the early morning sunlight. "Tell you what, I'll trade you. A ride for that there guitar."

"Afraid I can't do it," Carter said, shaking his head. "She's a family heirloom." He'd heard this line plenty of times when his mother made offers on antique furniture at flea markets. It was the seller's way of asking for more money. But for Carter, the guitar wasn't for sale. Not that morning, anyway.

"I'm making you a deal, boy. I'm offering you an air-conditioned ride to Tucson. For all I know, whatever you got in that case is a broken-down piece of junk," Darren replied.

"Sorry, sir." Carter's shoulders dropped. He turned to go.

Maybe back to the parking lot to see if anyone had California plates.

"C'mon now, don't hang your head like a beaten pup," the man called after him. "I don't want to spend the next six hours talking to myself. I ran out of conversation halfway to Albuquerque and I ain't got nothing new to tell myself on the way back." He laughed at his own joke.

Carter gave the man a broad smile. At this rate, he figured he might be able to get all the way to Santa Monica in a matter of a day or two.

They climbed into Darren's pickup. The truck roared to life, then settled into a pattering rattle. The Lius' SUV had been comfortable, but to Carter, Darren's old work truck was the closest he'd felt to home since the storms. It reminded him of his mom's. Dinged and scarred from dashboard to floorboard, each mark could likely tell its own tale of woe. As it pulled away from the curb into the lemony sting of the New Mexico sun, Carter had an itch to write another letter to Kaia. He'd hitched his first ride from the first person he'd asked. *Crazy*, she'd call him. But he was doing it, by the kindness of strangers.

"Are you a carpenter or something, Mr. Bartles?" Carter asked, poking his thumb in the direction of the tool boxes.

"Yup, and some electrical. You could call me a Renaissance man, a jack-of-all-trades." The man sure liked his own jokes. "And you can also call me Darren. Ain't nobody called me Mr. Bartles in a dog's age. Don't you start."

Carter nodded. "My mom has a carpentry business. Restoration and refinishing, mostly."

"And where might she be? Ain't often I come across a boy your age looking to travel state-to-state."

"Tucson." Carter looked away. Darren seemed decent enough, but if he knew Carter intended to make it as far as the coast, he might try to call the authorities. "I was just in Albu-querque visiting a friend at her grandma's."

"Uh-huh" was the man's only reply. Carter wasn't sure if he wasn't listening or just not interested. "And nobody thought a spell about how you'd get back to Arizona, once you were done with your little visit?" If Carter could convince the man to get him as far as Tucson, he'd be only a stone's throw from Califor-nia. He needed to keep his cool. Darren might even let him bor-row his cell phone to check in at the hospital along the way.

"My car broke down," Carter was quick to reply. At fifteen he looked old enough to drive, didn't he? "The transmission's been giving me trouble since last summer." Carter shifted on the broken vinyl seat, wondering if Darren was buying his story. If he hoped for the kindness of strangers, his mother would prob-ably say he had to give what he hoped to get. And nobody took kindly to liars. Carter coughed, his throat dry. He should've thought to pack a water bottle from the hotel.

"Maybe I could help?" Darren turned his gaze from the road to size Carter up. "What say we turn around and go back? This old pickum-up taught me plenty about transmission trouble." He spanked the broad dashboard of his truck lovingly. "Ain't ya, girl?"

Carter's eyes grew wide. They hadn't traveled more than a dozen blocks from the hotel, but heading back would dump him at square one, and with some explaining to do. Darren had the a/c cranked on high, but Carter felt uncomfortably hot in the truck's cab.

"Uh, my mom called a tow truck?" Carter said, wincing. Carter couldn't imagine his mother paying anyone to do work she could handle herself, but Darren didn't know that.

But Carter's story satisfied Darren well enough. He drove on without comment, veering left to merge onto the I-25 headed south toward Las Cruces.

Las Cruces?

"Hey, you took the south exit," Carter pointed out to Darren, but the man said nothing. He just kept his hand on the wheel, directing the rattling truck away from Interstate 40—and away from Arizona.

"What are we doing on Interstate 25?" Carter asked, loud enough to expect an answer.

Darren lifted the ball cap off his head and wiped his sweaty forehead with the back of his arm. Carter stared at his russet hair, so dense and plush he reckoned he'd skinned it off a red fox. Carter didn't like the image of Darren Bartles with a skinning knife. "I thought we were staying on Route 66. I mean the 40—"

He had to get out of there. Kaia was right, hitching rides was crazy. Carter pulled the lock open on his door and tried to imagine what it might be like to leap out of a truck going eighty miles an hour on the freeway. It worked in the movies. But real life was a different matter. Carter remembered what had happened to the guitars when they'd crashed to the floor back at Tommy's. Even if he somehow managed to make it, where would he run? There was nothing but dry, rural land, and uninhabited foothills beyond, on both sides. Fire warnings marked the roads, and his parched throat caused him worry there wouldn't be water for miles.

"Take the 40 to Tucson?" he repeated without looking Carter's way. "I said I'd give you a ride, not a scenic tour." Darren locked all the doors with a click of the automatic controls in his armrest. "A boy who lives—and, as you said, drives—around those parts ought to know as much." Carter pulled his guitar case into his lap, hugging it to him in a white-knuckled clasp. He was trapped.

Chapter Fifteen

CARTER KEPT HIS HEAD STRAIGHT LIKE HE WAS watching the road, but tried his best to study the man from the corner of his eye. He'd need to be able to identify Darren Bartles to the police, if it came to that. There had to be a way to stop him. He needed to get out of that truck. He considered taking a swing at Darren, but wondered whether slugging a grown man in control of the steering wheel while they were flying down the interstate would be so great for his health.

"A little ways down the road is a town called Truth or Consequences. I ain't kidding." Darren took out another cigarette and lit it. The cab of the truck was hot and stifling in the desert air and the cigarette smoke stunk. "They got a bunch of natural hot springs there." Darren had a habit of checking the mirrors, his head bobbing between the rearview and the side mirrors like what was behind them mattered as much as the road ahead.

Darren glanced over at Carter, taking him in from head to toe. "Don't suppose you thought to pack some swim trunks?" Sweating like a sinner in church, Carter swallowed hard. Darren laughed at his discomfort. He pulled his guitar across his lap, covering himself. "Hey, if you ain't into hot springs, we could always take a dip in Elephant 'Butt.' Nice and quiet there. Lots of privacy."

Carter reckoned the guy was just trying to rattle him. But they passed an actual state-erected sign reading "Elephant Butte Lake State Park." Darren was serious.

"Far as I can make of it," Darren said, "when it came time for naming places around here, a bunch of 'em met over a hooch still in a barn." Saying that must have jogged his memory because Darren motioned to Carter. "I hid some bourbon there under your seat. Take a swig and pass it over, little man."

Carter figured now was a legitimate time to panic. His gut clenched along with the tightness in his chest, his body a mess of knotted rope, but he remembered what his father had told him about stage fright: "The second terror hits you, leave your body. In your mind, float up to the ceiling and direct your body like a marionette, a separate being from your soul. Make it do what the audience came to see."

Carter put on an act, sitting back casually in his seat. He pretended he was enjoying Darren's humor, in on the joke. He opened the bottle of bourbon and sniffed it. The scent nearly burned his gullet double-wide. Pausing with the bottle near his lips, he pretended to savor a sip, then handed it over as they approached the off ramp to the lake. As they neared the lake exit, he tried to distract Darren, pointing out the windshield to bright green patches in the far distance. "Is that a golf course?" Carter asked, holding his breath while Darren took a long swallow from the bottle. "Crazy how they can make grass grow in the middle of the desert, huh?"

Sure enough, Darren missed the Elephant Butte Lake turnoff. He cursed every form of profanity Carter had ever heard, then tacked on a few new ones. "We missed the turn? Now we're never gonna shake 'em. It's a straight shot to Cruces, no place to hide."

"Shake what, Mr. Bartles?"

"I told you, don't *Mr. Bartles* me, little man." Darren glanced nervously at the rearview mirror. "Listen, I may have helped myself to a couple of tools at my last job site. Far as I can figure, they're making plenty of money and can afford to replace them." Bartles turned the brim of his ball cap to the back of his head, then brought it round front again. "But it seems they ain't got nothing better to do than come after me. Over a handful of tools; don't that beat all? The lake would've made a decent hideout, but you've gone and ruined that plan."

Darren drank himself uneasy, swerving over the white line dividing the traffic as he polished off the bottle. Occasionally, Carter grabbed the steering wheel to straighten it.

"We got another hour to Las Cruces," Darren slurred, "and I can't get tagged with another DUI. My work depends on my having a truck and all."

"*DUI?*" Carter asked, trying to place Las Cruces on the map in his mind. And where was Tucson in relation to it?

"Driving under the influence, stupid." Darren held the near-empty bottle up to indicate exactly what influence he was under, then pulled to a stop on the shoulder. "It's your turn to drive, little man," he said, his eyes narrowing to slits. "You told me you had your license. You ain't been lying?"

A chill ran up Carter's body, like a shallow dive into a frigid lake. He might know a thing or two about engine repair, but the closest he'd come to driving was a few motorcycle lessons out front of his house. His mouth clamped shut. He could feel bulges stand out around his jaw where he gritted his teeth. Carter kept his eyes on the man, not daring to breathe or even blink. Darren opened the driver's side door and hopped out, instructing him to slide behind the steering wheel.

Carter imagined himself peeling away, shooting back up the I-25 as fast as the truck could carry him. He tried to make sense of his feet, toeing around for the foot pedals. He put one foot on the accelerator and the other on the brake. It wasn't rocket science. But Carter just couldn't be sure.

Darren got himself into the passenger seat and punched Carter in the arm. "South, little man. I'll tell you when to stop."

Carter looked at the controls again. Tentatively, he moved the lever out of Park, the way he would on a motorcycle. The truck began to inch forward over the loose gravel lining the shoulder of the road. He squeezed the steering wheel in both hands and pressed all the way down on the right pedal, holding it to the floor. The truck jerked forward, squealing, dust flying all around. He slammed the other pedal quick and hard. The truck pulled to a fast halt. Darren nearly hit the dashboard with his forehead.

"Take it easy, will you?" Darren swore at Carter. "You got one job, stupid. Drive, straight forward. Any fool can do that."

Carter tried again, this time slow and easy. The truck picked up speed as he lowered his foot. He trailed an 18-wheeler in front of them, glints of sunlight ricocheting off the stainless-steel doors on its back end.

Darren tipped his hat brim lower to shield his eyes and rambled on, shooting the breeze about what he called "the greed of building contractors." Carter kept his eyes on the road, choking the steering wheel in his fists. He couldn't chat and drive at the same time.

Concentrating on holding the front wheel tight alongside the interstate's white line, sweat broke out around his collar. Carter didn't know who was chasing them, so every car, truck, van, and camper gaining from behind posed a threat. Many of the passing drivers startled him with a honk or an un-neighborly hand gesture, because Carter couldn't seem to keep the accelerator to the speed limit. Driving was harder than it looked.

Chapter Sixteen

AN HOUR LATER, THE TRUCK RUMBLED INTO
Las Cruces. Carter's T-shirt was sweat-soaked. Both the bourbon and the gas tank had run dry. Carter spotted a fuel station
and tried to pull off, but Darren wouldn't hear tell of it. He had a
particular station in mind, one with a tavern next door. Carter
swore he couldn't bear another mile in that truck.

The pickup sputtered and resisted. Carter slowed up, hoping
it wouldn't peter out on the side of the interstate. The only thing
worse than being chased by heaven-knows-who would be getting marooned in nowhere land with Darren Bartles for a companion.

Sure enough, up ahead he spotted The Little Yucca Tavern,
adjacent to a gas station. The Little Yucca had a tall wooden false
front, its name in Old West–style lettering. The dull, sun-
bleached paint, chipped and missing in several places, gave the
building a century-old feel. Neon lights flashed the names of
various brands of hard liquor in every window. It wasn't much,
but it was better than running for the hills and ending up dying
of thirst or bit by a rattler. Carter pushed away the worry there'd
be a whole mess of Darren Bartles types wasting the day in
there. More than ever, he was counting on the kindness of
strangers. He planned to make a break for it when Darren
stepped out to refuel the truck.

Carter managed to jockey the pickup next to a gas pump. He
cut the engine and pulled the keys. The truck's rattle fell silent,
but not the buzzing in his ears.

"You wait here." Darren stepped out, holding a cordless drill like a pistol. "Don't move or you'll get it."

Darren stumbled around the truck and opened the gas tank cover, but he was too muddled to coordinate the drill, the gas cap, the pump, and the nozzle. The drill fell to the concrete and Carter gulped a deep breath. *Now or never.* Grabbing his guitar and his backpack, he swung the door open and slid out in one fluid motion, sprinting for the tavern. He was halfway across the parking lot before it occurred to him it might be closed for business.

But Carter didn't stop or slow; he ran for all he was worth, pitching Darren's keys into a tangle of devil cholla cactus edging the gas station's parking lot. Darren left the gas hose propped in his truck and took after him, cussing a blue streak. When Carter was almost to the tavern's entrance, he clasped his guitar against his chest and slammed his body into the door. It was on saloon hinges and gave easily. Carter tumbled in, falling onto his side. The guitar case broke free of his grip when his shoulder hit the floor and skated across the broad wood floorboards into an iron footrail wrapping the length of the bar. Darren fell on top of him before he could make any sense of the place. "You ain't going nowhere, little man."

Carter tried to push the drunk man off his chest, but he was too powerful. The barkeep, an older gentleman who'd likely seen his share of fights, picked Darren up by his shirt. The gray-blond hairs on the barkeep's rugged arm glinted in a band of light streaming from the window. His fist reared back, then executed an effortless punch to Darren's gut. A knee thrust to Darren's ribs followed quickly, then an elbow jab to the drunk's nose. The barkeep caught Darren before he dropped to the floor and tossed him out of the tavern. If Carter had had second thoughts about taking a swing at Darren, he sure didn't want to get in scrape with that barkeep.

Sprawled on the hard-packed dirt outside, Darren spat and moaned, clutching his side where the barkeep's knee had been none too gentle. Carter kept his eyes glued to him, scared as a kitten in a dog pound that Darren would come barreling back into the tavern. The barkeep's cowboy boots stood right next to Carter, nearly as tall as his shoulder. He didn't dare make any sudden moves. Before Darren could catch his breath, a pickup truck with a home-builder's logo pulled up next to him and two burly guys hopped out.

The barkeep's hand thrust toward him and Carter ducked. "You all right, son?" The man motioned to take hold of his hand, and helped Carter rise to his feet.

Outside the tavern, Darren Bartles cursed up a storm. Carter nodded, said, "Yes, sir," and dusted himself off.

"Care to tell me what that was all about?" he asked.

"Thanks for—" He didn't want to talk about where he'd come from, or why. Carter figured a little truth was better than none. "I was hitching a ride to Tucson." He gestured to the parking lot, where Darren was unlocking the toolboxes in his truck bed while the two men collected their contents. "But my driver was more interested in the bottle than the road."

Pushing his hair from his eyes, Carter squinted in the dim light from the bare bulbs hanging in Mason jars from the rafters, his gaze sweeping every booth and table in the tavern. There wasn't a soul in the place. He could swear he heard music, but he felt so dizzy he couldn't tell where it was coming from.

"What's that sound?" Carter asked, confused.

"History," grunted the barkeep. He'd already resumed polishing glasses behind the bar and pointed with a towel to an old man strumming a guitar on a dusty, unlit stage in the corner. Carter relaxed a bit, having some distance between them.

The sound was raw. It had a bit of an aura about it, like the static you hear between a vinyl record and the record player's needle. The song was some kind of old-time rock 'n roll, maybe Roy Orbison or Bobby Darin; Carter couldn't place it. But the old man played the song like it hurt him, and the only balm to soothe the pain was to play it through.

A highway patrol car wheeled past the window, lights flashing. Carter edged behind a wood post decorated with old six-shooters mounted on wood plaques where he wouldn't be spotted. He held his breath, wondering whether Darren would point them in his direction. One thing was sure: He couldn't make any sense of what he was doing all by his lonesome in a bar in New Mexico. He hoped the police didn't come asking. He didn't even want to think about what his mother would do if he got hauled back from New Mexico in a police car.

As he watched the construction guys introduce Darren to the cops, Carter could feel the barkeep's eyes on him. He filled a tall glass with ice and Coke and placed it on the bar. "A cold drink fixes most things."

Carter wanted that drink, and about ten more after it.

Chapter Seventeen

THE OLD MAN ON THE STAGE JUTTED HIS JAW in Darren's direction. "We've seen him before," he said with a voice made of velvet and gravel. "He's about as useful as an ashtray on a motorcycle." Carter's thoughts flitted to the useless Yamaha V Star among the ruins of his home.

Placing his guitar on a stand, the old gent picked up a hand-whittled cane leaning at the edge of the stage. He teetered down the stage's short staircase and made his way over to the bar, slow and steady, like there was an expiration date on those old legs of his and it was drawing near. A life-size carved wood black bear wearing a bolo tie overshadowed the left side of the stage. A rusted 1930s truck bumper arched over a deserted drum kit. On the walls of the tavern hung out-of-date license plates and more than a dozen mounted sets of black-tipped steer horns. Carter's guitar was still under the bar, but the tavern was otherwise empty.

When the old man got himself on a stool, the bartender slid a glass of lemonade toward him without a word.

"Let's see what you've got in that guitar case, boy." When Carter remained still as a cactus, he added, "My name's Ledbetter. This is Mitch Keller, best bartender in the Southwest. We ain't going to bite."

Carter gave the two men a polite nod, but he'd had enough of making new acquaintances. They seemed nice enough, but so was Darren when he first met him. Hitch-hiking was plain stupid. Here he was, stuck in who knows where, and all he could think about was whether his mama weathered her surgery. There wasn't a thing he could do to help her. Carter needed to get out of there, and fast.

But if he hoped to get his hands on his guitar, this was as good an opportunity as any. Even if Darren Bartles and the cops weren't right outside, what was Carter going to do? If he busted out of The Little Yucca in a blaze of glory, he'd find himself penniless under the perpetual New Mexican sun, a few states right of his intended destination. He thanked Mitch the barkeep for the drink, then picked up his guitar case.

Carter set the case carefully on the long wood bar top, nicked, notched, and scarred in more places than smooth. He clicked open the latches and pulled out his father's guitar. The subtle scent of it calmed him. With the strap over his shoulder and his hand wrapped around the cutaway, the instrument gave him a sense of conviction, like its unlucky streak might be waning. If he was put on this earth to find his purpose, in truth he hoped his father's guitar could point him in the right direction.

"A left-handed Martin," the man called Ledbetter said, letting out a whistle of appreciation. "Now here's a man who knows what he needs to summon his own sound."

Was it? He played left-handed because that's the way his father taught him. It was a gimmick, a novelty to wow the crowd. Guess it worked.

"Just in time for auditions, too," Ledbetter added.

Above the bar hung a carved-wood sign, about a foot long, reading, "Musicians Wanted."

"How much do gigs pay, sir?" Carter asked. Maybe his luck was turning. "Judging by the size of this crowd, it's safe to say they're going to love me."

Mitch didn't crack a smile. "Won't be an empty seat in the house tonight," he grunted, "and none of 'em are interested in your jokes. Pass the audition, I'll pay you fifty dollars to open for my headliners."

Carter drained his Coke and stared up at the empty stage, wiping his mouth with the back of his hand. He couldn't be certain whether this was another kindness-of-strangers moment or if they were just messing with him.

"What you waiting for, son?" Ledbetter gestured to the empty stool on the stage with his lemonade. "Stage is yours. Let's hear what you got."

As Carter drew closer to the stage, he got a decent look at Ledbetter's guitar, a vintage Pimentel. It had a red and green motif on the rosette, the decorative ring encircling the sound hole, and it boasted the scars of a life on stage, a life Carter had hoped to know.

He was no stranger to auditions. Carter wasn't his daddy's boy anymore, either. If they ever locked horns about anything, it was because Eddie always had to have his way, and Carter was expected to shut his mouth and do what he was told. But Eddie wasn't shaking hands and making the deal that day. Carter could do things the way he saw fit.

Mitch's deal would be perfect. If Carter played three or four shows, he'd probably earn enough money to buy a bus ticket straight to his dad's.

"You got a better gig this evening?" Mitch asked from across the bar. Impatience was good, Carter recalled from his early training. A hungry audience appreciates a good performance.

Eddie said he knew the formula for becoming famous, and all Carter had to do was follow his direction. What Eddie didn't have time nor patience for was feeling the music. Getting inside it, making it your own. That was the part Carter liked best.

He took a seat on the stool, hooking his running shoe over the post connecting the legs. He gripped his guitar's neck in his fist and stroked the strings along the frets, warming them. "Just need a minute, sir."

Carter looked down at his fingers. A thatch of hair fell in his eyes. He brushed it away, considering his first move. He figured these guys would rather hear some country music or rock 'n roll. But he couldn't risk trying to pull off anything Ledbetter might play. He wouldn't do it justice.

"Let's hope the cat lets go of his tongue once it's out of the bag," Ledbetter chuckled to Mitch.

Carter closed his eyes and pinched the strings tight against the fretboard in a C chord. His eyes shot open and he checked himself. Garrett from Poly Virus had noticed how he was holding the Martin wrong, too far from his body. Carter corrected himself and strummed the chord again.

"Just because a kid has a guitar doesn't make him a musician," his father told him, "but technical skill will only get you so far." Carter's dad valued showmanship over everything. "It's how a musician plays that matters," he'd said. The ghost of Eddie's voice was in his ear, coaching him to beguile the audience, and not worry about whether he was any good or not.

This was his first audition, and he figured he wouldn't get two chances. Carter closed his eyes again, silencing his father, and strummed a D minor followed by an E minor, dragging the vibration as long as he could, calling out to Kaia across the lonely desert, back up Interstate 25 to Albuquerque. He let the vibration of his chords tap on her grandparents' front door. He imagined Kaia's smile, the feel of her warm palm pressed into his hand as they pulled into the airport the day before.

He played the sounds of what he pictured in his mind, trying to form her shape, like drawing in the dark sky with a lit sparkler on the Fourth of July. It felt good. There were songs inside him, he reckoned, in the form of memories. He didn't bother with showing off. He didn't even open his eyes. Carter Danforth was making his own music.

Ideas for chord changes came fast and furious. He could see the finger patterns in his mind, what was required of him to bring around the sounds in his imagination to the ears of the two men across the room. It was exhilarating and his heart raced. Soon his strumming hand fluttered over the strings like a hummingbird.

But his wrist felt stiff and tight. The notes jumbled together, falling to the floorboards below his feet. He opened his eyes and looked up, searching the dusty bands of afternoon sunlight for the faces of the two men.

Mitch was restocking a bar fridge with bottles of beer, his back to the stage. Ledbetter's seat was vacant. Carter glanced around the empty bar, looking for him. The door to the men's room opened and Ledbetter ambled back to his seat, cane in hand.

"I could use some help in the kitchen," Ledbetter suggested to Mitch.

"That's between you and the rock star," Mitch replied without turning around.

"Son," Ledbetter leaned on his cane and squinted at Carter, "you know your way around a deep fryer?"

Carter sighed and stepped down from the stage. The guitar wasn't his and was never going to be. The sooner he could get it signed and sold, the better. He needed to get back to his mother. If he could earn a few bucks feeding a hungry bar that night, he wouldn't complain. Carter needed money, and time to figure out his next move. He glanced sidelong out the window. About a hundred feet across the parking lot, Darren was being handcuffed by a highway patrol officer and tucked into the back of a cruiser. "I suppose I could learn."

Chapter Eighteen

CARTER RETURNED THE GUITAR TO ITS CASE AND followed the old man through swinging doors to a kitchen behind the bar. If a musician as talented as Ledbetter worked as a cook in this dive, just what kind of chops did it take to impress Mitch Keller?

While he was washing up over a deep stainless-steel sink, Mr. Ledbetter threw a folded apron at him. It landed on Carter's shoulder, and he put it on. The afternoon was spent hauling sacks of flour and frozen french fries, mindless chores that strained the old man's back. As he worked, Ledbetter got to talking.

"Poor technique," he said, one wrinkled hand palming the worn curve of the head of his cane. Carter lifted a questioning eyebrow, not sure what he'd done wrong. "Poor technique is the birthplace of some of music's most magnetic and relevant performances." Ledbetter gestured for Carter to pull a bag of onions from storage. "I'm going to show you how to make onion rings with mesquite flour. If you listen proper, I'll teach you how to break that nervous wrist of yours loose."

Carter worked hard and listened closely. The stellar lineup of musicians that evening surprised him. One after the other, sunburned farmers and tattooed biker guys plucked strings and pounded drums with masterful skill. Music didn't ask where you came from, Carter thought, but it made neighbors out of strangers.

Dropping onion rings in hot oil ought to have given him time to drum up an alibi to tell the barkeep and Ledbetter. Kindness of strangers was fleeting. It wouldn't be long before they'd want to know who he was and why he wasn't in school. Carter was thankful for the chance to make some money at the tavern, but he also needed a place to sleep that night. He was hard-pressed to make up a believable story; the music pouring from the tavern was too distracting.

Mitch Keller didn't take kindly to Carter hanging out by the stage. "Son, if you aren't twenty-one, you'd best make yourself scarce." Carter might have been tall enough to pass for sixteen, but could he pull off twenty-one? He wasn't fooling anybody.

Mitch saw to it that Carter made his way back to the kitchen. The boy could still watch the bands from behind the swinging doors, and keep up with the food orders as well. Mitch seemed almost satisfied, but something made him hesitate. He looked back across the busy tavern. The evening bar staff could hold down the fort another minute.

"Even prisoners ask for one phone call," he said, fishing his cell phone out of his pocket and offering it to Carter. "There must be someone you need to get in touch with."

Relief and gratitude washed across Carter's face. "Thank you, sir," he said, taking the phone. Mitch's sleek smartphone appeared downright futuristic in the old tavern. The barkeep nodded, satisfied for the time being, and went back to the bar.

Immediately, Carter began dialing his mom's cell number, then froze. He remembered her phone was destroyed, but worse, it reminded him of the night in Tommy's pawn shop, dialing her number over and over, hour after hour, without any response. And what was he going to tell her anyway, that he was working in a bar in New Mexico?

He didn't want to confess what he'd done. None of it. But he needed to know if she was all right. Carter stared at the phone's glowing screen for several minutes, planning what to say to his mother and how he might dodge her questions about why he was in Las Cruces instead of at Aunt Sylvia's. He came up with all of nothing.

Carter figured he'd better put the phone to good use before Mitch asked for it back. He dialed Felicitas Hospital in Tulsa and asked for Sandra Bermejo.

They wouldn't put him through; she was sleeping. But the nurse on call recognized his voice. "She's resting comfortably, bless her heart. On bed rest another few days while we watch for swelling. Your mother is the strongest woman I ever met, Carter. Too stubborn to let a little weather step in her way."

Carter smiled into the phone and thanked the nurse. He was about to hang up when he glanced over to Mitch and caught his eye. He was watching him. "What happens when she's released?" Carter blurted into the phone. "Where will she go?"

"We aren't ready to say our good-byes just yet. She's got a spell of recovery ahead of her. Another ten or fifteen days, likely."

Carter didn't know how he'd get in touch with her next, but he was sure glad she was on the mend. "Tell her I'm all right, will you, ma'am?"

"Sure thing, honey."

Backing into the kitchen, Carter slipped from Mitch's view. He wasn't sure when he'd get his hands on a phone again. It was as good a time as any to cement his decision to see his father.

His aunt picked up his call right away and went straight to wailing about him not showing up when Sandra said he would.

"Aunt Syl, I didn't mean you any trouble," he said, trying to calm her down. "Eddie—my dad—he wants me to stay with him.

Says we got a lot of catching up to do." If Sylvia talked to his mom when she came to, Carter hoped she might actually believe that.

♪♪♪

BY closing time, Carter was beat. Mitch stood in the kitchen's doorway, jangling a ring of keys. "You need a ride home?"

It was confession time; there was no way around it. Over the last plate of onion rings, Carter admitted he was broke. But he didn't want to give up, and he didn't want to go home, not until he gave seeing his father his best shot. Carter was rattled by the music he'd heard that night. Not one of those talented musicians on The Little Yucca's stage was itching for fame, but they played their darn hearts out.

Clearly, Eddie had been right about showmanship, at least when it came to securing gigs. Without it, he'd failed his audition. Carter decided to try his hand at his father's tuned and oiled bull-crap machine and prove that hitchhiking to California wasn't a mistake. Carter needed to sell the two men on his bright idea; he was worried they might call the police. Or worse, send him back to Tulsa.

"I think my father's guitar is trying to tell me something," Carter said, solemn as a TV preacher. "I need to get back to the man who marked it with Creativity, Victory, Heart, and Discipline." Ledbetter seemed to like that a lot. When a kid brings to mind the mystical, folks nod like he's got more than his years.

He couldn't figure whether Mitch Keller was a good guy or bad, but the hour was growing late, so he gambled on Mitch's kindness. "Mr. Keller, sir? Would it be all right if I spent the night in The Little Yucca?" Carter gestured to a bank of padded benches along one wall. "I'd be sure to have Mr. Ledbetter's onions chopped for y'all in the morning."

Mitch didn't like the idea. "Any kid who falls into my bar within inches of getting his face dented by a drunk," he said, "shouldn't be left to his own devices."

Ledbetter had a ramshackle trailer permanently parked out back. He offered the boy the use of his settee for the night. "I'll keep an eye." He nodded at Mitch, tapping his cane handle tip gently against the brow over his right eye.

Ledbetter's trailer sat on cinder blocks, the wheels hovering motionless over hard, red earth. Carter could tell it had had a custom paint job; maybe it was once green, but the New Mexican sun had broiled it to a near-white gray. Ledbetter grabbed a handle bar next to the door and hoisted himself in, beckoning Carter to follow. It was dark and stuffy. A stale, musty odor hung in the air. The windows were shut tight and blinded by dust, but Carter could make out a small sink and counter and a mini fridge. There were boxes of records and old magazines under a tiny kitchen table and rows of books that looked older than the dirt baking under the trailer's wheels.

Carter's body ached for sleep. He had no clue what a settee was, but when Ledbetter showed him, it turned out to be a small, lumpy love seat, roughly a thousand years old. He wished he could've slept by himself in the tavern. When Ledbetter turned in for the night, Carter kept a light on and pretended to browse a bookshelf, afraid of sharing the darkness with the old man.

Once alone, Carter grabbed his notebook and Kaia's sparkle pen. *Today is April 7*, he wrote, followed by everything she'd need to know to send the cops, starting with his exact location, in case anything went wrong. It was ridiculous, he thought. He had to tell her this info that instant or it was useless. He tore out the page and clicked shut her pen, staring at the blank page after it. How long would it take a letter to get to her grandparents' house? He needed a phone. Why hadn't he called her when he had the chance? Then the worst occurred to him: He hadn't deleted the numbers he'd called from Mitch's cell. So much for privacy.

On the other side of a curtain dividing the bedroom from the living area, Mr. Ledbetter was making snoring noises. Sleep wasn't going to find him anytime soon, so he opened the pen again. Carter wrote about the bands he'd heard that night, and the cash Mitch had paid him under the table—fifty bucks for six hours of kitchen labor. He couldn't help but brag how he'd driven Darren Bartles's truck, all by himself. In the middle of a car chase on the interstate.

On a third page, he tried to capture the sounds Ledbetter could pluck from his old Pimentel guitar. Words weren't enough, so he sketched a drawing of the old man and his old guitar on the dusty old stool in the old tavern.

He stared at his pages for a long time, wondering whether it was worth it. What did he have to gain from holding back? The whole truth and nothing but the truth, that's what he'd want from Kaia. So that's what he ought to give her, right? He began a fresh sheet, describing his audition. How he'd pictured her, and how he drew her image with sound. And how Mitch turned his back on him. He found himself promising her he'd practice, become good enough to make an entire roomful of people hear her with their own ears.

Chapter Nineteen

WHEN CARTER WASN'T SWEEPING UP OR prepping the kitchen for the nightly crowd, Ledbetter made him practice on the Martin. Carter could hardly contain his irritation. He just wanted to make enough money to get to California. Once he convinced his dad to sign the cursed instrument to increase its value, he could go back to Tommy's and sell it, and get on with his life. He was worried sick about his mama, and besides Carter didn't need any practice. He wasn't a musician and he'd never be one. It was pointless. And it hurt, too. Having old Ledbetter nag him about rehearsal rekindled the happiest days of his childhood. Those days were far behind him, and every strum of his fingers was a reminder that it'd been a long time since he could honestly say he was happy. The only reason Ledbetter thought he cared about playing his daddy's old guitar was because it was part of his bull-crap story from his first night at The Little Yucca, so Carter had to keep up the act.

"Your elbow ain't playing the instrument, son," Ledbetter scolded him. Carter wondered if the old man was off his rocker. "When you play a single string, the motion comes from your fingers. With a chord, the strum is born of the wrist." Ledbetter demonstrated. "Either way, the elbow is motionless."

Carter nodded. "Right, the motion doesn't happen at the elbow," he repeated, plucking a few strings to get a feel. It was just like when he was a kid and his dad expected him to do as he was told.

"Easy now, son. The pick needn't travel more than a quarter inch for a single note."

Lots of rock guitarists made big windmill motions. He saw it all the time in music videos. If there was one thing his father had drilled into him, it was that showmanship trumped subtlety. An audience expected a show, and the performer was paid to deliver. Any technical weakness could be buried under either style, or conviction. The problem was, performing with conviction meant diving into the music and reawakening all the feelings he was trying every day to hold down. Carter tried to appease him by playing several notes slowly but found himself picking up speed to show he was getting it.

Ledbetter sat back in the wooden chair he'd pulled up to the stage and pinched the wrinkling skin between his eyes. "No one likes to hear this, but you got to slow down, boy. Fast comes when you're ready, but you're far from ready. Keep a pace you can control. Don't rush."

Carter tried to follow Ledbetter's instructions, but his hand wouldn't listen. The second he gained "control," he strummed faster.

"No, son. Take your time. Practice. Over and over, until it's perfect. When it's perfect, then you can jump the pace."

Carter wanted to get it right the first time. The man's notions of technique were older than his Pimentel and twice as sentimental. Like a vintage roadster, Carter reckoned Ledbetter was among the last of his breed. Stylish back in his day and fierce when the engine revved, but too old to win the race.

Worse, Ledbetter had a habit of making faces. He often stopped for long pauses, punctuating his sentences with a deep grimace. At first, it seemed the polite thing was to look away. The wrinkles and ridges on Ledbetter's face seemed to move on their own, telling secrets too painful to put into words. Or maybe he was trying to clear gunk from his teeth or fighting some intestinal trouble. What did Carter know from old people? The only family he had was Mama.

"Modern music harkens back to the earliest days of rock 'n roll," Ledbetter said, squinting into the distant past, "when legends like Chuck Berry and Bo Diddley established its roots and carved its shape. You'll get your style by studying the masters."

Carter didn't tell him the left-handed guitar was supposed to pay tribute to Jimi Hendrix, an incontestable master. The truth was that style didn't matter to him. For Carter, music was about expression, a way to say something about yourself. Carter figured he'd take what he could from Ledbetter's teaching, but only until he made enough money to get a bus ticket out West.

After the lesson, Ledbetter shuffled out to his mobile home for a midday nap. Carter put the letter he'd written to Kaia in an envelope and worked up the nerve to approach Mitch. When the old barkeep saw he was desperate enough to put pen to paper, maybe he'd let him borrow his cell phone again.

Something was biting at Carter, but it wasn't panic or even fear. What troubled him most was causing his mom worry. If she caught wind of his getaway, she'd pitch a duck fit with a tail on it. He knew he needed to explain himself, and a letter wasn't going to cut it. He needed to talk with his mom.

"I reckon writing letters is kind of lame," Carter said, sliding Kaia's sparkle pen into his pocket to hide it. "It's why they invented telephones, so no one would have to spill their sorrows in permanent ink. Any chance you might lend me your phone?" Aside from the gas station next door, there weren't many signs of human life around The Little Yucca. He hoped Mitch would tell him there wasn't one lonesome mailbox this side of Route 66. He didn't want to tell him about his mother's condition because Mitch would say what he already knew: that he ought to be in Tulsa taking care of her. But Carter knew the best thing he could do to help his mom was sell the guitar for the highest price.

"Son, whatever you've written, I'm willing to bet you meant every word," Mitch said, standing a full four inches taller than him, his arms crossed over his massive chest.

"Nah, not so much." What he'd written the night before seemed too personal now, and he didn't know what Kaia would think if she saw it. "But I do need to let my friend know where I am. Safety first." He tried half a smile, but the hard line of Mitch's brow stopped him.

"I gave you that opportunity last night. Don't suppose you squandered it?"

"No, sir. I called my mom, first thing. My aunt, second."

"Good. You minded the important business." Mitch held out his hand, and Carter gave him the letter. Mitch held it at arm's length and considered the address, then handed it back. Carter's gaze wandered to Mitch's cell phone, sitting on the counter next to the cash register. "I'm no axman," Mitch continued, "but far as I can tell, writing letters is good for building finger dexterity. There's a mailbox a quarter-mile south, outside the drugstore." Mitch picked up his phone and slid it into his pocket, then turned and headed toward the storage room, like the conversation was over.

He was going to get that phone, one way or another. Finger dexterity, he'd said. If Carter could show him he was writing letters and putting in practice on his guitar, he'd have to let him use it.

Carter set out down the road a piece, keeping an eye out for a drugstore.

Chapter Twenty

THAT NIGHT, CARTER FOUND OUT LEDBETTER was more than a fry cook, he was a local legend. He watched Ledbetter butter up the crowd with his mellow, Latin-influenced songs. His facial expressions were an integral part of his music, casting a spell over the crowd. A coolness softened the heat of his sound, smooth as fresh-whipped cream melting on hot apple pie. Halfway through his set, he swapped his acoustic for more insistent, hard-edged rhythms on an electric guitar. Carter and The Yucca's waterholing regulars nearly brought the house down with cheers. For Ledbetter, rock 'n roll wasn't a hobby. It was a way of life.

Exhausted from feeding the late-night crew and hanging on every chord change from Mr. Ledbetter's skillful hand, Carter crashed out on the settee, another fifty dollars closer to scoring a bus ticket out West. Maybe he'd pay a little more attention to the old man at his next lesson. It wouldn't hurt to perfect a song or two to play for his father. He didn't have much else to offer.

After breakfast the next morning, Ledbetter taught Carter licks and techniques from rockabilly, blues, old-time rock 'n roll, and western swing, playing T-Bone Walker, Buddy Holly, and Janis Joplin albums on a record player sitting on a shelf in the kitchen. Carter decided to make the most of it by choosing one to learn for when he came face to face with Eddie. "Listen close for patterns, boy. You hear how chords tend to move in fourths? Nail that, and soon you'll be playing any song that hits you right." Any song? Seemed unlikely, he thought.

Carter couldn't believe he'd never noticed those patterns before. Alternating between songs on Ledbetter's old records and dialing in stations on an AM/FM radio, Carter listened. There they were, loud and clear. His ears were opened. The tough part was wrangling his hands to play what he could see in his mind. He pulled the Martin closer to him, focusing on replicating the music's exact structure.

He looked over at Ledbetter with a grin, but he'd nodded off to sleep in his chair. Carter spent the afternoon studying selected songs from Ledbetter's collection, and painstakingly imitating each and every note, mimicking the artists' timing. It was powerful, always knowing which pattern came next. He was in control for once in his life. With some real practice, he'd sound as good as any musician. He could accomplish what his father always wanted from him: flawless execution of rock's biggest hits. Maybe there was a chance he'd make it as a performer after all. Maybe he had a future worth working toward.

Ledbetter's callused fingertips stilled Carter's hands on the strings, surprising him. The man had been dead asleep.

"You got to connect what's happening here," Ledbetter tapped his lined brow with his cane handle, "with what's going on here." The old man thumped the top of his cane into his heart, the way a soldier might've loaded gun powder into an old Civil War cannon.

"But I'm finally getting somewhere," Carter argued. "That was 'flawless execution,' like Janis Joplin was right here in the Yucca with us," he said, using one of his father's favorite phrases. "You're the one who told me to learn from the masters."

"And I stand by word. But you gotta give it your own signature and style." Ledbetter leaned toward Carter on his cane.

"Listen, it used to be that painters trained by making replicas, copying their famous teachers, Michelango, Matisse, Picasso, Rembrandt—all the greats. But does history remember the fakers? No." Ledbetter pulled a stool next to him and sat down. "You got two choices, boy: you can follow or you can fight."

Shaking out his fingers like a wet dog, Carter wondered whether fighting had ever done right by him. All his life, he'd ignored what people told him and tried to do things his way. It brought to mind the "Hour of Freedom" song he'd written on his hand that day he got up the nerve to buy his daddy's pawned guitar. He wasn't supposed to have that guitar, and look at the mess of problems it'd brought him. If there was one thing Carter had never done, it was what he was told. Maybe if he'd just listened to his father in the first place, his life would be completely different.

"I'm near enough a man," Carter said. "If it comes down to following or fighting, I choose to follow."

Ledbetter's graying head tipped forward, but he nodded like he could see Carter's point. Arranging his fingers on the strings, Carter tried again. Ledbetter placed his hand on the boy's shoulder and waited for him to look him in the eye. "You're wrestling with a pig in the mud and the pig likes it," Ledbetter said, when Carter finally met his gaze. "When you're ready to make peace with yourself, with who you are, we can continue."

Carter didn't want Ledbetter to go, but if he kept doing things his way, all he'd end up with is more mistakes and bad decisions. He knew he'd best be moving west soon. Ledbetter rose off the stool and headed out to his trailer. Before he made it as far as the kitchen, Carter spoke up. "I need to find out how much a bus ticket to LA costs," he said, sliding the guitar strap off his shoulder. "I've earned a hundred dollars. That's plenty for a ticket, right?"

"Sure, I suppose," Ledbetter replied, folding back the cuffs of his button-down shirt. "I spent a good while traveling this country in tour buses back in my day," he said, contemplating an invisible map of the American Southwest in the air in front of him. "Las Cruces to LA is a decent trip. If you like rock formations."

♪♪♪

MITCH couldn't argue about lending his phone to call the bus station. It meant getting the boy off his hands. Turned out, a bus ticket to Los Angeles cost little more than one evening's work in the kitchen. Carter reckoned he'd soon see his father. Even better, it meant he had a head start on paying his mom back for the guitar. The trouble was, the bus company had all sorts of limitations when a traveler's seen less than seventeen years. The operator told him he needed an adult vouching for him at the start and finish. Even if he had a grown-up he could count on at either end, unaccompanied minors were limited to trips eight hours or less, nonstop, between sun up and sun down. From New Mexico, it was impossible. Carter's simple plan to get out of The Little Yucca was melting like a popsicle in a hot spell. He couldn't be stuck. There had to be some other way.

Carter quickly researched airplane ticket prices, and learned they cost way more. He'd only earned a portion of the money he'd need. Even when he made enough, there was also the problem of how he'd get back to Albuquerque Sunport, the closest airport. Carter had no choice but to collect more kitchen pay, hatch a plan for getting back to the airport, and stay out of Mitch's way in the process.

Panicked, he sat and stared at the dusty stage for a long while. Long enough to realize he wanted another crack at it.

Chapter Twenty-One

CARTER HAD NO CHOICE BUT TO STAY PUT AT The Little Yucca until he earned enough money to buy a plane ticket, but he sure wasn't going to squander his time. Mr. Ledbetter was inarguably the best musician he'd ever met. He wasn't a bad teacher, either. They may not have seen eye to eye, but Carter reckoned the old man had opened his ears. More than that, Ledbetter had given him hope. Carter's plan to get his father to sign the guitar to help his mother was good. But if there was a chance he could make a living as a musician, have the future his daddy had groomed him for, he was certain it would be a much bigger help to her.

It was nearly time to turn in for the night. Carter found Mr. Ledbetter in the kitchen in his saggy bathrobe, stooped at the counter over his collection of vitamins and supplements. Only an hour before he'd rocked The Little Yucca with energy and authority. The tavern nearly shook with the power of his rhythms. "It seems you become a whole new person when you're on stage," Carter said, trying to show his respect, "like the music takes over."

"Might say I'm reborn," Ledbetter replied, with half a smile. "Music has a way of suspending time. And it ain't tightfisted when it comes to handing out second chances."

A second chance, that's exactly what Carter wanted.

♪♪♪

THE next morning, Ledbetter set Carter on a stage stool for the day's lesson. He had a theory about the spotlight becoming a performer's shrink, a safe place to unload demons. Carter couldn't make sense of it. By the way he played his Pimentel, Ledbetter sounded like an angel.

"You know why my Pimentel guitar sounds so good?" Carter watched him hobble back to a table, coordinating a tall glass of ice-cold lemonade and his cane with an efficient swagger. "Because it's family-built. A guitar that runs in the family holds a special sound," Ledbetter added, sliding into a chair.

Carter swallowed hard. "My dad had this Martin custom-made," he said, running his fingertips along the stained inscription that read, Creativity, Victory, Heart, and Discipline.

Ledbetter nodded. "Family, that's a bond ain't nothing going to break."

Carter tightened his jaw and shook his head. His own family was sure broken.

"Mitch has a daughter out in Tucson he visits most Sundays," Ledbetter continued. "She's a full-grown woman now, owns her own joint just like The Yucca. But Mitch still looks out for her, 'cause she'll always be his baby girl. That's family for you."

If Mr. Ledbetter was trying to make him feel better, it wasn't working. Eddie Danforth had left him when he was a little kid. He'd plucked the guitar out of his dreams and pawned it. With or without music, Carter still needed his father to look out for him, but where was he? On the other side of the country, playing Daddy to someone else's kids. Probably already cut an album with them. Now he and his mama needed Eddie's help more than ever. If there were only two choices, following or fighting, he couldn't tell which would serve him best. If he followed what was expected of him, he'd be in Reno with his Aunt Syl, and not on his way to getting his father to sign the Martin.

Against all logic, music breathed life into old Ledbetter's singular sound. If Carter followed exactly how the masters played, copying them note for note, would he experience the miracle of rebirth every time he played?

♪♪♪

To pass the time during Ledbetter's afternoon naps, Carter wandered the sun-bleached ridges around The Little Yucca, spotting the fossilized footprints of various reptiles and insects. Heading southwest, he scrambled over boulders to discover long, wavy lines where rocks and rubble formed a dry creek bed. If this was what his mom grew up around, it didn't seem so bad.

Carter wished he had word whether Mama was okay. He thought about her all the time but always found an excuse not to call. One moment, Mitch would be in too foul a mood to risk asking to borrow his phone. Another moment, he'd picture her reaction if she had any clue of his whereabouts. She'd be in quick need of a heart attack doctor, and she already had more than enough medical bills. But the longer he went without calling, the worse he felt. In truth, playing the Martin made him realize how sad he'd been all those years without it. He wondered how many of the troubles he caused were from not knowing he was just sad.

Carter sat for hours in the shade of a boulder, practicing his guitar and writing to Kaia Liu, often two letters in a single day. There were too many squabbles in his head, duking it out. Should he play the music he felt bubbling up inside him, or, knowing the most important audition of his life would be with his father, keep practicing 'flawless execution'? Scratching his pen across the page, he let it all out: everything he felt about his dad, everything he'd learned on his guitar, everything he hoped might change, and everything he hoped might stay the same. She couldn't reply to a single word of it, so he wrote without second-guessing what he knew to be true, real, and necessary.

At the drugstore, there was a pay phone out back with a handwritten "Out of Order" sign covering the coin slot. The scotch tape holding the sign had clung there so long it'd turned brown as dirt. Carter mailed his letters and stocked up on envelopes and stamps, and treated himself to chocolate bars and issues of *Guitar Player* and *Guitar World* magazine. He still needed another three hundred bucks to buy a plane ticket, but it felt good to have a bit of cash in his pocket.

♪♪♪

AFTER a week in Las Cruces, Carter relaxed into the deep cushions on Ledbetter's settee, writing Kaia to beg her not to tell anyone where he was, hoping it wasn't too late. *My mom would freak*, he wrote. *Best thing for her right now is peace and quiet. Give her a chance to get back to her old self. It wouldn't do her any good to be worrying about me.*

It was already the fourteenth of April. It was just past closing time, when Mitch finished locking up and filled the entrance to the kitchen with his imposing frame. "Don't you think it's time you called home, son?"

Carter dug his hands into his jeans pockets and waved his hair out of his eyes with a swish of his head. He tried to act casual about the worry he carried day in and day out. He wanted to talk to his mama like his life depended on it, but he was scared she may not be feeling better and it was easier to imagine her healing up fine. He was scared of what she was going to say about him skipping out on Aunt Syl's, and he was scared of what he had coming to him for running away. If he could just explain, he'd tell her he didn't run away. He was running to. "I've been busy, sir. Working hard in the kitchen, practicing lots, and writing letters, too."

Mitch reached into his pocket and fished out his phone. He held it out and waited, leveling his cold blue gaze on the boy.

Carter took the phone from him, imagining the heap of trouble he was going to be in for not calling sooner. "Thank you. I won't be long."

"Give her my regards." Mitch went back into the bar to finish calculating the evening's receipts.

Mr. Ledbetter had already turned in for the night, so Carter found some privacy in the storeroom. He dialed the hospital, hoping for something he might consider good news. The attending nurse put him through to his mother's room, and Carter held his breath, surprised by how excited he was to hear her voice.

Chapter Twenty-Two

LOLA MAY LEGGITT BOOMED THROUGH THE phone. "Cotton, how you been, darling?" She said everything like there was a studio audience watching and half of 'em were hard of hearing, the other half deaf. What was she doing at the hospital?

"I'm just fine, Lola. May I speak with Mama?"

"I'm sorry, sweet pea," Lola said. "Sandy's down in rehab. They have her doing exercises to get her strength back. Doctor says your mama's going to be right as rain and discharged the day after tomorrow." This was the best news Carter could hope for. "She's been eager to hear from y'all. How are you and your Aunt Sylvia getting on?"

Carter stared at the phone in his hand. His mama didn't know he was missing. He could spin a tale; it would be easy to lie to Lola May.

It was lucky Mama didn't know he'd ditched Aunt Syl, but she was going to learn the truth some time. Carter wagered the news might sound better coming from her best friend. In one breath, he let off the ten-gallon load on his shoulders. Carter stuck with the high points.

"I'm not at Aunt Syl's, Lola May. But I'm safe and snug in Las Cruces, New Mexico. I'm even earning wages working in a restaurant kitchen, just down a ways from the Lius." It didn't make much sense to call it a *tavern* or a *bar*; she might get the wrong impression. "And when I earn enough"—and get the nerve up—"I'm going to knock on my daddy's front door in Santa Monica and ask him to help us out."

Lola May nearly broke the phone in two trying to holler some sense into the boy. "Cotton, you had better be telling a tall tale. Are you kidding me? Las Cruces? How in the name of—" Lola fell silent, without completing her sentence. Lola and silence, those two just didn't mix.

Carter dropped his forehead into his hand, and tried to talk to her like a reasonable adult. "I bought my dad's old Martin guitar out of hock. I know it sounds crazy but I've gone back to playing music, Lola. And I'm not half bad, either." Once he admitted he had the guitar, he needed to make some kind of sense of it for her. Lola wasn't around much back when his dad was still in the picture, she didn't know Carter could play. "I'd all but forgotten what it felt like, making six lonely strings work together to create something from nothing. Making music on my dad's old guitar's got me thinking he might just help us, if we ask." The news of his disappearance would be enough to send his mother into a fit of worry, and he didn't know what she'd do when she found out he was playing his father's guitar again. Ain't no way he'd have had the nerve to tell her all that in person. It was bad enough over the phone. "How is Mama doing, Lola? I can't tell you how happy I am that she's back on her feet." Carter wished he'd thought to send his mom a letter.

"Hold your horses, Cotton," Lola said. "Now you listen to me. Your mama is going to be worried sick when she hears about the stunt you've pulled. I'm coming to get you, you hear? Give me your address."

Carter froze. He should have known better than to hope Lola May would soften the blow for his mom. There she was again, acting like she was kin or something. He didn't want her thinking he needed her help, not when he hadn't even reached out to his father yet, not properly. What he wanted was to talk with his mom. He needed to hear from her directly that she was all right. He needed to explain himself. Buying the guitar and going to see his father was his responsibility. Maybe she'd understand.

"Cotton, can you hear me," Lola May asked again when he didn't reply.

He wasn't going to give her The Little Yucca's address, no way. Carter reckoned Lola could turn two flies circling a cow patty into a melodrama. He tucked behind a stack of bar napkin boxes and whispered hard and loud. "Lola, I need to speak with Mama. When she gets back to the room, have her call me, please."

"I'm not going to tell her a word about this. You can do that when you see her, because I'm bringing you home. Now are you going to give me your whereabouts?"

He ignored her question. "Where will she go when they discharge her? Our house is nothing but scrap and rubble."

"I told her I'd put her up in a hotel. But she insists on going to the shelter." Carter shook his head. Just like Mama, he thought. She had to do everything her way and never ask for help. "Doesn't want to owe me, she said," Lola May continued. "I can't convince her there's nothing I wouldn't do for her. But you know what they say about Sandy, cain't never could change her mind. So," Lola May sighed and fussed like what she was about to say was none too pretty, "I'm going with her."

He pointed out the obvious: "You'd just as well stay home with Wayne."

"Wayne ain't home for me, Cotton." The way she said it, the word *home*, stung Carter's ear like an off-key note. He knew shacking up with a bunch of strangers in a high school gymnasium was the last thing Lola May wanted, and yet she aimed to do it. She was putting his mama before herself, and even though he couldn't make her understand right then, that's exactly what Carter was trying to do by going out west to find his father. "Lola May, I'm sorry. I—"

"Tell me where you are, Cotton," she said.

He leaned against the cool storage-room wall in silent refusal and waited for Lola May to give him what for. He couldn't go back. What would going back do? He couldn't fix anything. He messed up too badly, but he aimed to set things right. A minute ticked by. Then another.

At last, Lola May spoke. "Cotton, did I ever tell you how I got into home renovation?" Carter frowned into the phone. She had a fondness for telling parables starring herself. Now wasn't the time. "Growing up in Little Rock, I was the middle child in a house with seven kids. Near invisible, you might say. My daddy did what he could to support us, but most people didn't expect much from him, and frankly, he delivered exactly that." Lola May's voice sounded like a bruised peach, soft, dark, and fuzzy. Why was she telling him a story when she was mad enough to have him skinned? "When I was just about your age, our congregation was called to turn the pastor's dank, dirty old basement into a meeting place for Bible study. Someone put a power tool in my hands and before I knew it, I'd helped transform it into something beautiful."

Carter swallowed hard and shut his eyes. He never thought about what people might have expected of Lola May when she was growing up. Probably not a career in carpentry. Carter whispered to her in the dim storeroom. "That's how playing guitar feels." He couldn't be entirely honest with her, but he owed it to her to admit, "It's like you said, *transformation*. But of me, you know?"

"Sandy's done a fine job raising you up. She just wants you to be safe."

"You always been good to me, Lola May." Carter couldn't believe he was saying it, but it was true. "And I don't reckon I ever said thanks." He told her he'd ask Mr. and Mrs. Liu to bring him back to Tulsa so she wouldn't have to leave his mother's side.

"Y'all need anything, just holler at me," she said.

Carter knew it was time he spoke with his father. Maybe his daddy would come to him, if he asked.

Chapter Twenty-Three

THE NEXT MORNING, LEDBETTER SHUFFLED sleepy-eyed into the kitchen. Carter was already at the kitchen table with the Martin, Kaia's sparkly pen, and his notebook. He strummed a few chords, then picked up the pen to transcribe the notes into his notebook. Lola May expected him back in Tulsa, but he couldn't go, not until he spoke with his father. It would be hard enough to ask him for the favor of signing the guitar. Carter wanted more than the man's signature. He wanted to see if he still cared. And he wanted to prove that Eddie Danforth should not have given up on his son so easily all those years ago, and the only way to do that was to perform for him. Carter couldn't reach out to his dad until he was ready to rock.

He woke early that morning short on time but not on inspiration. He reckoned he could build a bridge between fighting and following by perfectly executing his very own song. Step one was getting the melody down on paper. Ledbetter leaned against the counter and considered the boy strumming and writing, writing and strumming, for a long while. On the stove, Carter had a pot of fresh eggs simmering in salted water.

"What in the—? Son, you ain't left-handed."

"Nope. But Jimi Hendrix was," Carter said. He ran his fingertip over the stained letters of the word *Discipline.* "My dad used to say if I hope to impress an audience like Jimi did, I'd have to practice twice as hard."

Ledbetter began rummaging through three drawers full of

guitar strings, mumbling to himself. When he found what he was looking for, Ledbetter sat down at the table and fished a pair of eyeglasses from the chest pocket of his Western-style shirt. "Trust me, boy." He held out his hands for the Martin.

Carter handed over his beloved instrument. Truth was, he did trust old Ledbetter. A new set of strings would add to the instrument's value, too.

Ledbetter flipped the left-handed Martin over and set to restringing it.

Carter watched Ledbetter's wrinkled knuckles move across the strings as masterfully as they did when he played. For a moment, he felt comforted knowing the Martin was in experienced hands. His comfort quickly disappeared. As Ledbetter loosened the tension on the first tuning peg, the string made a startled, offended-sounding twang. Then the first low E string moved in where the sixth high E string had just called home. "That's not how it was strung. What are you doing?"

"Restringing it for a righty like yourself, of course," Ledbetter said without looking up, bumping the string's bridge pin out and inserting a new, unfamiliar string.

Carter couldn't sit still. He hopped out of his chair and paced the floor. "But then it'll be just like any old guitar," he said. "What you're doing, it ain't natural. Stop." Before Carter could get to him, Ledbetter had another peg loose. Another sad twang filled the kitchen. He was already halfway to ruining Carter's most valuable possession.

"I said stop it." Carter regretted raising his voice to Ledbetter. He didn't want to fight the old man.

Ledbetter set the guitar down, removed his eyeglasses, and raised a solitary eyebrow at the boy.

Carter was breathing hard, like a fight had already started. "You're wrecking the thing that makes it special."

"You think the order of strings is what makes a guitar special?" Ledbetter had a deep, throaty laugh. He might have been a smoker when folks were still allowed indoors with a cancer stick. This was no laughing matter. "Son, you don't owe me any thanks for putting them back where they're supposed to be," Ledbetter began, "because I don't care to restore this instrument to what it once was. The past is past. I'm fixing the strings to fit you."

Over Carter's shoulder, the pot of eggs over-boiled, spilling hot water across the stovetop. A cloud of steam filled the kitchen. Carter scrambled to fix the mess, keeping one eye on Ledbetter's hands as he resumed his work. Carter had enough to contend with; if he was going to play for his father, he needed all the frontman tricks that went into a memorable show because his daddy always said performing was ten percent sweat, ninety percent style. At six foot, he had no notions of climbing back in his daddy's lap for a music lesson. But he wanted the man's respect.

Carter drained the eggs in the sink and poured cold water over them. He didn't know what to make of Ledbetter changing the guitar to fit him. Hadn't he made it clear he planned to sell it anyway? He couldn't dare think of the Martin as his. It wasn't. He owed too much for it. The whole thing was just like Lola telling him she was coming to get him. Ledbetter was trying to do something Carter secretly wished his father would do and it made him lonesome for his dad and that didn't feel right. It would be a whole lot easier if he could just stay mad at his father and not care one way or another what he did.

Dragging himself back to the kitchen table, Carter sank into a chair, frowning as the next string loosened with its own pitiful twang. He swished his hair out of his eyes, but it fell back in the exact same place. He sat stone still, letting Ledbetter carry on to the finish, heat rising around his neck. Stopping Ledbetter now was as useless as having second thoughts halfway through a tattoo.

At last, Ledbetter rose from the table and offered the guitar back to him. "New strings need to stretch a little. No more than a day or two."

Carter sniffed and grabbed the guitar, bolting toward the kitchen's back door. He cursed himself for sticking around at The Yucca. When Lola May told him to get his butt back to Tulsa, he should have gone.

"You're welcome," Ledbetter said as the door slammed behind him.

♪♪♪

CARTER threw the guitar strap over his shoulder and stormed past Ledbetter's trailer into the desert. He didn't slow up or stop until he made it as far as his secret spot by the dry creek bed. He was too angry to cry and too freaked out to turn back and give old Ledbetter an earful. Situated under his shady boulder, Carter examined the new strings. They were heavier than the ones he was used to, and strung so tight they looked nervous. The guitar was his one hope for paying back his mother and rebuilding their life back home. But more important, Carter hoped he might make amends with his future in music. Mr. Ledbetter had no business altering the instrument.

He strummed out a chord, assessing the damage. The sound, clean and pure, caught his breath in his throat. He tried another chord, and then another, sliding his hand up the fret. He'd have sworn Ledbetter had given him a new set of ears. Launching into Poly Virus's "Shotgun Candle," his fingers found the melody, swift and easy. Something shining hot and bright burst in his chest, connecting his mind to his heart, igniting his fingertips and tickling his ears. He broke out singing. Maybe it was the full, clean sound, the gauge of the strings, or the straightforward ease of playing right-handed guitar with his right hand, but Carter realized he'd been working against himself, trying to play his father's way. Making do. It was like what Lola had said about transformation. Ledbetter had transformed the guitar into something that worked for him, and with him. The guitar fit him, just like Ledbetter said it would.

Carter rose up from under his rock and met the day's full sun. The instrument felt lighter in his hands, an extension of his body. He knew he wouldn't have it much longer, and it pained him to think that music would be another too-short moment in his life, but he wasn't going to waste a second of it. He strode back to The Little Yucca, strumming and singing loud enough for Ledbetter to swing open the kitchen's back door to have a listen.

"Now the hard work begins," Ledbetter called to him, ushering the boy into the tavern. Ledbetter said it was time he learned how to set up the mics, foldback speakers, amplifiers, and cables for the evening's entertainment. Carter didn't complain. He was choosing to fight for what he wanted.

Chapter Twenty-Four

CARTER OFFERED MITCH A FULL DAY'S PAY FOR the use of his phone. He was running out of time. Lola May and Mama would pitch twin fits if he wasn't home soon, but he had no way of getting back. He already knew he couldn't take the bus, and he hadn't figured out how to get himself back up the 40 to Albuquerque Sunport to catch a flight to Tulsa. Above all, he didn't want to admit to Mitch the fix he was in.

It was a steep price, but Carter wagered he couldn't turn him down. Mitch held out his hand with a grunt. He counted his hard-earned bills into the barkeep's oversize palm.

While Ledbetter rehearsed for his set in the bar, Carter found some privacy in the mobile home out back. He entered the phone number by heart. He'd practiced speeches for his father over the years, some anger-fueled, some wishing for understanding, some plain lonesome. But now he wasn't sure what he wanted to say. Carter quickly ended the call before it rang through.

He took a deep breath and tried dialing again. He didn't make it past the area code. What if one of his daughters answered again? Or worse, Camellia? Carter considered waiting until tomorrow.

He'd paid good money to use Mitch's phone. Call now or hitch a ride back to Albuquerque, he told himself. The last thing Carter wanted to do, ever, was hitchhike again.

Carter dialed the number and squeezed his eyes shut, pressing the phone too hard to his ear.

His dad answered on the second ring. "Hey, it's Eddie."

"Dad, Eddie? It's me, Carter." He sank into the settee, folding his long legs under him. "Sorry if I'm calling at a bad time." He wasn't sorry for calling, just nervous as a long-tailed cat in a room full of rocking chairs. "You mind if we have a word?"

"Who? What in the—?" Carter could hear muffled voices in the background. "Hang on, I'm just finishing up in the studio," his father said. "Trying to record a jingle for Ma Joad's restaurant chain, but it isn't going so great. The commercial's got everything but a heartbeat." Shuffling noises were punctuated by unintelligible whispers. His dad seemed irritated. Maybe it was a bad time. Would his father drop the call, block the call?

"You sound so grown up," Eddie said at last, confusion weighing his words.

Carter wondered how he expected him to sound. "I'm fifteen." Clearly, Carter had been the only one counting the days and nights they were apart.

"Has it only been six years?" his father said. "It feels like a lifetime."

"Sure does, sir," Carter replied, swallowing a hard lump in his throat. He pulled the phone from his ear and double-checked the number. The man on Mitch's cell didn't sound a lick like his father. Carter realized then that he'd lost his Tulsa accent. It seemed his dad had left everything behind.

"I've missed you," Eddie said.

Carter hung his head, shaking it in amazement. "Dad, I've missed you, too." He thought about all the make-believe conversations he'd had with his father over the years. Carter wanted to tell him everything he wished he'd been able to say, but figured he'd best get straight to the facts. "The hospital says Mama'll be back on her feet now that she's had her operation, and the insurance company is going to help us get another house."

"Operation? Insurance?" Eddie let out a long breath, like this information was out of nowhere and none too easy to swallow. Hadn't Camellia told him about Mama's call?

Whenever he hit a sour chord or lost his momentum, Mr. Ledbetter would tell him to back up a little and pick up a few bars from where he'd dropped off. Seemed like the right approach with his father.

"Remember the left-handed Martin?" Carter nearly kicked himself for bringing it up like that. He wanted to try and make peace with his father before admitting it wasn't a lefty anymore. "I'm doing guitar lessons again."

If his dad didn't know about the storm, maybe he wasn't 'too busy with work' to care for him after all. What Carter wouldn't give to hang out with his dad in his music studio. Carter kept going.

"Our house was totaled in the tornado outbreak a few weeks back. You didn't hear about it?" It was hard to stay on one topic. This wasn't how he'd pictured catching up with his dad. "Mama got hurt pretty bad in the storm. I don't know how we're going to manage her hospital bills, let alone get a new house." Carter couldn't figure how to stop everything from coming out at once. "Rock and blues mostly, the classics, you know? We never asked you for anything all these years but we sure could use your help now. And—"

Eddie spoke up. "You're still playing my old Martin?" He let out a low whistle. "I always imagined I'd hand that old girl down to you. Your mama let you keep her?"

Let him keep the Martin? He couldn't very well ask his mother's permission when the thing cost more than her savings. Carter was getting mad. "Why didn't you just leave it for me instead of pawning it?" Eddie had no idea what that one decision had cost him.

"I'd never pawn a beauty like that. The only pawn I ever handled was in a game of chess." Carter remembered his daddy used to play chess backstage between sets, but he couldn't be sure if Eddie was bluffing. His voice sounded so different, like Los Angeles got in his lungs and washed out the Oklahoma. "Pawn shops were Sandra's thing."

Carter's throat caught with a hot sting. He couldn't trust what he was hearing. "But you sold it," he managed to choke out.

"I made some dumb-fool choices," Eddie muttered, "but I would never sell that guitar." A silence fell between them. Carter hoped his father meant to say that leaving him had been a dumb-fool choice. It felt impossible to ask for his dad to see him, and sign it. He sure wasn't going to admit his plan for selling it when he got back home.

"Your mother told me to stop sending presents because you didn't need anything," his dad added, as if Carter hadn't wanted anything the man tried to give. "But I would've liked to hear from you. I'm glad you finally called."

"What presents? I never got any presents." It was just like his mother to say they didn't need anything, but she wouldn't hide gifts from him. *Would she?* "How come you never told your daughters about me?" Carter didn't want to pick a fight with his dad, but once he turned the ignition, his engine was revving.

"I couldn't. Your mama wouldn't let me have one weekend with you. I didn't want the girls missing something they'd never have."

Carter's heart pounded like a hailstorm. He wanted to believe him, but if he did, it made his mother a liar. "You didn't even try. Just left Tulsa and never looked back."

"I wanted to do the right thing," Eddie said, his words shot full with anger but damp and mushy. Must be what folks called anguish, Carter reckoned, listening for more than what his father had to say for himself. "She ripped my heart out, showed it to me, then baked it in a pie. But I knew if I fought Sandra in court, she'd get buried by lawyer fees and shackled by debt. I couldn't do that to her."

It didn't add up, not after all this time. But he sure wanted to believe his father had loved them. Carter took a deep breath, trying to keep all his feelings from running catawampus. He searched for something to say, but he was caught between longing to be closer to his father, and wishing he'd make right all the years they'd spent apart. Before Carter could open his mouth, his father said, "You're growing up a musician. Don't that beat all." His voice was recovering some of its old Okie flavor. "How about you play something for me?"

Carter brushed his hand through his hair. He'd been writing something new, practicing for just this moment. But wasn't his father going to ask about his mom? The house? And if he did, what then?

Music. It was the only thing that made any sense to Carter. The only thing he could stand behind with any certainty. "What do you want to hear?" He pulled his guitar strap over his shoulder, centering the Martin in front of him.

"Give me some music from back home." He liked that his father referred to Tulsa as home.

Ledbetter had drilled in him daily to face a challenge full-bore, but Carter didn't want to push his luck. He was only starting to catch hold of the music he'd discovered inside himself back at Shoretown Inn in Albuquerque. He decided to choose an old favorite of his mama's. She was big into country music, and even though his father used to tease her about her crooner crushes, Carter knew there were a few songs his dad also liked. He started playing "In Lonesome Dove," an old favorite by Tulsa-born Garth Brooks. "Music can transport a soul back to a place and time as though it were yesterday," Ledbetter had told him. "Memories," he said, "it's what we're made up of. All of 'em, good, bad, crazy, or copacetic." Carter didn't know what *copacetic* meant, but Ledbetter must've been right because he'd spent most of his life chasing after his memories.

The mechanics of the song were inborn. Sandra's old favorite was a landmark in their lives, grounding their family like a blessing before Sunday dinner. Carter played it through without using a guitar pick, the new strings already at home under his fingers.

"Son, you've got it," Eddie's voice came low and solemn. "I always knew you'd be a musician. You picked it up so easy and natural. Shoot, you're still my boy wonder."

Carter stared at his own hands, nearly as big as his daddy's had been when he taught him to play. There were calluses forming on his fingertips, just like his dad's. He'd have to give a proper thanks to Mr. Ledbetter for making him work so hard. "Thanks, Dad. But c'mon, you're on the pop charts and all." Carter could almost hear his father smiling through the phone. "I just want to play, you know?"

"No, I don't know," Eddie replied. "What do you mean, 'just play.' Are you a solo act or frontman to a band?" Carter knew Eddie didn't trust much in teamwork. As far as he was concerned you were number one, or you didn't count.

"I'm on my own," Carter said. For a moment those words made him feel plenty lonely. But then he remembered Ledbetter, and Mama, and even Lola May, and he knew he had people who believed in him.

"A solo act. That's my boy," Eddie said, recovering his good spirits. "Hey, you know what it takes to make it to the top?"

Carter's gaze fell on the instrument. He slid his rough fingertips across its smooth custom stain. "Yeah. It's right here on the Martin."

"Read it."

Carter didn't need to look at it to know the words: "Creativity, Victory, Heart, and Discipline."

"See? I had it custom-made when you were born. I hoped you'd fall in love with music as much as your old man."

Carter shook his head, not understanding. "Isn't it just your musical creed or something?" What did a few words of wisdom prove?

"Look at the first letters, CVHD."

Those were Carter's initials. Across the phone line, electrical signals from New Mexico to California bouncing to some outer space satellite and back to earth, they both spoke his name together: "Carter Vaughan Hendrix Danforth."

"I wanted your first name to be Vaughan-Hendrix. Hyphenated, you know? How cool would that be? But your mama didn't think it'd be fair, like you'd have to live up to Stevie Ray and Jimi, rock's greatest guitarists. Because what if you turned out to be a dentist or something?"

Carter broke out in a laugh, surprising himself. His dad was proud of him. And he was more than a little relieved his first name wasn't Vaughan-Hendrix-with-a-hyphen. He owed his mother a world of gratitude for that save.

"Hey, what do you say to coming out and helping me record this jingle for Ma Joad's pancake house? We can produce a father-son thing that'll crush the internet. The restaurant chain is all about family values. They'll eat it up."

Carter couldn't believe what he was hearing. He was ready to pack up his guitar and leave that night.

Eddie was quiet a moment, and then he added, "I know your mama won't accept any help from me. But I can get you compensated for performing on the jingle, and you can use the money to help her out, okay, son?"

"Dad, that would be amazing, thanks. I'd love to."

"Cool. I'll look into flights from Tulsa to LAX. We just gotta clear it with your mama," he said. A silence fell between them nearly a minute. Carter hadn't been honest with Eddie about where he was or how he got there. If he went home now, his mother would want him to move into the shelter with her. He was already in trouble for not going to Aunt Syl's. There was no way she would let him get on a plane to California, not when he still owed her money. He'd been dishonest, and as much as he wished he could fix all his mistakes, he wanted to see his father again more than ever. His mother didn't know Carter had found his way back to music and that for the first time in his life, he knew music was who he was.

"Listen," Eddie said, "maybe it's best you ask her?"

Carter wasn't sure he could. He'd used up the last of his nerve dialing his old man's number. "I'll see what I can do," was all he could offer.

Chapter Twenty-Five

CARTER COULDN'T SLEEP THAT NIGHT. HE'D given back Mitch's phone before he remembered he was supposed to ask Mr. and Mrs. Liu for a ride back to Tulsa. He wasn't even sure they were still in Albuquerque. He wasn't sure of much, and the worry of it kept his eyes from closing. Mama was moving into the high school gymnasium the next day. He needed to see for himself if she was all right, help her however he could. Good thing Lola May was there. But one image kept popping front and center in his mind: sitting next to his father in a recording studio. Sure, all they'd be playing was a little ditty about pancakes and sausage links. Truth was, he wouldn't care if they sang about two bullfrogs mating in a river bog. He just wanted to make music with his daddy again.

His mother wasn't going to like Eddie's plan, and she sure wasn't going to want Ma Joad's money. All Eddie cared about was "his personal gain," his mama used to say. Back when Carter was just a kid, his parents used to fight about it all the time. Sandra thought Eddie was only using Carter, "his little trained monkey," trying to get rich off him. When other children were going to birthday parties and baseball games on the weekends, Eddie was hauling Carter around the countryside to perform at county fairs, bars, and even on street corners, hoping to get discovered.

Carter grabbed his notebook and Kaia's pen and tried to sort it all out in a letter to her. Nothing came out right. No matter what he chose, helping Mama or helping his dad, he was letting someone down. Whether he went back east to Oklahoma, or out west to California, he had a bunch of explaining to do. He couldn't figure where he was needed most. As the morning sun rose over the golden hills, it was the first time he gave up trying to write a letter to Kaia.

Carter sat in silence in the kitchen. He didn't have any stomach for breakfast. He'd been at The Little Yucca coming on two weeks, and he knew it was time to move on.

Mitch's boots were loud on the linoleum, but Carter didn't turn around when he heard him come into the kitchen. "Well, good morning to you," Mitch said, pausing before the boy. Carter was too worn out from trying to figure his next move to offer anything more than a nod. Mitch held out a crisp white envelope to him.

Carter recognized the oversize, loopy handwriting on the envelope immediately. It belonged to none other than Kaia Liu. He held back a moment before taking it from Mitch. Carter had told her pretty much everything that came to mind every day he'd been away, and he couldn't help feeling close to her for having shared his heart. But seeing her letter reminded him he didn't know her well enough to guess what she might have to say in return.

Carter tucked the letter under his arm and slipped out back to read it in private. Sometimes he wondered if his daily scribblings and sketches ever landed in her grandma's mailbox or just disappeared in the darkness of the drugstore's postbox. Getting a letter in reply made him feel like she was listening. Part of him hoped she somehow had answers to the questions he hadn't had the nerve to ask the night before.

She'd typed up three whole pages, alternating between font styles and colors. She said she loved hearing about his audition and how he'd tried to draw her image using sound, and gushed about how "cute" he was writing with her sparkly pen. Carter couldn't help but grin. He kept her pen with him at all times, safe in his pocket. Cute or not, it was special to him.

Kaia had searched The Little Yucca's address on her grandmother's computer. She'd found the tavern in pictures taken by a satellite in outer space, and set about exploring the natural world beyond Mr. Ledbetter's mobile home, just like him. Carter looked up into the cloudless blue sky and waved. Carter wished she'd offered some reassurance about all the secrets he'd dared to write her. Instead, she dedicated two pages to her thoughts about the edible flowers of the Southwest. If she were there, she said she'd try her hand cooking with exotic petals. There were forty-nine species and twenty-four subspecies of yucca, she explained, but the ones you could eat bloomed only once a year. In spring, as it happened. Big talk for a girl who'd sworn she'd never cook without a partner.

Kaia's letter read like she wished she were there with him. She didn't say he was crazy or wasting his time or downright stupid for getting stranded so far from his intended destination. She liked that he was making friends with music again, and she actually wanted to hear him play again one day.

Ledbetter's mesquite onion rings were a big seller and gave Carter an idea for cooking with Kaia, even though they were miles apart. When Ledbetter turned in for his afternoon nap, Carter snuck into the kitchen and helped himself to a long, serrated bread knife. He tucked it carefully down one leg of his jeans and headed out to the desert for the afternoon. Once he was out of sight of the tavern, Carter hiked up to a blooming yucca plant. He squinted at the stalk of dense white flowers, nearly as high up as he was tall, stretching upright to heaven. The yucca was a freakish twist of nature, Carter reckoned, like an exploding firework growing square out of the dry dirt. He fingered the sharp tip of one of the long, pointy leaves, spinach green and shaped like a sword. If Carter hoped to collect the flowers, he had no choice but to wade in to the center of the yucca.

Weaving in between the spikes, Carter reached up along the base of the flower stalk, feeling for the right place to chop it. The pointy spikes held close to his body, thick and springy. No matter how careful he was, the sharp tips poked through his T-shirt, scratching him. The sun shone hot and unforgiving. A sweat broke out on his forehead and dust climbed his legs. He thought of Kaia dreaming of a chance to cook with rare ingredients. What were a few scratches? He was hurting a whole lot worse on the inside. He knew Kaia was too, and he hoped getting the yucca blossoms would help her see she wasn't alone. Carter wasn't her brother, the one she wished was still around, but that didn't mean she had to give up on cooking.

Carter bent his cheek to his shoulder and wiped the sweat from his brow. He drew back the knife and, with a groan, brought it down hard into the center of the rosette, cutting out the stem. Carter moved from yucca to yucca, collecting bushels of white flowers, his sides, belly, and back streaked red with scratches.

Firm and slightly crunchy, Carter thought the petals tasted a bit like green beans. Back in the kitchen, he went to work chopping the stems away. Among the smooth, long petals something wiggled and skittered, and then flew up in to Carter's face, surprising him. He swatted at the tiny critter, blowing air out of his nose and clamping his mouth shut. Dozens of yucca moths wormed loose from the petals, dropping to the countertop and onto the floor around his feet. Carter squealed like a stuck pig, grabbing the whole mess of blooms and hustling them outside, where he pitched them to the dirt. He threw up his hands, shouting at an invisible satellite miles from earth, "Hey, Kaia! You still hankering to cook with these?" For all he knew, she'd tricked him into going on a fool's errand.

He thought about dumping the heap, bugs and all, in the rubbish bin. But giving up on the flowers felt a whole lot like giving up on Kaia. Or daring her to give up on him.

Carter gathered the blooms in a wash bucket with fresh water and took his time cleaning, cutting, and de-mothing the flowers. Back in the kitchen, he stacked the petals three at a time, dipped them in Ledbetter's mesquite mixture, and dropped them into the deep fryer, determined to make a dish worth all his trouble. Mitch busted in and threatened to dock his pay for wasting Ledbetter's stock. Mr. Ledbetter wandered in from his nap, woken by the commotion. He took one look at Carter, buried in a snowdrift of white petals, with wheat flour up to his elbows and smudged across his face, and showed the boy some pity. Ledbetter found a bag of rice flour ordered by accident and let him have it.

Later that night, Carter Danforth's deep-fried mesquite yucca flowers with hot sauce catapulted to the most popular item on The Little Yucca's menu. Mitch grumbled and cussed, wishing he'd thought of it himself.

"You're welcome," Carter said, brushing a curl of his hair from his eyes.

He put the recipe in an envelope and addressed it to Kaia. He placed a stamp on it and set it aside till his next trip to the drugstore. He knew the recipe was nothing fancy, but he never would've done it without her. Her letter had made him feel as if he might be managing better than he'd reckoned, and yet he wasn't sure she was right about him. He'd been excited to get a letter from her, and he was thankful he took her up on her challenge to cook with the petals, but he didn't want to pretend he was bigger than his britches when he was only trying to make it through each day.

Mitch found the envelope on the counter. He didn't take a shine to Carter's flimsy, one-page offering.

"Mr. Keller, it's kind of you to let stay me on at the tavern, and you know I'm ready to help out around here however I can," Carter dared to argue with him, "but my letters are none of your business."

Mitch's face went from dead serious to plumb angry. "If I ask you to lift a finger around here, I'm asking for ten. Same goes for writing home."

It was a pointless fight. Carter wished he could find more words to say, but they weren't in him. He loved learning music with Mr. Ledbetter, but he couldn't stay there any longer. His mama needed him, but even if he were a doctor, they still didn't have a place to live. His dad, for once, wanted to see him, play music with him. That gave Carter the kinds of feelings he couldn't even admit to Kaia. He sure couldn't tell her he was scared as a knee baby about where he would go next.

"I can't write anymore, sir. Practicing my music is all I have a heart for."

Mitch held firm. He insisted something more go out.

Carter refused, claiming he'd promised Ledbetter he'd get some practice in before it was time for his kitchen chores.

Playing the Ledbetter card worked. Mitch gave an inch, saying it didn't have to be a letter; he could record his music. But he had to send it; "The Little Yucca is no hideout."

Carter shook his head, but he knew he couldn't win.

Mitch shot some videos on his phone of the boy practicing his guitar on the old, dusty stool on stage. Texting the videos to Kaia saved Carter from having to find the words only music could say. She'd said she wanted to hear him, and Carter reckoned Kaia was in the habit of getting her way. Even though it reminded him of his mother, he liked that about her.

Chapter Twenty-Six

LEDBETTER AND CARTER HAD ESTABLISHED AN easy rhythm, rising in the morning to fix breakfast, then picking up the lesson they'd left off just hours before, playing late into the night. Ledbetter was a devout believer in the "sweet spot" offered only in the sanctity of late-night jam sessions, but he wouldn't abide by late sleeping. "The sun is new each day," he said, "and anybody who wakes up breathing gets a shot at becoming better than yesterday." Carter needed to tell Ledbetter his plan, but he was sure going to miss the old bluesman.

Carter laid out long strips of hickory-smoked bacon on a platter, still hot and greasy from the pan. "I talked to my father," he began. Carter had come to trust Ledbetter enough to confess the whole mess he'd gotten himself into. "He wants me to come out to California, and record a commercial with him. Trouble is, he thinks I'm in Oklahoma with Mama. But I can't go back to Tulsa because Mama will never let me go out west. So I'm just going to go," Carter took a deep breath, "to my dad's. Without telling anybody. But you, of course."

Picking up an egg and cradling it in his hand, Ledbetter's fingers curled around the delicate shell much the way they framed the neck of his guitar. It seemed to Carter that Ledbetter's hands were permanently curved that way, like they were ready to jam any time, 24–7. He searched the boy's face like Carter had left something important out of his confession. "And how do you feel about this plan of yours?"

"Honestly sir, it's the scariest thing I could ever think of doing." Carter wandered over to a shelf near the storage room and pulled down a jar of shellac. He needed a moment to give it more thought. "Is it weird that the scariest thing also feels like the right thing?"

Ledbetter shook his head. "A song is just a piece of music if it ain't got feeling."

Carter knew Ledbetter's ear could be trusted to listen. He didn't preach about what Carter ought or ought not to do.

Ledbetter cracked one egg after another right into the blistering bacon fat, a half-inch deep. "You know why musicians write songs about women?" Dredging the raw yolks in the sizzling fat dulled them to brownish beige and gold, the same colors as the hills around The Yucca. "Because nothing else stirs up so many emotions. Desire, jealousy, longing, regret—the kinds of feelings a man can't easily uproot and be done with."

Carter began polishing his Martin with a salve of handrubbed shellac, listening. It was coming on the end of three weeks' worth of lessons and he was used to Ledbetter talking as such.

"Now, I'm guessing a man your age hasn't been married and, more to the point, divorced," Ledbetter continued. "And I'll wager you never lost your lady to another." The old man leaned forward and corrected Carter's polishing technique. "The blues is only a game, some folks say, and it's true." The old man worked his jaw in a series of grimaces. "And the Grand Canyon is only a hole in Arizona."

When the guitar was shining, and the strings adjusted, Carter put the strap over his shoulder. He'd been stuck. Halfway between two places and neither one could he call home. So he just stayed put and learned. And practiced and cooked and cleaned up after himself. In the short time he'd been at

The Yucca, he'd learned enough to find out he wasn't through learning.

"You may not have women troubles, but you're out in the middle of nowhere on your own, with a daddy who doesn't even know you're on your way." Ledbetter held his gaze on Carter's, flat and square. "Play that."

Carter looked away. He'd been trying to follow Ledbetter's instructions, and he'd been trying to copy the familiar melodies of the old songs he taught him. But now Ledbetter was asking him to improvise.

He'd tried that once, too. On The Little Yucca's own stage, when he'd attempted to capture a vision of Kaia. Maybe he wouldn't be good enough to improvise until he faced the sharp pains of stealing from his mother, and leaving her to find his father. In his heart, he was doing it to help her. But he wasn't sure how much help he was giving when it hurt as much as it did to be away when she needed him. Or, maybe he did have a case of the blues from a lost love? The love he longed for was miles away in LA. If he ever managed to get there, Carter couldn't even be sure that love was his anymore. The least he could do was look his pain in the eye instead of running from it. Ledbetter said the blues could free him. Or they were freedom. He wasn't sure which, but there was only one way to find out.

Carter shut his eyes. He tried to strum the form of his father this time, but he couldn't remember exactly how he looked. It had been six years since his dad left, and Carter was only a kid at the time. Instead, Carter remembered what it was like to hold his guitar while his father held him. In his mind, he let himself return to the unshakable belief in his own family, back when he had no idea in the world his daddy would ever leave his mom and him. He played the memory. Not as the child he once was, but with the years that stood empty between those days and these. He strummed it out, found its shape, and once he had it, he discovered it had been with him all the time. He heard it on the patio at sunrise at the Shoretown Inn back in Albuquerque.

"You found them. The blues, son," Ledbetter told him.

It was time to come clean, if only to make room for the music growing inside him.

Chapter Twenty-Seven

CARTER COUNTED HIS MONEY. HE'D EARNED almost seven hundred bucks working in The Little Yucca's kitchen. He could finally buy a plane ticket to Los Angeles. All he had to do was figure a way north to ABQ airport. And say good-bye to Mr. Ledbetter.

It was just coming on dinner time and The Yucca started to get noisy with hungry patrons. Mr. Ledbetter tied his apron and adjusted the temperature on the fryers.

"It's time I move on," Carter said. He pulled Kaia's pen from his pocket and leaned against the counter to write down every phone number and email he could think of: his own, his mother's, his father's, and even Kaia Liu's. He looked at Ledbetter and admitted, "Riding shotgun next to a random and shifty Darren Bartles put me off hitchhiking for good. But I don't see any other way of getting back to ABQ airport." Carter swore he'd never get in the car with anyone. No way. "But more important, I don't know how you thank you properly, Mr. Ledbetter. You've been a great teacher. And an even better friend." Carter bit his lip, crossing his arms over his chest. He wanted to give the old man a hug, but Ledbetter was already busying himself wrapping napkins around sets of cutlery.

"You want to thank me?" Ledbetter asked without looking up from his work. "I suppose there is one thing you could do for me. Make peace between Mitch and his daughter Piper. I've been trying to help those two see eye to eye for years. You're young, maybe Piper will like you better than she likes me."

Piper was living with a man she hoped to marry out in Tucson. Ledbetter said Mitch had his doubts about the guy and made it a habit to drop by to check up on her, a habit she didn't appreciate. "The passenger seat in Mitch's truck is yours if you want it," Ledbetter assured him. "Besides, a plane ticket to LA is a whole lot cheaper from Arizona."

"I'd do anything to show you my gratitude, but I wager it'd be safer hitching a ride with some transient wanderer than asking a favor of Mitch." Carter started wrapping cutlery by Mr. Ledbetter's side. "You know I had to pay him to use his phone?"

"That was your idea, not his. All he asked you to do was practice and write letters," Ledbetter pointed out. "Son, I trust Mitch Keller with my life." He put his hand on Carter's shoulder and Carter turned to meet his gaze. "You had a bad scare with that Bartles good-for-nothing, and I can't blame you for thinking twice before accepting a ride. But Mitch'll do right by you, I swear it."

Carter nodded. He didn't like the idea, but he didn't want to let Mr. Ledbetter down. He'd let down too many people he cared about and it was time he learned to fight for what was right. "If it means that much to you, sir, I'll do my best," he promised. How hard could it be to bring a little peace between a man and his daughter anyway, Carter wondered. That's all he wanted with his own father.

"I'm gonna miss you, son. You'll always be welcome at the Yucca."

Carter couldn't hold back another minute. He gave his old friend a hug.

♪♪♪

MITCH wasn't so easy-going about Carter's plans. He wanted to know the logistics of how Carter expected to land at his father's doorstep once he made it as far as Piper's restaurant. They searched for flights out of Tucson International Airport, and Carter found a great deal for just under two hundred bucks leaving the next evening. After years of saving and never feeling like he had enough, he was suddenly flush with cash. He bought himself the ticket and did something he hoped would set right all his mistakes back home. He sent four hundred dollars addressed to his mother to Lola May's house. He kept the remaining one hundred bucks for incidentals along the way to his father's.

♪♪♪

IT was a good four hours to Tucson and Mitch didn't offer many words on the drive. Carter didn't mind. He kept one eye on the highway's marker signs and the other on Mitch. Mitch's truck was clean and comfortable, but brought to mind too many bad memories of riding with Darren. Shifting in his seat, Carter kept reminding himself that old Ledbetter asked him to do one thing, that was all. Getting Mitch reunited with his daughter was the only way Carter could show his thanks. Mr. Ledbetter changed his life, and this trip would also get him one step closer to his dad.

Packing for the trip had been easy. The only possessions Carter had to his name were his guitar and his backpack, Kaia's sparkly pen, a Poly Virus tee, and his last haul of yucca petals.

After a while, Mitch requested a song to pass the time. This small gesture assured Carter he'd made some decent progress over the three weeks he'd spent at the tavern. Carter pulled out his guitar and threw the strap over his shoulder. He knew Mitch had a taste for the classics, so he started with Bob Dylan's "Like a Rolling Stone," which gave him the idea to move on to The Rolling Stones.

"Maybe once you learn your way around that thing, I'll let you try The Yucca stage again," Mitch said with a wink.

He was still a long way from impressing the barkeep, but Carter couldn't help but smile. "I wouldn't take a gamble until I've got the chops to open for Mr. Ledbetter."

Mitch laughed. Carter could tell he appreciated his respect for Mitch's old friend.

"You're a smart kid, but you don't know your fists from your feet. Remember how I made your acquaintance? You were about to get your butt whupped," Mitch said, adjusting his cowboy hat. "Even if I play chaperone all the way to the Pacific Ocean, you ought to learn to protect yourself."

Carter put his guitar away, remembering how Mitch had handled Darren. He'd like to have skills like that.

"Size doesn't equal strength. My daughter, Piper? I taught her how to look out for herself."

"You taught her to throw a punch, sir?" Carter curled his hands into fists and punched the air in front of him.

"I did indeed. And how to run a restaurant, too."

"So you bought her a deep fryer and some frozen burger patties?" Carter dared to tease the man the way Mr. Ledbetter might. Mitch shot a glance at him, cocking one brow. He wasn't one for jokes and Carter wished he hadn't tried to pull one on him.

"Those jabs are about as lethal as a butterfly in pollen season," Mitch said. Carter dropped his hands into his lap. "Eyes, groin, neck, and knees," Mitch added, staring at the long stretch of freeway ahead of his late-model truck.

Carter bolted up in his seat, alarmed. He knew hitch-hiking brought nothing but trouble, but Ledbetter had said Mitch could be trusted. "Excuse me?" The man never mentioned anything about groins back at The Yucca, and Carter wasn't interested in the topic now that they were alone.

"Try this," Mitch told him, taking his right hand off the wheel. "Imagine an attacker is in front of you. As fast as you can, flick at his eyeballs with your fingers, like you're trying to get water off 'em. It's effective and it's painful."

Carter practiced flicking his fingers in the direction of Mitch's face.

"Good. Next, bring your knee up as hard as you can. A blunt shot square in the groin will take out any man."

Carter flinched. He'd once accidentally smashed the center bar of his bike into his crotch and the memory of that pain hadn't faded.

"You want to throw a punch? Aim for the neck. Knock the wind out of that sucker."

Carter nodded. Mitch wasn't trying to hurt him; he was trying to help.

"Now listen, if an attacker gets you to the ground, kick at his knees. Knock him down and run for your life," Mitch continued. "You're young, you're agile, you can move fast. Get out while you can." He took a good long look at Carter. "Do you understand what I'm saying?"

"I get it. Eyes, groin, neck, and knees." Carter repeated the pattern a few more times to himself, committing it to memory. "Thanks, Mr. Keller."

When they reached Tucson, Mitch pulled his truck into the parking lot of a restaurant. Over the front entrance, a simple painted sign read "The Desert Willow."

Mitch stepped inside and glanced around the place, pressing

a finger to his lips while searching for the words to describe it. "What in the—? She must have redecorated."

Wooden tables no more than a foot tall were scattered around the restaurant. There wasn't a chair in sight, only cushions, each and every one made with a different material, like a caravan of gypsies had crashed a quilting bee. The place in no way resembled The Little Yucca. A handful of customers lounged around a few tables, grazing from heaping plates, a low-key murmur blending with soft acoustic guitar music. There was no sign of Mitch's daughter, Piper.

Mitch directed Carter to a table and lowered himself to a cushion with a grunt. His legs, unaccustomed to bowing the distance, quavered as he neared the floor. His scuffed and worn cowboy boots wouldn't fit under the low table. Mitch wasn't doing a good job of hiding his irritation with the restaurant's new décor.

Carter plopped down in one motion onto a pillow covered in a reclaimed blanket with a woven Navajo motif. He set his guitar on the floor next to him, the top of the case laid over his thigh like the chin of a loyal pup.

Waiting for Mitch's daughter to show, Carter had a look at the menu. Where meat dominated at The Little Yucca, The Desert Willow was plant-based. The words *organic, locally sourced,* and *vegan* laced the strange menu. While The Little Yucca attracted the night crowd, the Willow served only breakfast and lunch.

"How's my baby girl?" Mitch said, beaming, when a young woman appeared at their table. Mitch got to his feet a lot easier than he had to his bottom. Carter tried not to stare. Piper didn't look anything like him. It wasn't just her piercings, olive skin, and chopped, lavender-streaked hair. It was her slumped shoulders and the way she held her chin like she was about to spit.

Mitch opened his arms to her but she ducked away, busying herself with stacking three or four cushions in a high tower. She took Mitch by the arm and helped her father to sit. Carter got off his cushion and scurried over to assist. Mitch made a fuss; he didn't like being treated like an old man. Squatting over the cushions, the back of Piper's T-shirt pulled up around her apron strings. Across her lower back, he spotted a storm cloud of bruises, black and blue and in some parts pea-soup green. A sourness caught in his throat. He pushed it down, but it refused. How did she get bruised so badly?

"Carter Danforth, this is my favorite restaurateur, Piper." Carter leaned back a bit on his cushion, trying not to stare. Mitch squeezed Piper's hand lovingly, but nothing changed in her empty, faraway look. It was strange for Carter to see this side of Mitch, the gruff and stern man going soft over his kin.

"Did you marry another woman with a kid or something?" she asked.

"Your mother will always have my heart, rest her soul," Mitch replied, the phrase like the familiar refrain of an often-repeated song. "Carter's just passing through on his way to his pa's in California. I was due for a visit to The Willow and he joined me for the ride. You know I can't go long without seeing your beautiful smile."

"You don't need to come all this way, Mitch. I don't know why you put yourself out on my account," she said without a hint of a smile, beautiful or otherwise. Carter glanced back and forth between the two of them. Why did Piper call her father *Mitch*?

"I'll bet Carter here would love to try your vegan chocolate brownie with walnuts," Mitch said, brushing off her remark. Was he going to ignore her bruises, too?

"What if he has a nut allergy?" Piper asked, without making

it sound as though she cared either way. "He might eat it and die," she added, as an afterthought.

"As a matter of fact, I came about a bit of business." Mitch might have ignored her nasty comment, but Carter didn't let it go so easily. "Mr. Danforth here has crafted a recipe that's right up The Desert Willow's alley. I'm going to buy it from him and give it to you as an early birthday present, sweetheart."

Carter's eyes shot open to twice their normal size. Mitch hadn't said anything about selling his recipe. What did yucca flowers have to do with Piper's restaurant?

Piper stood over him, her hand on her hip. "Well, what have you got to say for yourself, little man?" Carter bit his lip. He didn't like the crack. It reminded him of Darren Bartles.

"Deep-fried mesquite yucca flowers?" Carter responded with a question, half-expecting her to cuff him on the head.

Piper did nothing and said nothing. So Carter rambled on, explaining his recipe and technique. "The customers at The Little Yucca said my deep-fried mesquite yucca flowers were so good, 'They make your tongue slap your brains out.'" She stared blankly through him, or perhaps past him.

Finally, she said, "Let's get some lunch into you and then you can show me in the kitchen."

Did Mitch really expect him to go into the kitchen with Piper? Where there'd be sharp knives and oil boiling in the fryer? Far as he could tell, the woman seemed to feel nothing. What did crime shows always say? *The killer lacked remorse.* He'd already earned enough money to get to LA. No reason to hang around. Getting her to warm to Mitch was too tall an order.

"Uh, I'll have whatever your dad is having. Thank you, ma'am," Carter stammered, looking pointedly away.

"He isn't my father. My last name's Piedra. It's not Keller and it never will be," she replied, her words drier than cracked cement. "And don't call me 'ma'am.' Were you raised by an army sergeant or something?"

"No, ma'am," Carter dared to reply, then wished he hadn't. He ought to shut his mouth before she dished up a whupping. Whoever put those bruises on Piper was probably in far worse shape for having crossed her. He pictured her the ring leader of some Southwest all-girl Fight Club. It made sense that Piper wasn't Mitch's own flesh and blood. Carter couldn't help but smirk that Piedra was her last name. It meant *rock* in Spanish and Piper was, he reckoned, a stone.

Another server brought their meals. Piper ignored them while Carter and Mitch ate. "I married her mother when Piper was just about twelve," he explained in a low whisper between bites of a grilled veggie sandwich. "Her father was a drunk. Unemployed and violent. Couldn't keep his fists to himself. I'm just glad he up and left them before he—"

A flush of anger rose around Mitch's shirt collar. "What the women I love have been through—" He exhaled a deep breath and took a long sip of his iced tea. If Mr. Ledbetter were here, he'd show Mitch a way to tell his own blues, Carter thought. He wished right then he knew how to do that, use music to help a friend.

Mitch wiped his mouth with a napkin and readjusted his sprawling legs. "You can see for yourself, Piper's doing fine now. But she never shook that hurt."

Carter chewed his sandwich in silence. He couldn't see that at all.

Chapter Twenty-Eight

AFTER THEY FINISHED LUNCH, MITCH PULLED his cowboy hat down over his brow and looked directly in Carter's eyes. "I don't suppose I told you how much I appreciated your help around The Yucca."

"It was nothing, sir," Carter said, surprised. He busied himself with folding his napkin, realizing he didn't want to be left alone. He was short on time for getting Mitch and Piper back together, and he could tell the road to a father-daughter reunion was one-way only. Mitch wasn't the problem, Piper was.

Mitch walked Carter out front and pointed north toward the I-10. "You can take the city bus from the stop on the corner to Tucson International Airport. It's not far from here, maybe seven, eight miles."

Carter reckoned it'd be best to give up on a hopeless case like Piper and go to the airport right then, even though his flight wasn't till after ten that night. If Mr. Ledbetter hadn't been able to get through to her over the years, what could Carter do in an afternoon?

Mitch reached into the back pocket of his sun-washed jeans and pulled out a brown leather wallet. He counted out two hundred and fifty dollars and folded the stack of bills in half, offering it to Carter. "For the recipe." He nodded and placed it in Carter's palm. "It'd mean a lot to me if you showed her how to make it."

The money made him feel like he'd accomplished something of value, all on his own. When he finally made it home to Mama, he was going to be more independent and, better yet, capable, able to take care of his own. He'd never steal from her again. "Thanks, Mr. Keller, for everything," he said, meeting his eye. The money was the smallest portion of what the man had given him over the past three weeks. The truth was, Mitch had been a real friend to him from the moment he'd fallen into The Little Yucca. All he'd ever asked of Carter was to give his best effort.

But Carter had to ask one question, "Why do you do it?" He gestured through the window of The Desert Willow. "She says she doesn't want your help, but you keep giving it."

Mitch's gaze followed Piper as she moved from table to table. At last he replied, "Love doesn't walk away."

If Mitch was right, Carter wondered whether showing up on his father's doorstep would be hard or easy. "I never met anyone like you, sir. And I reckon there ought to be more Mitch Kellers in the world."

Mitch squeezed his shoulder. "You're a good kid. We hope to see you around The Yucca again someday."

Carter's smile faded. He wasn't a good kid. He'd stolen money from his mother and he was as homesick as a knee baby, but he couldn't call his mom because he'd have to lie to her again about where he was. Maybe it was best he refuse the recipe money.

Mitch saw the doubt on his face and pulled the boy into a hug with a good thump on his back. Short on words, he turned Carter by the shoulders and nudged him back toward The Desert Willow's front door.

Inside, Piper was straightening up after the lunch crowd. For just a moment, Carter was jealous. If a man like Mitch had married his mother instead of Piper's, he'd sure be grateful for having a stepfather who actually cared about him.

Paying it forward: Carter knew that was when you did someone a favor because someone else did something to help you. It was kind of Mitch to pay him for his recipe. He knew he ought to teach it to Piper simply because Mitch was a good man, and he couldn't let down Mr. Ledbetter either. "I've got it from here, sir," Carter said at last. Mitch tipped the rim of his cowboy hat and walked back to his truck.

When Carter stepped back into the restaurant, Piper motioned for him to sit down. A plate rattled on the low table in front of him. On it sat Piper's infamous fudge brownie with might-kill-you walnuts. She went back to spraying down tables, humming to herself as she worked. Carter picked up the fork and dug in. It was perfect. Granted, he hadn't eaten a home-baked brownie since before the tornadoes, but this one was special. Moist, and dark as a starless sky. Something went off in Carter's brain—fireworks or carnival game bells or the velvet explosion of holding Kaia's hand in his, Carter couldn't tell which and it didn't matter. This brownie was her secret weapon, he figured. The mysterious jewel luring customers back when Piper's personality made them swear an oath never to return to The Desert Willow.

In the kitchen, Carter demonstrated his recipe from memory. Piper made notes on ingredients, measurements, and cooking time. She asked how he went about harvesting petals, and Carter lifted his Poly Virus tee to show her the scratches on his midsection. Nothing worth doing came easy.

By late afternoon, the restaurant was empty. Piper's quiet hum in the dining area morphed to full-on singing in the privacy of her kitchen. Carter knew she wasn't singing for his benefit. He was pretty sure she didn't care what he thought of her one way or the other, but he liked her sound. It made her seem less of a psychopath, at least by a small measure.

"Any chance Mr. Ledbetter taught you to sing like that?" Mitch may know a thing or two about how to run a watering hole, but Carter couldn't imagine him breaking out in song.

"Is that old has-been still hanging around?"

Her comment caught Carter by surprise. He couldn't imagine anyone saying a bad word about Ledbetter and came to the old man's defense. "What do you mean, *has-been?*"

"He used to be a big studio musician, toured with all the old rock legends back in the day. But he never kept a dollar in his pocket. Blew all his money," she said, her words bitter as a raw yucca petal. "Mitch likes to play Lord and Savior to the desperate and pathetic."

"He was there for me when I needed him." Carter felt himself getting angry. Was she calling him desperate and pathetic? "And from where I stand, Mitch Keller's still there for you."

"Yeah?" She gave Carter a long, hard look that told him that conversation was over. "Well, I don't need his help."

He wanted to argue, but earlier that morning he would have agreed with her. "I thought his idea of help was beyond annoying when I first met him. But he surprised me, you know?" Making peace between Mitch and Piper was going to take patience, and patience required time he didn't have. His flight took off in five hours.

Piper nibbled the fried yucca flowers, considering the boy. "What I do need," she said at last, "are creative ideas like this recipe of yours. Rice and mesquite flour are both gluten-free; my customers will like that. So, did you serve them on a plate or upright in a cup like fries?"

"Neither. Served them in a plastic basket lined with parchment."

She rolled her eyes slower than cream rising on buttermilk, then selected some dishes of varying sizes and shapes from a shelf. "To the customer, half the flavor depends on how it looks," she said. Carter nodded. It sounded like something his father would say about faking confidence on stage.

Arranging the petals into a tiny sculpture, Piper made Carter's dish look like art on a plate. Carter tried to create his own design, but his looked more like he was arranging kindling for a campfire.

A shadow appeared in the slit of light under the closed kitchen door. Piper twitched. Just a slight nervous squirm, but Carter caught it. The door swung open and a man stepped in. At first Carter thought he was a cop. His hair was cut close to his scalp and tanned biceps stretched the short cuffs of what looked like a police officer's starched white uniform shirt. Built like a brick wall everywhere but his face, Carter couldn't help but stare at his double chin squeezing over his starched collar.

Under her breath, Piper told Carter, "Playtime's over. Clean up your mess." She stacked all the dirty dishes, rattling them as she scurried over to the dishwasher.

"Where you been?" said the man.

Had Piper called the cops on him? Carter thought about making a break for the door. He couldn't miss his flight. The big man moved toward him and Carter hurried to patch together an adequate explanation for why he was halfway across the country without parental supervision.

Chapter Twenty-Nine

PIPER REACHED UP ON HER TIPPY-TOES AND kissed the man's cheek. "Hey, babe. How was your day?" Her voice spiked an octave higher. Carter held his breath, hoping maybe he was Piper's boyfriend and not a cop after all.

"Same crap, different day," he replied, swinging open the kitchen's large stainless-steel commercial fridge and grabbing a beer. Nope, not a cop. Reflective wraparound sunglasses sat backward on his broad shoulders, holding on for dear life to his flabby, sunburned neck. He tossed the beer cap over the trash can and into the sink Carter had just begun scrubbing. "Who's the brat?" he asked, taking a sip that drained the bottle by half.

"My stepdad's new kid," Piper lied. "Name's *Crater*." She laughed a cruel laugh. "Isn't that right, *Crater*?"

Piper had a bully streak and Carter didn't like it. He cleared his throat, unsure what to say.

"Your big-boy words stuck in your throat, Crater?" The man laughed, throwing a polyester suit jacket with an embroidered security company logo onto the disinfected countertop. Above the left breast pocket was the name *Willard*.

"I hear y'all are fixing to get married," Carter managed at last, picking up his guitar case and eyeing the door. Best he found that bus Mitch had told him about, and sooner rather than later.

"Yeah; what of it?" Willard asked. "What else did Keller tell you?"

"Nothing. Just being polite is all." Carter got the feeling the guy was picking a fight. *What's his deal?*

"Bet he didn't tell you people around here call me a hero." Piper's fiancé finished the bottle and grabbed another beer. "Saved Piper here from a misdemeanor assault with potential felony endangerment written all over it, but even that wasn't good enough for old Mitch Keller."

"Willard, sweetheart?" Piper said, her voice barely a squeak. "I'm running short on inventory, babe." Where was her couldn't-care-less attitude? Carter wondered. Where was the voice that carried her singing strong and true? And what was with all the *babes*?

He set the bottle down, but Carter could tell it bugged him. Willard busied himself with scratching at the peeling sunburn on his forearm with ragged fingernails bitten down to nothing. When he noticed Carter's eye on him, he took it as a challenge. Willard picked up the bottle again and pulled a long swig. "I'll drink whatever I want to drink when I want it," he said and chugged the rest, setting the empty bottle on the counter, this time right in front of Piper.

Carter swept his hair back from his eyes. There was a part of him that was curious. He wanted a reason to like the man, if only for Mitch's peace of mind. "Mitch didn't tell me that story. But I'd like to hear it if you got the time."

Willard didn't need much in the way of encouragement. He edged toward Carter, demonstrating his moment of glory. "I spotted two shady-looking losers who had this chick cornered in a parking lot at the mall, right? I didn't know Piper back then, total stranger." Willard stood a few inches shorter than Carter but carried twice the boy's weight in muscle. "I heard her scream. One of them had her by the wrists. I ran fast as I could, pulled my five-fingered weapons," he showed Carter his clenched fists, "and laid waste to both of them." Even though Piper was all the way across the room, she cowered from his raised hands. "Piper learned fast to respect what these hands can do. We've been together ever since."

Carter stood still as a cactus against the kitchen sink, looking back and forth between them. Lola May's ex-husband Wayne liked to solve problems with his fists, too. Carter wagered the bruises on Piper's back were Willard's doing. But it didn't make sense. Mitch said he taught Piper how to fight.

"I saved this girl's life and delivered justice on the spot. And what was my reward? Got kicked out of the police academy and served time for aggravated assault. Judge sent me to jail; can you believe that? Our justice system protects the criminals, but it won't stop me from setting things right." Willard's doughy face twisted into a grin. "You can tell your buddy Keller that Piper's had enough bad men in her life to know a good one."

If Mitch were here, he'd sure set things right, Carter reckoned. Taking a deep breath, he tried his best Mitch Keller voice: "You use those fists on Piper, too?"

Willard leaned into Carter, glaring. "What did you say, *Crater?*"

He could smell Willard's beer-stained breath. Carter held his shoulders square, his knuckles white around the handle of his guitar case. Mitch had stood up to Darren Bartles for him without question. Time to pay him back. "She's tough as a claw hammer swinging both ways," Carter warned Willard, low but clear. "You better watch yourself."

Willard laughed, the way a giant might laugh before crushing a bug under his boot. "She's smart enough to stand by her man and do what she's told," Willard told him through gritted teeth. "Another word and I'm going to teach you who's in charge here." The guy readied his burling arm to throw a punch. "C'mon, just one more word."

"Willard, he's just a dumb kid." Piper inched toward them, her gaze on the man's upraised hand. "He doesn't know a watch from a warning."

What had Mitch told Carter? Neck, belt, nose?

"Why don't you get on home," Carter said as calmly as he could. He might be a kid, but he wasn't dumb.

Carter ducked Willard's punch when it came at him. The man swung with all his body weight, well over two hundred pounds, and the punch landed, hard. There was a sound of bone meeting bone. He hit Piper, knocking her to the rubber mat lining the concrete kitchen floor.

"I'll call 911," Carter breathed and raced to a phone on the wall.

"Kid, are you crazy?" Piper grabbed Carter's ankle, stopping him, her other hand still holding the cheek where Willard's fist had landed. "Babe," she reassured Willard, "no one's calling the cops. I'm fine; it was an accident. Let's just lock up and head home. Okay, baby?"

Willard ignored her, turning to Carter in a rage. Before he knew what was happening, Willard threw him over his shoulder, firefighter style, and hauled him out to the parking lot. "Look what you made me do," he said with a growl.

Carter held tight to his guitar, kicking and pounding on the man with the wide end of the case. Willard threw him down in the parking lot, and Piper raced up behind him. "Babe, stop. Someone will see you," she said, her voice so thin and tight that all that got out was a high-pitched whisper. "You don't want to get busted again." From the parking lot, Carter could see couples and families strolling along the well-lit sidewalks in the early evening.

"He isn't worth it." Willard spit at the ground in front of Carter's feet. He rose quickly and brushed off his jeans. "Get your helmet, Piper."

She locked up the restaurant and put on a silver motorcycle helmet without another word, staring straight ahead, hard as rock. *Piedra.* Willard threw his leg over a black Harley-Davidson Softail, and fired up the motorcycle's engine. Piper slipped onto the back and they peeled out of The Desert Willow's parking lot.

Carter took off walking as fast as he could in the direction of the bus stop. When he reached the intersection, he paced anxiously waiting for the light to change. Piper was nuts. What was she doing with that guy? Why didn't she use the fighting skills Mitch had taught her? Eyes, groin, neck, and knees. Oh great; now he remembered. Carter should have dropped Willard to the floor and run, taking Piper with him whether she wanted to go or not. She was the dumb kid, not him.

The light changed and Carter crossed the road, moving as fast as he could away from The Desert Willow. He shook his head, trying to make sense of what just happened. When a bad guy like Darren Bartles stole some tools, the cops came after him. Willard just hit Piper. Maybe that punch was meant for him, but Piper's bruises told him Willard didn't often miss his target. What do they call that kind of bullying, assault or battery? Piper shouldn't marry Willard; she ought to drag the guy to jail.

Carter's Converses came to a dead stop on the sidewalk. Wayne had dislocated Lola May's shoulder once. If his mother hadn't been there to stop him, it could've been worse. She'd helped Lola understand that she didn't need to stay with the wrong man because she was strong enough to make it on her own. It was what friends did. He had to do something. Maybe this was his chance to help someone other than himself. He owed it to Mitch.

Chapter Thirty

CARTER PACED THE STREET, MUTTERING SOME choice words he wished he'd said to Willard—and a good lot for Piper, too. He thought about calling the police but he didn't have any idea where she lived or even her phone number. His mother would've known what to do. He considered calling Mitch, but it was clear that Piper wouldn't accept his help. Carter was sure that if Piper told Mitch what Willard was doing to her, there sure wouldn't be one solitary bruise on her back. She was keeping the abuse a secret.

Carter found the bus stop Mitch had pointed out, and sat on the bench. Across the street was a weedy, vacant lot between a dry cleaner and a liquor store. Carter wondered why no one ever filled the gap, or at least tended to the property in some way. He reckoned those weeds pushed themselves up toward the sun, died, and new weeds took their place. He was sick and tired of feeling like a helpless kid tossed around by circumstance, trying to get to the place that caused him the least amount of burden. He was fortunate to have met Mr. Ledbetter, and finding out Mitch Keller wasn't a bad guy after all was nothing but a stroke of luck. Lola had said his mother raised him right. It was high time Carter did as he was taught by his carpenter mother: fix what was broken.

If there was one thing he'd come to see was broken, it was him. Losing music had crushed him. It was like old Ledbetter said, he had two choices: follow or fight. When he got angry enough to buy his daddy's guitar back from Tommy, that bit of gumption paved the way for him fall in love with the Martin all over again. Music was the only thing he understood or could count on anymore. His father said the instrument was meant for him; his dang name was on it. No way he was ready to sell it, not at any price.

The bus to the airport rounded the corner and headed for his stop. Carter needed to make a decision.

The money Mitch gave him for the recipe was enough to buy another plane ticket. He didn't want to miss seeing his father, but the only way Carter reckoned he could help Piper was to convince her to reach out to Mitch herself. He shouldn't have let her go. Willard probably had her making his dinner under the shadow of his fist; Carter didn't know. The plane ticket in his pocket mocked him, taunting him to give up and get on that flight and forget what he saw.

A billboard over the vacant lot featured rates for a local motel. Carter knew well enough they'd ask for a credit card or a driver's license before they'd give him a room. He'd do just as well sleeping behind The Desert Willow. He could talk to Piper first thing in the next morning, or at least try. It was still fairly hot, even as the sun began to drop. He reckoned it couldn't get too cold overnight in Tucson in April. But he'd been wrong about the weather before.

Carter adjusted his backpack and his guitar and walked away from the bus stop. He was making plans faster than he could reckon if they were any good. At least he had cash. That was good. Carter decided to get himself some dinner before hiding out behind The Willow. Several of the restaurants along the street had open-air patios. When he rounded the block Carter spotted a tavern, The Crusty Maiden, with a sign reading, "Live music."

He wasn't old enough to be in a bar, but it was still early. If he slipped in with the dinner rush, he could linger a bit and maybe catch the first act.

As he stepped in, he felt right at home. The Crusty Maiden had the raucous, bouncing spirit of The Little Yucca after dark. But this place was more punk or rockabilly than Mitch's southwestern-flavored roadhouse. Where cowboys and steer horns held court at The Yucca, tattoos and black leather ruled at The Crusty Maiden. A server in lace-up motorcycle boots, with jet-black hair fringed by short, cherry-tinted bangs, stepped out in front of Carter before he could make it to a table. A tattoo of a spider's web encircled her chest and neck. On her left shoulder sat a life-size and too-realistic-looking tat of a black widow spider.

"You looking for your mama, honey?" she asked, chewing a tiny wad of pink bubble gum. She couldn't have been much older than him, and he was plumb tired of getting treated like a dumb kid.

"You looking for your daddy?" Carter answered her question with a question and tried to appear taller.

She laughed. Carter didn't know what was so funny, but he couldn't help but prefer her smile. "You look more like jailbait to me, honey," she said with a wink, looking him over from head to guitar case. "My name's Bet. Let me show you to a table."

Bet sat Carter at a table in the corner by the stage. He was starving, and a quick glance at the menu she gave him made him hungrier. He couldn't decide between the Maiden's roadkill burger or chicken tacos, so he ordered both, along with french fries, potato salad, and a big slice of chocolate cake.

Carter listened to the sounds of boots tramping the old planks of the wood floor and the clinking of glasses on the long bar, sometimes harmonizing with a pinball machine in the corner. The waitstaff had a neighborly way of cussing out the clientele. Grabbing his notebook from his guitar case, he sketched the bank of blood-red vinyl booths and strings of Christmas lights twinkling from open-beam rafters. He began writing to Kaia again. Having something to say to her renewed his hope a measure, made him feel like he was making his way again, charting a path to what he wanted and what mattered. He wrote about The Crusty Maiden, but he found himself telling her about meeting Piper and how she'd swung from fierce to flimsy. When he tried to explain what had set Willard off, he couldn't make sense of it. All Piper had done was ask him not to take a second beer. Weird. He stared at the next line on the page, empty, his pen soaking ink into the pores. He dared himself to write: *I'm going to play my guitar here tonight.*

This was a big declaration. Could he really convince The Crusty Maiden to let him onstage?

Bet came by with his check. "How you doing, Jailbait? Can I get you anything else, honey?"

"When's the show?" Carter pointed to the stage with a jut of his jaw, trying to be cool.

"Another hour or so."

He pulled out enough cash to cover his meal plus a healthy tip and placed it on the table. "With a name like Bet, I reckon you'd be interested in a little wager."

Bet put her order pad back in her apron and tucked her pen behind her right ear. She raised one sculpted, painted-black eyebrow at Carter. "Who could resist those puppy-dog eyes? What've you got in mind, Jailbait?"

"Give me the stage for ten minutes and I'll guess your favorite song," he said. "If I can't guess it, I'll buy you a slice of cake."

Bet placed her hand on her hip and sized him up. "I'll give you five minutes and not a second longer."

Carter flushed with relief and grabbed the handle of his guitar case.

"But I can tell you right now," she added, "you don't stand a chance, Jailbait."

"We'll see." He grinned, rising from his chair. Carter leaped onto the stage without bothering to use the side stair. The nervous tendency to clear his throat chased him, but he kicked it to the floor.

He unlatched his case and pulled out his guitar. "Play to your audience," Ledbetter had told him, "the way only you can." *Forget Dad's idea of 'flawless execution,'* he thought, *play what they'd like, my way.*

His wrists were tender from mixing mesquite and rice flour with cornstarch all afternoon. They felt loose, too tired to strain or resist. He played the familiar chord changes of "Ring of Fire" by Johnny Cash. The song sounded good in his ears. In his mind, he pictured his plane ticket to California flaming up in a ring of fire, and it made him feel powerful, in charge of his life for once. Carter brought the tempo up to a faster rock version. The chords bounced along, unfettered and free. His fingertips peeled with soreness from practicing guitar for hours by the riverbed back in Las Cruces and he couldn't press the strings against the fret as tightly. To his surprise, that improved the sound. The music was lighter, less forced.

It was a give and take, pleasing the audience while remaining true to himself. Carter dragged the notes where his heart pulled him, both toward Santa Monica and away. He played for Piper's biological father, wherever he was. As he strummed on, his thoughts unfolded. When that man lost his family, Mitch gained a wife and a daughter. You find out who your family is, and sometimes blood's got nothing to do with it, he decided.

Cash's lyrics weren't about any of those things, but Carter

had practiced the song until he knew it too well to get it wrong. Bet leaned against the bar, giving the stage her full attention. When he caught her eye, she shook her head, a playful smile telling him she'd won. It wasn't her favorite song. But she didn't move to stop him either. Meeting her gaze made him feel less alone behind the microphone.

At the end of the song, Carter moved directly into "Juvenile Delinquent," a rockabilly tune, without lifting his fingers. Ledbetter said it was an old favorite that would save his butt when the haters told him he was too young to rock the house.

When she recognized the tune, Bet hooted and whistled, cheering him on. An older woman with white-blond hair sweeping across her shoulders and a Crusty Maiden tee torn to a deep valley sidled up and said something to Bet, pointing at Carter.

He pulled his gaze away, daring to make eye contact with other patrons for just a few beats, nothing big. What a difference. Random strangers scattered about the room assembled around him, called forward when he looked them in the eye. He wasn't alone. They shared the music together. Carter played on, an unceasing stream of all the old rock 'n roll songs he'd learned alongside the little record player on the kitchen shelf back at The Yucca. He played the familiar songs his way, with his own arrangements, singing with an honest voice, and no one turned their back. When he ran out of the old favorites, he tried a few alternative rock songs he'd always liked. His five minutes onstage melted away and soon became an hour. It felt so good now that his wrist was freed, he didn't care if he had a goofy smile on his face.

After his set, Carter made his way over to Bet. Hands from the crowd extended toward him for high-fives, handshakes, and fist bumps.

"How about that cake, Jailbait?" she asked.

"Yeah, of course," Carter said, catching himself before tagging on "ma'am." If it didn't fly with Piper, chances were good it wouldn't fly with Bet. "Mind if I ask what your favorite song is?"

Bet winked. "Goes with me to the grave." She counted out twenty-five dollars from a pocket in her apron and handed it to him. "Your pay for tonight's show. Boss says she wants you back tomorrow for another happy-hour set."

Carter couldn't find the words to express either his surprise or his gratitude. He threw his arms around her, squeezing her in a hug.

"C'mon now, get outta here," Bet said, giving him a sisterly pat on the head. "You're gonna break hearts when you come old enough to fill a man's boots," she added with a shake of her head. "We'll see you tomorrow."

Out on the sidewalk, Carter's feet carried him back to The Desert Willow without his slightest effort, like he was floating between the ground and the stars. If this was what it felt like to perform, he was hooked. LA could wait one more day.

Chapter Thirty-One

BACK AT PIPER'S RESTAURANT, CARTER THOUGHT about his mom and how the only thing she needed to deal with the crazy Wayne ordeal was courage. There was no light around the restaurant save the glow from The Desert Willow's sign out front. He couldn't find a decent place around The Willow to crash. He tried the back door to the kitchen, but it was locked. The front entrance was bolted shut. He checked all the windows; no luck. Picking his way around the perimeter of the pueblo-style building in the dark, a square stucco cube with round air-ventilation tubes poking out just below the roofline, he found a metal ladder attached to the building and climbed up to the roof.

There was nothing up there but a pool chaise longue and someone on it, covered by a large, lumpy wool blanket. He froze, holding his breath.

"Who's there?" The lump bolted up, alarmed and alert. He recognized Piper's voice. "Don't take another step. I have a knife."

"It's me. Carter." He dared to step toward her. A knife jutted out from under the blanket. Carter shuffled out from the shadows so she could get a better look at his face.

"Shouldn't you be on a plane?" The fear in her voice was replaced with irritation.

"Shouldn't you be home in bed?"

Piper pulled the blanket down and crossed her arms. "What on earth are you doing on my roof?"

Carter couldn't figure out how to explain himself without making her mad. He toyed with bragging about Bet giving him a reason to stay. But the truth was, he'd come back to help her. Of course, she probably didn't want his help any more than she wanted her stepfather's. Piper waited for him to say something, anything.

He was done telling stories and hiding the truth. Whatever went on with Willard that night, Piper was safe for the time being, far as he could tell. So he unloaded. Once he got started, he didn't hold anything back. Carter told her how his daddy up and left, taking his future in music with him. He told her about the night he'd spent in the pawn shop, when his entire neighborhood disappeared, along with his mama. He gave her the play-by-play of searching the soggy remains of all their belongings for two whole days before a relief crew found him. He admitted he should have been at his aunt's house days ago, and his shame of promising Lola May he'd go to stay with his mama in the shelter.

"Sometimes I'm terrified of being on the run. But the only thing scarier than being alone is trying to figure out who I'm supposed to be." Carter knew his mother believed his father had used him, and as much as he wanted to make money recording the Ma Joad's jingle, he couldn't help but wonder if that was still true. But he couldn't go back to the way things were, drifting through each school day wondering how any of what he was learning mattered. Or building his skills in carpentry and engine repair with his mom, knowing his hands only wanted to play guitar.

Piper didn't try to comfort him. There was no "poor you" from her. He didn't want her pity anyway. The bruises on her back spoke on her behalf.

"Why do you want to see your father again?" Piper asked at

last, her voice muffled under the blanket she held snugly around her shoulders. "He left you."

Carter didn't need to be reminded. "Well, at first all I wanted was to destroy his guitar and make the past go away. And then I wanted him to sign it, so I could sell it for more than I'd bought it." Carter didn't care to mention how much he owed his mother for stealing. "But now . . ." Carter looked Piper in the eye. "I guess I just want to show him I was worth staying for. In truth, I want him to be my dad."

The dark sky hung like a black burlap curtain with a hole where a bright moon peeked through. Before Carter could drum up the nerve to ask what Piper was doing up on the roof, she whispered, "My dad was home a lot, but all he did was beat up on Mom and me." She tucked a loose wave of her lavender-streaked hair behind her ear. "When he finally left for good, my mom had to work two jobs. She only came home to sleep or get drunk."

"And then she met Mitch Keller and he changed all that?" Carter was hopeful that if her story turned around, his might, too.

She had a bitter laugh. "Is that what he told you?"

"He didn't tell me much of anything. Just that he loves you a lot."

"Yeah, he's famous for his sweet talk. Most bartenders are. No surprise my mom married a guy who owns a bar, right?"

Carter got defensive. "Mitch is a good man."

"Maybe his guilt gets the best of him." She shrugged. "He probably thinks he owes me because he killed my mother."

"What are you talking about?"

"Drinking and driving," Piper explained. "She died in a fatal collision, coming home from The Little Yucca."

Carter didn't know what to say. He knew how bad it had felt

when he thought he'd lost his mother after the tornadoes. Piper's loss was for real. Forever. "I reckon there's no way round the pain," he said, as much to himself as to her. "Nowhere to go but straight through it."

Piper glared at him and pushed herself back into the chaise longue. "Shut up. The last thing I need is some random runaway's pity," she said, her voice flat and final.

Why'd she always have to be so mean about everything? Carter wasn't a runaway; he was a running-to. "I'd sooner be home in the Sooner State," he said, trying to act like she wasn't getting on his last nerve. "I just have unfinished business with my dad, is all."

And no home.

"How'd you get those bruises on your back?" he asked, but it sounded more like an accusation.

She looked at him like he'd just smacked her face.

"I'm so sorry," Carter rushed to apologize. What was he thinking? He'd come back because he thought she was in danger and now he was the one hurting her. "I had no place saying—"

A tear escaped her eye, but she brushed it away quickly. She said nothing, her lips shut tight, her mouth flattened to a straight line. Carter wanted to reach out and touch her shoulder but hesitated. What did Mr. Ledbetter and Mitch do when he found himself in Las Cruces, broke and plumb out of bright ideas? They gave him his space. And a chance to make his own way.

Carter stretched out next to Piper on the cold tar-paper roof. Together, they stared up into the black burlap sky without speaking. The loss he felt on Mitch's behalf was bigger than Carter could explain. He'd said Piper's mom would always have his heart. He'd said Piper "never shook that hurt." But Mitch was the one showing up every Sunday.

Carter needed to go to his father. He needed to call his mom. Be honest. Help where he could. It seemed all too easy to fall into the habit of hurting. Carter aimed to do something about it.

Chapter Thirty-Two

THE SUN ROSE OVERHEAD AT AROUND FOUR-
thirty. In the golden light, Piper's brown eyes showed bits of
green and gray, like pebbles under a clear stream. They'd spent
the night telling stories about The Little Yucca. Carter had only
a handful, but Piper shared plenty about how she grew up
singing with Ledbetter in the kitchen and learning to cook.

Piper whipped up stacks of buckwheat pancakes. Carter
pulled a stool up to the kitchen counter, smeared his pancakes
with vegan butter and maple-flavored agave syrup, and dug in.
The steaming flapjacks were so soft and delicious, they tasted
like dessert.

"Why vegan?" Carter asked, his mouth full.

"If I said health reasons, it wouldn't be lying. I didn't want to
inherit my parents' bad habits. Besides, Mitch told me to cater to
the demand of a local niche, to 'play to my audience.' There's a
good lot of health freaks around here."

Carter wasn't any health freak, but he sure loved her pancakes. He'd eat them whether they were good for him or not.
After his third helping, he sat back and patted his swollen
tummy, satisfied. He told Piper about his gig at The Crusty
Maiden, harkening back to the thrill of performing, and how
he'd been invited back that night. Because he had to kill the
day waiting, he offered to make himself useful in the kitchen
before catching a red-eye flight into LA County after his gig.
In truth, he needed time to figure out a plan for helping her.

"Willard will come round looking for me," she assured him, as though chasing after her proved he cared. If he's so wonderful, Carter wanted to ask, what was she doing up on the roof last night?

While prepping the yucca flowers, his thoughts lurched and wavered like a tree in a Tulsa tornado, with nothing but the soggy soil to keep it from flying into the eye of the storm. The people he cared about, all of them, were in some kind of pain: his mother, Kaia, Piper, Mitch, even Mr. Ledbetter. For all he knew, his dad had the blues of some sort.

"Here, try this," she said, pouring a tangy-smelling amber liquid into a shallow bowl. "It's apple cider vinegar. It'll soothe those calluses on your fingertips."

Carter let her take his hands and drop them in the bowl. "Willard can be real sweet, Carter. He saved me, and I'll always be thankful," she began, her shoulders curling inward. "You just don't know him. He lost his way after getting kicked out of the police academy. One minute the news people were calling him a hero and the next he was serving time. All for teaching a couple of nasty no-goods right from wrong. You can't take the law in your own hands. He knows that now."

Piper stared into the bowl between them, avoiding Carter's eye. "I keep telling him there's something better than being a cop, he just hasn't found it yet."

The ounce of kindness she was showing with his fingers gave him a measure of courage to speak his mind. "I reckon music says the things words can't. And it feels real good, too." Carter didn't have bushels of time to get to the point. "Music doesn't leave any bruises."

"Well, if I met a man who made me feel like music does, I'd marry him," she said. "But there's no such thing, is there?"

"Can't say as I know," Carter replied, thankful she didn't get mad again. She was right about the vinegar; it felt good. He hadn't realized he was so sore. "Mitch said he taught you to fight. So why don't you?"

"Fight Willard?" She twisted her face like he'd suggested she kick a kitten. "Sometimes he uses his fists to say the things he can't find words for, but he promised he'd never set out to hurt me. Unlike my father. I know I can show Willard he's better than that. If I'm just patient—"

"What if you ran away?" He cut her off, daring to look her in the eye. "You could buy yourself a plane ticket, go places you always wanted to visit. Before Willard even figured out you split, you could move on to anywhere."

When Piper didn't say anything, he took it to mean she was hearing him out. "I watched where my mom hid her savings. I don't know why, but she doesn't much trust the banks." The vinegar must have been some kind of truth serum because Carter heard himself telling far too much of his worst secret. "I didn't have enough money to buy my father's guitar and I wanted it so bad. I just wanted to be free from the past, you know?"

"You didn't steal from your own mother?"

Carter was surprised. It wasn't like Piper had a gracious word for parental figures. But even though she was disappointed in him, he was glad to see she cared. Carter lifted his fingers out of the apple cider vinegar, but Piper pushed them in again. "So you think I ought to abandon my business? Walk away from everything I built with my own two hands? This is my life, Carter."

He nodded, embarrassed. She couldn't just up and leave; running never solved anything. *I ought to know*, Carter thought, glancing up at Piper's face. For all her tough talk, there was a goodness about her, like a perfectly ripe apple with a wormhole through it.

"You really think I'm tough as a claw hammer swinging both ways?"

"Yes, ma'am," he replied. The word *ma'am* made her lips crumple at the edges, not quite a smile. "I can tell you my mom wouldn't stand for a lick of sass. Any man who raises his hand to her should hope he gets to keep it."

"Hey, why don't you use that smart mouth to call her already?" she shot back. "From everything I'm hearing, you owe your mother a phone call. And a big fat apology."

Piper handed Carter the phone from her office and sent him up to the roof, where he could speak in private. He'd been through every possible conversation with her in his head. As much as he wanted to hear his mother's voice, he was worried she would have his hide for not being home yet. He didn't know if she could ever understand his wish to see his father again. In a strange way, he hoped she had the strength to give him what-for. He couldn't shake the nagging worry she might not be doing well, and it made him feel even guiltier about being so far from home.

Chapter Thirty-Three

HE SAT ON THE EDGE OF THE ROOFTOP AND looked out to the horizon. Kaia would probably like Piper, he reckoned. He jotted a quick letter to her. *There's something special about Piper's menu,* he wrote. *She's got her own flair. Slices of jicama here, chopped cilantro there. Some say there's nothing new in music, but every artist mixes their own flavors.* Carter hoped Kaia might try cooking with him some day.

There was no putting it off any longer. Carter dialed Lola May's number, then held the phone tight to his ear.

"Hi, it's me. I—" He stopped himself, realizing he ought to open with some respect straight up. "I know I owe you an apology and a whole lot more." The weight of worry made his words sound wooden and formal. "Mama's well enough to talk, I hope?"

"Well enough to be out of hospital going on a week, and even doing some minor carpentry around the shelter. But stubborn 'ol mule that she is," Lola emphasized the word *mule*, clearly for his mother's benefit, "she still won't let me move her into a hotel." As Lola passed the phone to his mom, Carter drew in as much of the big, open Tucson sky as he could hold.

"Mama, are you okay?" Before she could get a word in, he blurted, "I'm sorry. I've missed you." He let all the air out at once.

"Cotton? Oh, thank goodness. I've been so worried about you." Her voice felt as familiar, warm, and close as a Tulsa summer rainfall. Cleansing. The events of the night before, the day before, the week before, and every moment since he'd stepped into the Albuquerque airport, disintegrated. She was a part of him, the only part left that he could honestly call *home*.

"What were you thinking, sending me money?"

Carter paused, unsure how to reply. She didn't sound happy about it.

"I hated the idea of sending you to Aunt Syl's, and I certainly didn't take a shine to reaching out to your father," she went on. "But now you're in the middle of nowhere with no one to look out for you. Working in a bar, of all places." Sandra's voice turned a sour note. "I don't want your money, Cotton. I want you home, safe."

"Are you okay, Mama?" Carter couldn't believe she wasn't impressed by how responsible he'd been on his own. She did need his money. Sure, he'd made his share of mistakes, but didn't she trust him to make good?

"My head's still on my shoulders. But you've got some explaining to do." Carter had seen his Mama get mad, but never this mad. "I don't know what kind of stunt you've pulled staying on in Albuquerque, but you best pack your things. Your aunt's been pulling her hair out with worry, and I'm not faring much better. You told Lola May the Lius were bringing you back to Tulsa but they haven't heard one word from you." Her words were coming faster now, lining up like they might finish with a month-long grounding. Carter glanced at his guitar, looking for some sort of reassurance.

His first instinct was to argue. His music lessons with Mr. Ledbetter turned out to be one of the best things that ever happened to him. But Carter reckoned the reason he'd called in the first place was to be honest with her. "I'm in Tucson now, Mama."

"Tucson? You told Lola May you were in Albuquerque."

"I hitched a ride."

"This isn't a game, Cotton. You're a fifteen-year-old boy." Mama sounded mad enough to knock him into the middle of next week looking both ways for Sunday. "I should've plunked you down at a temp shelter myself." Carter tried to get a word in, explain that he was okay and that he had a plan, but Mama wasn't having it. His chest sunk. Turned out, they were having the conversation he'd expected. "Let's not forget you've got schoolwork to do. I don't suppose you've given that any thought? No, you thought you'd take a nice little vacation for yourself. What's gotten into you?"

"I'm not on vacation." Carter wished he could find the words to make her understand how none of what he'd done was easy. He wished she were there with him, to see how much he'd learned and grown. He was only trying to make things right. "The last thing I wanted was to get stuck in the middle of nowhere," he managed to choke out, but his words didn't ring true. He didn't feel stuck anymore. Sure, he would've liked it a whole lot better if his father had sent for him to begin with, offered up the cost of his ticket and a warm bed to sleep in back when he first tried calling from the hospital. But he wouldn't have met Piper or Ledbetter or Mitch. He wouldn't have learned his way around the kitchen, and he might've already sold the Martin. His dad's guitar had come to mean the whole cotton-picking world to him and as much as he loved her, as much as he was sorry, he wanted to keep it.

"Mama, don't freak out. I talked to Dad and everything's going to be okay. I'm catching a plane to his place tonight. It'll be fine." He sure hoped that was true.

"Carter, I don't know what to believe. One day you're my sweet boy and the next you're hitching rides across the country? There are some crazy, unstable, and dangerous people in this world, son. You may be six foot, but I would have your hide, I'm so sore at you."

It was safe to say his mother was near recovered.

"Mama, I won't hitchhike again, I promise. I've made some good friends and I'm learning to play—" Carter shut his fool mouth and thought hard about what he had to say about his father's guitar. "All I have left in the world is Dad's guitar. I started playing it again. It feels right. Dad said he got it for me, and Mama, I want to keep it. I want to write my own music, become a musician. I reckon it's what I was born to do."

Sandra fell quiet on her end. That was bad, he figured. He expected her to fire back, ground him until high school graduation for his sass mouth. Her silence was unbearable.

"Cotton," she spoke up at last, "let's leave the past where it belongs. Behind us."

What was she on about? His mom had built her whole business around refinishing antiques, resurrecting what was lost or left behind. There was nothing Carter wanted more than to go back to the way things used to be.

"Eddie knows you're in Tucson?" She sounded hurt that his father knew more about Carter than she did. "And he sent you a plane ticket?"

Carter was caught. He couldn't lie to her, not again. "Well, not exactly. Dad thinks I'm in Tulsa. But I have enough money to buy my own ticket. I earned it—"

"If you have money to buy a plane ticket," she said, her words solid and immovable, "you're coming home tonight."

He was sorry he hadn't called her, and he aimed to fix that. But give up on reuniting with his father?

"No."

He could almost hear the expression on her face, some mutation bent between anger and surprise. He'd never stood up to her before and he was sure she wasn't ready for it. As far as Carter was concerned, his mother had some explaining to do herself.

"I'm going to Dad's," he told her. "He invited me to play a duet with him for a Ma Joad's pancake house jingle, and he's even going to pay me for it. I'm doing it for us, Mama. We need the money." He was afraid to tell her he also wanted to see his father, be with him again.

"Cotton, Eddie's all hat and no cattle." Carter knew she thought his father was all talk, and not the genuine article, but it wasn't true. The man's own rock ballads and love songs showed up in the pop charts, just like he always wanted. Carter knew he was a showman, and a bit of a show-off, but even Mama couldn't deny he'd made a success of himself.

"He claims he sent presents and you told him not to. Is that true?" Carter stroked the bumps along his jaw where he was gritting his teeth. One of his parents was lying.

"If you count autographed promo pictures of himself. All he cared about was his own success. His way of loving was to make you think he's the greatest in the world, but he never reciprocated that feeling."

He disagreed. Carter's family was his world. And that included his father.

"When I told him to leave, I meant for good. He didn't need to send his guilt in a package."

"You left him?" Carter's legs buckled. He sank to the pool chaise, holding his forehead in his palm, a loud clanging sound pummeling him between his ears. How could she make that choice for him?

"Son," she began. "Eddie and I," she added, rationing her words like one too many might snap the last thread holding them together, "we loved each other. But just when I thought we were building something to last, he went off chasing another one of his schemes, trying to get famous. He made poor choices for us, his family. It was up to me to protect you."

"But he is famous. He caught what he was chasing, Mama."

"And I'm happy for him. But he wasn't a good father. I couldn't stand by and watch what he was doing to you. All those sketchy places he took you to perform, keeping you out till the wee hours on a school night. Shady bars, deals under the table because you were underage. Making you his little dancing monkey."

"I wasn't his 'dancing monkey.' I loved playing music," Carter argued. "You aren't a musician, you wouldn't understand."

"No, but I am a mother. Don't you remember all those weekend county fairs he dragged you to? You'd spend the whole day crying your sorry eyes out because Eddie wouldn't let you ride the roller coaster and the Ferris wheel. His idea of parenting was making you a source of revenue."

"As I recall, the audience always loved it when I played. I got standing ovations." Carter thought about telling her how it felt to play his set at The Crusty Maiden. Or about the song he was writing. He needed to make her understand.

"Oh they thought you were born to play the blues all right," she said, a bitterness staining her words. "Red-faced and snot-nosed from crying, your 'blues' came from missing out on your childhood. I tried to protect you from that life, and what do you do? Run away and find work at some run-down tavern in Las Cruces."

Carter hadn't forgotten those fairs or how much he'd longed to go on just one carnival ride. But what stung him was how he found the blues with Ledbetter. By remembering his childhood.

"That's why I pawned the guitar when he left," she added.

A bright flame snapped to high heat in Carter's belly, the

blaze surprising him like a kitchen grease fire. "You pawned the Martin?" At fifteen, he was mature enough to be thankful to her for watching out for him. But it wasn't okay to deprive him of his music.

"When did you buy it out of hawk from Tommy?"

Carter wished he could explain. Stand up and choose the life he wanted to live. That guitar had come to mean everything to him. It was his past, present, and, he hoped, his future. But he'd had to steal from her to get it. He'd left her, broken in the hospital, and he'd lied. He had no explanation. Only one question.

"Why did you pawn it? It was hard enough when Dad left. But I loved that guitar."

She pressed on, determined to make him see things her way. "I've done right by us both. Eddie was putting his wants and wishes ahead of your safety and well-being. I didn't want you to turn into your father. I begged him to ease up on you, but he didn't pay me any mind. You know I'd rather be on my own than put up with a lick of sass."

Lick of sass? He'd give her a bushel.

"Get over yourself, Mama," he heard himself say. "You've always wanted me to follow in your footsteps, and you taught me plenty. But Dad wanted me to fall in love with music. And I did. Twice now, by my count." Carter stood up and glanced over the side of the roof to the ladder. He wanted to make sure Piper wasn't listening. "I always thought you were strong," he said, quieting to a whisper. "Truth is, you think you're always right. And plenty of the time you got good reason. But you took away my father, and my guitar. Why?"

He could hear Lola May fussing in the background, begging her to "go easy on the poor kid."

"Your father was shiftier than the weather. Every time he failed—and he failed plenty—he never took responsibility for himself. Just pretended he was someone he wasn't." Carter thought about how his father had dropped his Tulsa accent. How he'd failed to mention his own son to his new family. "You were too young to be working, thinking about making money and getting famous. It was up to me to give you a stable home, a chance to be a kid. When he got it in his head to move west, chasing whims instead of getting a proper job, I was plumb out of patience." Sandra's voice softened, pleading with him. "Trust me, Cotton. I know what's best for you."

Carter let the phone drop from his ear. He held it in his lap, distancing himself from her. What a waste of time, being mad at his daddy all those years for pawning his guitar. This definitely was not a conversation he'd imagined. Carter willed his lip to remain still. If he let the quiver have its way, tears were sure to follow.

He put the phone back to his ear, steeling himself. "I best get on my way. I love you, Mama."

"Sweet pea, please come home tonight. I want to see you with my own two eyes, make sure you're okay. I understand Eddie is tempting you with that Ma Joad's jingle but we can make our own way without him. I promise."

"I got to go," he choked out. He'd heard that promise before, and they always made do. But maybe she was only part way right. Carter reckoned it was time to find out the truth about his father for himself. "I'll call you tomorrow when I get to Santa Monica."

"Cotton, I love you."

"Be safe, Mama. Take care of yourself."

Chapter Thirty-Four

CARTER HID OUT ON THE ROOFTOP A WHILE. Whatever bright hope he'd had for himself before talking to his mother was gone. Going to his father's in California was stupid. Eddie thought he was still in Tulsa. His mom wanted him back in Tulsa. He should just go back to Tulsa, he thought. But what about Piper? He wasn't one tiny step closer to convincing her to reach out to Mitch. She was still in harm's way and he'd made a promise to Mr. Ledbetter. If his mom had just listened to him, maybe he could have asked her advice about how to help. But she only wanted one thing: for him to get his butt back to Oklahoma where it belonged.

Throwing the guitar strap over his shoulder, he pulled out his notebook. He'd been putting it all together, note by note, lyric by lyric, the song he'd first caught an inkling of back at the Shoretown Inn. Carter let out a long breath and closed his eyes on everything weighing him down, going back in his mind to the pool deck at dawn. Picturing the Sandia Mountains reawakened the melody from deep within him. He hoped writing might quiet the chaos between his ears.

Carter started a fresh page, penning the chords, strumming, then writing more of the song he'd been working on the morning Ledbetter changed his guitar strings. He could feel the shape of it now and he knew the words he had to write. The melody and the lyrics fell in line together like they'd been friends all along but kept missing each other in the confusion of Carter's pressing forward and hanging back. He had to make a decision, and soon. Would he get a plane to Tulsa, or head out west to surprise his father? He was starting to see how songwriting could be about conflict, taking two opposing things and putting them together to see what happened. There was harmony between home and away. Maybe he'd given up or maybe he'd grown strong-willed, he wasn't sure which. But he could play it through until he figured it out.

Piper appeared at the top of the ladder with a sandwich. "Your song is really good, Carter. I see why Ledbetter took a shine to you." Carter shrugged like it was no big thing, but he couldn't help but smile. He helped her onto the roof and she took a seat on the pool lounge. "Taste this." She held out the plate to him.

Carter had prepped enough dishes that day to know it was her mashed pesto chickpea salad sandwich. His mother had tried to serve him chickpeas once. It was an experience he didn't want to relive. But Piper wouldn't take no for an answer.

Carter had always thought of himself as a meat-and-potatoes guy, but Piper's combination of flavors tasted bright and alive and satisfying. Familiar, yet entirely new. "It's earthy, but I like it." He took a seat next to her and dug in.

By late afternoon, Piper sent her employees home. Carter helped her scrub the kitchen. He planned to catch a bus to the airport right after his early gig at The Crusty Maiden, and he if couldn't convince Piper to come to her senses about Willard, he'd call Mitch himself.

A band of light below the door to the dining area went dark. They both knew who stood on the other side. Piper stiffened, eyeing the low snake of shadow. Even if Carter had some idea of how to help her—and he didn't—he wasn't sure Piper would let him come between them. The door swung open. Willard's hulking form dominated the frame.

"What's the kid still doing here? This place a daycare now?" Willard walked past Piper and opened the refrigerator. He helped himself to one beer, pausing to consider a tray of fresh brownies. "Why you got to put walnuts in them, Pipe? You know I'm allergic."

Piper lowered her eyes, toying with the ends of her apron strings.

Willard rambled on about his job minding the security cameras from a darkened room in an office building. It sounded like the dullest job in the world. But Carter couldn't help feeling a measure of pity. He knew all too well what felt like, being on course toward his dream job, when the winds suddenly changed. Carter wouldn't even join band at school, it hurt him too much. Security work was as close as Willard would ever get to becoming a police officer, but at least he was trying. Then it hit him. What Piper needed was security. Carter knew just where to find it.

"Hey, I got a gig tonight at The Crusty Maiden," Carter told him. "I'd appreciate some friendly faces in the crowd. Want to come?"

"The Maiden's letting some toddler brat onstage?" Willard narrowed his gaze on the boy. "We got better things to do. Piper wants to watch me clean and adjust the chain tension on my Harley."

Carter whistled like he was impressed. "Prettiest bike in America, I reckon. Best if her rider knows how to maintain her." He tried to get a read on Willard. His doughy face didn't give away much emotion. "C'mon and watch my show. I'll buy you a burger if you'll tell me what it's like to ride a bike that fine. I got my learner's permit and took a few lessons on my neighbor's Yamaha. Wish I could ride a Softail like you. Must be nice."

Willard yawned, scratching his fingers along the reddened

scalp visible under his buzz cut. "That oughta be good for a laugh, huh, babe?" Willard unbuttoned his uniform shirt and handed it to Piper. "I could go for a cold beer and a burger." Underneath he wore a plain white T-shirt, large sweat clouds drooping from his armpits.

"Yeah, should be a good laugh," she replied. Piper threw Carter a puzzled look.

Carter jutted his jaw toward the door. "Why don't you guys go on?" she said, catching on. "I need to file some receipts." She backed toward her office, angling the dirty shirt away from her nose. "I'll meet you there in a few."

"Sure, see you," Carter nodded, urging Willard out the door.

Chapter Thirty-Five

"JAILBAIT!" BET CALLED OUT WHEN WILLARD and Carter sat down at a table. From around the room, an echo of Crusty Maiden servers, security staff, and bartenders called out, "Jailbait, what's up, man?"

Willard scratched at the short hairs on his scalp, frowning at Carter. "You been in town for, what, twenty-four hours? And you got Bet on your good side?"

Bet sidled up to their table and pulled a pen from behind her ear. "What'll you have, honey? Chicken tacos again?"

"Do you have anything vegetarian?" Carter asked. One day in Piper's company had made his taste buds eager to find out what they'd been missing.

"I'll see what I can do for you, Jailbait." She winked. Piper arrived at the table, a large tote bag over her shoulder. Carter rose from his seat and pulled an empty chair for her to join them. Willard rolled his eyes and closed his menu.

"How you doing, Chef?" Bet greeted her. "Can I get you something?"

"I'd like an iced tea when you have a moment, Bet."

"What about you, Javelina?" Bet asked Willard.

"Cheeseburger, double. With bacon, double," he said, his voice like gravel. "The kid's buying. Hope it doesn't take as long to get to the table as it did to take my order."

"Get bent," Bet replied and turned on the heel of her black biker boot and stomped off.

Carter leaned across the table to Piper and whispered, "What's a javelina?"

She angled her face close to his ear and held a hand in front of her lips. "A peccary; a hairy skunk pig."

"It's a badge of honor if a Crusty Maiden gives you a nickname," Willard said, too loud. Piper and Carter exchanged a smirk, but only Bet had the mettle to rib him that way.

Carter still couldn't believe his mother had been the one to pawn his guitar. It was too much to wrap his head around. It was good that Mama was recovering, that much he could hold onto.

He set about planning which songs to perform, and Piper was kind enough to throw some ideas his way. If Willard was grumpy when they sat down, he only grew grumpier. No one bothered to ask him what music he wanted to hear. He choked down his burger then stood, the legs of his chair skating across the floor. Still chewing, he left them to sulk by the pool table. Carter was glad he'd taken his storm cloud with him.

The music Piper liked was alternative rock and lesser-known indie acts Carter followed on the college radio station back in Tulsa. Thinking about home reminded him he hadn't finished his letter to Kaia that day. Carter pulled a folded piece of paper from the back pocket of his jeans and opened it on the table, flattening it out. It was the song he'd been working on. Grabbing his pen from his backpack, he held his hand across the top, trying to come up with a title.

"Love Doesn't Walk Away," he finally wrote, stealing a glance at Piper. She stroked her bottom lip, avoiding his gaze. Carter wondered if she was stifling a smile. The song held everything he could possibly hope to say, more than he could write in a proper letter or even a whole book. Piper shot a photo of it with her phone and Carter quickly emailed the image to Kaia. Then it was time to hit the stage.

Grabbing his guitar, Carter took his place on a single stool. "Hey, everyone," he said, adjusting the microphone, "thanks for having me back." A weak round of cheers went around the room. It was early yet, and only the die-hard regulars, the ones who practically lived at The Crusty Maiden, had any clue who the kid with the mahogany guitar might be.

"I spent my whole life in Tulsa, Oklahoma," he told the audience. Carter wasn't sure when or if he'd get another chance to perform, and hoped to make the most of his gig. Storytelling, spreading good vibes, that was the way Ledbetter did it. What did he have to hide? All that time he was laying low in New Mexico, the letters he wrote to Kaia were as honest as the ties between his fingertips and his guitar. The truth prevailed, like an unstoppable wind.

"Anyone here from the Sooner State?" he asked. Not a single Okie in the place but him. "Well, a tornado took the only home I've ever known, so I set out on the road. I was in Albuquerque a few weeks back," he continued, trying a few chords. He noticed Piper wandering over to Willard like a cursed mosquito to a bug zapper. "You'll never guess who I met: Poly Virus." The crowd offered a few murmurs of approval as Carter started strumming the opening bars of "Shotgun Candle." Launching into the lyrics, he figured the worst they could do was make fun of his accent. Better to be true to himself. If they didn't like it, it didn't bother him a lick. Far as he could reckon, he was born alone and that was the way he'd die, so he'd best be his own shotgun candle, because sometimes your own family let you down.

Carter shut his eyes to concentrate. He'd practiced over countless hours. Playing guitar had become part of his nature, something he didn't have to think about, just allow. He remembered Garrett and the way he held himself. *Front man* colored his every move.

But he couldn't let go. He was worried about Piper. He couldn't stand being out of sorts with his mother. And truth be told, he was downright afraid of facing his father after all these years. A note in his song misaligned, and then another, like they'd fallen out of rhythm with his own heartbeats. He was watching his finger patterns, trying to correct his chords, when his vocals slipped out of tune. He could only maintain one thing at a time. But music was anything but one-dimensional. Around the bar, customers resumed their conversations. Bet penned an order on her pad, paying him no mind.

He knew he had to free himself in the music, blend the thousand different ingredients that made up a song. Worrying would have to wait. No, that wasn't it. He'd have to face every burden, every unknown, every worst-case scenario the way Ledbetter had taught him to treat the blues. Bring 'em on; let his pain, worry, fears, and sadness bleed into every note and lyric.

The tune was still a hair off, so he slid off the stool, opening himself. Standing in the spotlight, tall as nature made him, he played on.

The room fell quiet. Carter's sound flushed clean, pure and honest. At the bar, Bet leaned toward the stage, watching the song find its home among the strings under his fingers. Giving up the pads of his fingertips was a small sacrifice. His unruly hair fell over his eyes as his head lolled forward, following the wild beat. He swung his head back to get it out of the way, then it rolled forward again, like every hair on his head was a wave on the ocean of his music.

A small group of girls in platform heels and crop tops sat at a table to the right of the stage. When Poly Virus's familiar chorus came back around, they chimed in, singing along with Carter. The evening crowd began filing in, brightening the room with laughter and good spirits, even as the sun sank below the horizon.

Carter poured his Creativity, Victory, Heart, and Discipline into every lyric, chord, strum, and pluck on the strings. Piper watched him, mesmerized. He held the attention of every set of eyes in the house. Everyone's except Willard's, who was too busy stink-eyeing his fiancée, a dark scowl pulling down his thick face.

At the end of his song, Carter leaned into the microphone and paused, unsure whether it was too early to share the song that'd been biting a hole in him since that sunrise in Albuquerque.

"This next one goes out to a girl I never knew back home. But she sure knows a thing or two about me," he said, his breath too loud in the mic. "It's called 'Love Doesn't Walk Away.' I hope it's as good as it sounds on paper."

Chapter Thirty-Six

PIPER PULLED AWAY FROM WILLARD. KNEELING in front of the stage, she held up her phone to Carter, recording a video of his song. Drawing near, she shot a close-up of his hands strumming furiously with a mind of their own. Carter's eyes met hers over the top of her phone and he sang the chorus line, the reason Mitch kept showing up every Sunday. Belting out the lyrics with all his heart, Carter caught a glimpse of his mother's choice to go her own way, too. And his father's respect for her space. But he was still lost in the middle.

Willard didn't like all the fuss Piper was making with her phone. "Time to go home." He took hold of her upper arm. "I've had enough of this dung heap." He grabbed the phone from her hand and thumbed a few icons. Carter could tell by the cruel edge to his grin that he'd deleted the video. It didn't matter. The song wasn't ready yet anyway. Couldn't be, not when the people he loved were still walking away.

Carter brought the song to an end. "Bet, can you help me out a second?" he called to his favorite server. He wasn't about to let Willard take Piper anywhere, not if he could do something about it.

Too brazen to miss a beat, she answered him from across the loud bar. "What can I do for you, honey?"

"I'd like to place a wager," he said into the mic, faking a grin. Dead center in the spotlight, he had to make it seem like what he was about to do was part of the act. "A slice of your famous chocolate cake to Ms. Piper Piedra here if she'll get up and sing with me."

Bet let out a long hoot and a whistle. Willard stopped short and glared at Carter, still gripping Piper's arm. "Been down that road, honey," Bet told Piper, sidling up to the stage. "I'd like to say I came out a winner. You might as well take your chances on this snip of trouble with a guitar."

"Stop wasting everybody's time," Willard grunted into Piper's ear. He pulled her toward the front door. "Let's get out of here." Stooping like a whupped pup, she glanced sidelong at Carter with sorry eyes and poor excuses: *I don't even want cake. It's probably not vegan here.* Carter knew it was up to Piper to stay or go. If she wasn't ready to take a stand for herself, there was nothing he, or Mitch, or anyone could do. He sure hoped she'd fight and not follow.

Bet lifted a fishnet leg onto an empty chair and hoisted herself up onto a table surrounded by tattooed and bearded regulars. Cupping her hand around her blood-red lips with one hand and waving a bar towel with the other, Bet booed Willard for hassling "The Crusty Maiden's newest singing sensation." Following her lead, Carter rallied the crowd in a chant, then pulled a second microphone next to his. The girls who sang along to "Shotgun Candle" joined Carter's chant straight up. Faster than a metronome set to speedcore, they had the whole crowd chanting, "Pi-per, Pi-per, Pi-per."

When Piper dared to turn back to Carter, he met her eye. He hoped Ledbetter had made the stage a safe place for her the way he had for Carter. He held out the second mic to her and waited for her to choose which way she wanted the wind to blow.

Piper pulled away from Willard and slumped toward the stage, rubbing at the back of her arm where he'd held her too tightly. Bet lowered the bar towel to her side and the crowd quieted down. All eyes followed Piper. Securing the second mic in a stand, Carter sat down on the stage stool. When she reached the stage, she hesitated in the dim shadow at the curved edge of the spotlight. He nodded to her, asking her to take the last step to join him. She stood frozen in the shadow and he wondered whether he was making another mistake.

Carter stole a glance at the crowd and centered his guitar in position, strumming a chord to signal another song was on the way. He didn't know Piper from nothing and maybe all this was stupid. Or, from the looks of Willard, darn near dangerous. Bet stepped down from the table and edged toward Piper, concern pinching the high arch of her painted brow.

Choosing a familiar melody, Carter slowed its tempo, strumming out an agonizing wail of Patsy Cline's "Walkin' After Midnight." The song was a gamble, but he had to take a chance. Piper found the steps to the stage in the dark, joining Carter. The din of the crowd settled. He repeated the intro a few times to prepare her.

Clutching the mic, she stared at the wall behind the bar, straight past Willard's angry glare, listening.

Carter abandoned the intro and transitioned to the melody. All hesitation gone, the song's familiar old lyrics poured from Piper, filling Carter's heart with relief and gratitude. She sang of the sorrow of wandering in the night and her lonesome hideaway atop The Desert Willow. Night winds seemed to whisper through Piper's voice, blending with Carter's bittersweet longing for the highway waiting ahead and the miles behind him. Carter watched her, the spotlight unloading Piper's inner demons, just like Ledbetter said it would.

Carter and Piper were different as night and day, no doubt about it, yet Carter recognized they shared the same musical core, the kind of DNA replication he'd learned about in Mr. Russell's science class back at Bob Bogle High School. If Carter believed Piper should be brave enough to leave Willard, give up the familiar in favor of the unknown, he ought to, too. He needed to go see his father.

Watching Piper transform before his eyes, feeling the music flow effortlessly from his hand, and witnessing the transfixed crowd drawing closer to the stage, Carter was beginning to believe in his own transformation.

By the end of the song, Bet was smiling up at the two of them from the foot of the stage. "Jailbait, you are something else. How'd you know that was my favorite song?"

He hadn't. Shrugging, he tried to make sense of it. "The Desert Willow reminds me of the weeping willows back home in Oklahoma," he said. "Weeping willows remind me of 'Walkin' After Midnight.' And Patsy Cline reminds me of another music legend—my buddy, Mr. Ledbetter." Carter grinned. "Seeing as Ledbetter taught Piper here to sing, I reckoned she might be familiar with the old song."

For the first time, Carter witnessed Piper's smile.

Song requests drifted from the floor. Piper found her mojo and the audience loved her. The downswing of her slumped shoulders straightened, opening her heart to the crowd. She loosened her choke hold on the microphone.

Soon Piper led the music, calling the playlist on a whim, song by song. Their set lasted just over an hour. Carter had been raised to stake his claim as a solo act, but performing as a duo gave him a sense of belonging. He liked how their individual offerings fell together in harmony. Performing the Ma Joad's jingle duet with his dad seemed only natural now.

Every passing minute multiplied the flush of red climbing up Willard's neck from the collar of his T-shirt. He didn't look so good. Pushing past other customers and shoving against chairs, Willard stumbled toward the stage. "You already spend the better part of the day running that hippie dive. If you think you're going to start singing at night when you should be home with me," he said through gritted teeth, his words staggered and blurred, "you better believe I got something to say about it." Carter glanced with worry at Piper, but she didn't falter. An empty bottle sailed across the stage, nearly whacking Carter on the forehead. Surprised, Willard turned and squinted into the darkness to see who'd pitched it.

"I knew I'd find you, little man."

Carter silenced his strings, the cold terror he'd felt behind the steering wheel of Darren Bartles's truck flushing over him like a full-body brain freeze. With the spotlight in his eyes, he couldn't make out faces in the crowd.

A wiry body burst from the shadows, pushing Willard aside and barreling toward the stage. Carter caught hold of Piper's hand, pulling her out of harm's way. Darren Bartles leaped onto the stage, grabbed Carter by his shirt and yanked him forward, choking him with his free hand. "Thought you could run away? You still owe me that guitar for the ride," he said, squeezing Carter's neck. "It's a beauty. Should cover the cost of those tools I lost, and for the fines I had to pay." Darren pulled the boy close enough for Carter to get a whiff of Darren's whiskey stink.

Bet summoned the bouncers. A tight crowd surrounded the stage. Darren grabbed for Carter's guitar, but Carter swung his arm up and around, elbowing Darren square in his nose. Willard toppled a chair to the floor in his hurry to get to Piper. He marched up the steps to the stage, taking hold of her by the arm and dragging her toward the back exit. She must not have been too keen on going,because her knee came up hard to his groin. When Willard yelped and covered his hands over his crotch, Piper punched him in the neck and kicked at his knees, knocking him to the floor. Mitch would be proud of her.

Darren came at Carter again. He swung his guitar over his back and flicked his fingers in Darren's eyes. His fingertips sprang lightning fast after plucking at the strings for the past hour and the effect sure made an impression. Darren fell back, pawing at his eyes. Two bouncers broke through the cheering crowd. One hooked Darren around the arms and the other tackled Willard. They escorted the skunk pig and the tool thief out to the sidewalk in front of The Crusty Maiden, accompanied by a round of cheers.

Carter packed up his guitar quickly and Piper grabbed her tote bag. Bet ushered them out the back door. "Best you get yourself somewhere safe, now. We'll see you tomorrow?"

"Sorry for the brawling and carrying on," Carter said, looking away. Tomorrow he'd be in California and he didn't much care for good-byes. His bigger worry was what to do about Piper.

"You didn't start that fight," Bet pointed out. "But you sure finished it."

Carter turned to her and threw his arms around her in a hug. "I owe you a world of thanks."

"You're a decent kid, Jailbait."

Piper grabbed Carter by the hand and they raced up the sidewalk to her restaurant. "LA. Tonight," she panted with shining eyes. "You and me?"

Carter broke out in a grin. "I'm ready if you are."

Piper pulled a spare key for Willard's motorcycle and turned the ignition. "I make the payments on it," she said with a shrug. "I should get to ride it."

"For real," Carter agreed.

She handed him Willard's helmet. Piper strapped hers on

and jumped on the bike, flipping the Run/Stop switch to Run. Nothing happened. She flipped it again, pitching her body forward, as though the motorcycle might take off on its own.

"You got to squeeze the clutch with the bike in neutral," Carter told her. "You ever ridden this thing before?"

"I watched him plenty," she said, a threat in her tone. Nice Piper was fading quickly.

She glanced back over her shoulder toward The Crusty Maiden, her face wrung with worry. "You think you can handle it?" she asked.

"I can get us out of town, then teach you once we're safe."

Chapter Thirty-Seven

Piper directed him to head west on Interstate 10 toward Los Angeles. They had a seven-hour drive ahead of them, but Carter was so pumped with excitement, he felt as if they could nearly make it in two.

The lights of Tucson faded behind them as they sailed across the desert. For a long while Carter stared ahead to the endless dark highway, his thighs hugging the bike. He found having a passenger to counterbalance made the ride seem more stable. Scenes from The Crusty Maiden played out in his mind. They'd only been onstage an hour, but time sure had stood still. It was one of those one-with-the-universe moments, and it had come out of nowhere. Over his shoulder, Piper broke into a raucous laugh of freedom. Wild freedom and abandon.

"I just sang in front of one of the toughest crowds in Tucson. And they liked it!" She let out a long howl, the kind that might attract a coyote in spring. "And I left him." She smacked Carter's back good-naturedly. "I didn't just leave. I fought that big, dumb javelina. And I won."

Carter started laughing, too, happy to see her happy. Piper squeezed his shoulder with one hand. "You're all right."

Over the next three hours, they recalled the high points of the evening. Carter couldn't believe she'd planned to go to California with him before she even set foot in The Crusty Maiden. He was going to face his father at last, thanks to her. He'd wanted to save her, but she'd saved herself. Piper grew quiet a while. After a spell, she spoke up. "I know it wasn't easy calling your mother. I'm sorry if I pushed you." The roadside lamp-posts illuminated the bike in intervals, dark and then light. He could see her eyes in the rearview mirror before they fell into darkness, and then he met her gaze again.

"Well, now it's your turn," he said.

"Mitch?"

"Yup."

♪ ♪ ♪

THEY pulled in to a service station to fill up. Piper didn't say much when she spoke to Mitch. Turned out, it was enough for her to call. Mitch told her to take her time in LA, sort things out for herself. He promised he'd step in at The Desert Willow, give the assistant manager a task list for the week, keep him accountable.

"Thanks, Mitch," she said. "I'd feel better knowing you were there. You got a way of bringing out the best in people."

Carter reckoned that right there, on a long scratch of highway under an ink-black sky in the American Southwest far from home, he and Piper were probably the bravest they'd ever been.

Back on the road, he started singing, beginning with the songs they'd performed earlier that night at The Crusty Maiden. Piper sang along, her voice determined and unwavering.

Over the miles, Piper's voice gently faded to quiet. This bike ride was one of the best moments of his life and he planned to remember it in a letter to Kaia.

They'd left Tucson around nine. Piper said that would put them in Santa Monica at four or five in the morning, depending on LA traffic. Carter didn't want to show up in the wee hours of the morning and disturb his father's new family, but he didn't want to risk missing him before he went to work either. Then there was the tough business of calling his mother again, to let her know he'd made it. Carter sure wished he'd had the chance to tell her all the good that'd come of his travels. If he'd gotten a word in about the yucca petals, she might have been impressed. The real problem was the guitar. The thing that meant the most to him, the promise of his future, and the life breath of his right now, she could never understand. He'd stolen from her to get it because she'd never have agreed to his having it.

They still had miles ahead of them before the I-10 reached Los Angeles County, and Piper wanted to say a proper good-bye to the desert. They decided to kill some time at Joshua Tree National Park, just outside Palm Springs. There would be plenty of room for riding lessons.

Piper hopped off the bike and had a look around. Carter hung back, admiring the gorgeous machine. A ride like that belonged with Piper, he reckoned. He squinted into the darkness to see where she'd gone. The highway buzzed with passing cars, but beyond the shoulder of the road there was no division between the land and the sky at night. It was all one, a great big seamless universe without boundary. A kid could get lost out there.

A fat moon hung alone in the borderless desert sky. The trees there were unlike anything Carter had ever seen, like an oak tree in a cactus costume, arms raised to the sky to polish the moon. Piper explained that the Joshua tree was actually a type of yucca, the result of the combination of two desert systems, the Mojave and Sonoran. "They call them Joshua because some religious folks thought the ragged bark and bending branches reminded them of an Old Testament prophet," she said. Carter asked her to repeat that, then wrote it in his notebook. He couldn't put off his schoolwork any more. It was time to take responsibility. Maybe he'd do his independent research project on the types of yucca native to southwestern deserts. They'd witnessed his journey, they'd fed him, they'd helped him earn his way. He wondered what Caleb and Landon were writing about back home. He felt older than them now. Like he'd seen some things, enough to call himself a man.

"When we get to my dad's, we should play 'Walkin' After Midnight' for him." Carter grinned at Piper. "Hey, he may be a pop star now, but he's still old school in his blood."

She'd pulled off her jacket and bundled it into a pillow, stretching out and staring up into the night. Carter joined her, resting his head in his arms. She didn't move or turn to look at him. "I'll go with you as far as your father's. Then you're on your own."

Carter coughed, clearing his throat. "You're not going back to him, are you?"

"No, honey. Me and Willard are over. I just need time to myself. You need time, too, to bond with your father and all that."

Carter felt able to take on anything with her by his side. But he couldn't count on her, or anybody, to live his life for him. "What are you going to do?"

Piper shrugged. "I'm going to get familiar with doing things my way."

Carter was quiet for a while, hushed by the enormous expanse of desert sky twinkling over them. Under those same stars, his mother trusted herself to make good with what she had. Under those same stars, his father had a new life, too, and soon he would be part of it. He wondered what Piper was thinking about. She would tell him if she wanted him to know, he figured. He just hoped they would make music together again one day.

Bright headlights and the crunch of gravel under wheels startled them. Piper jolted to a sitting position and Carter rolled over to find a cube van pulling to a stop next to the motorcycle. Four guys jumped out the back and dropped a ramp. They laid siege on Willard's motorcycle, wheeling it into the van. Carter took off running toward them, but he felt like he was running in slow motion while they were moving in triple time. Before he could reach the road, the cube van's doors slammed shut and upturned gravel pelted him from its squealing tires. Willard's motorcycle was gone.

Chapter Thirty-Eight

THE DESERT'S ENDLESS DARKNESS CREPT close around them. Goosebumps prickled the skin on Carter's bare arms. Even though the evening was warm, Piper folded her arms tightly across her chest. "I should've known that was coming. Can't be happy for one night, can I?"

"Where'd they come from anyway?" Carter asked. She wouldn't look at him; she wouldn't even answer.

What Carter was worried about was whether they were alone or if there was someone out there. Training an eye on the sprawling, endless darkness, he watched for any subtle movements or shadowy shapes. The Joshua tree looked a whole lot like a man's body with two outstretched arms.

The closest town, Indio, was up ahead another twenty-five or thirty miles. Carter picked up his guitar and began walking the gravel shoulder like he could see it at a hundred paces. He hoped Piper'd get off her sorry behind and follow.

Along the flat stretch of highway, he kept his head up, shoulders squared, faking confidence to cover how terrified he felt inside. From behind him, he could hear the approach of oncoming traffic. Carter stole a sidelong glance at each passing vehicle. Could be they were all thieves on the prowl. Or maybe one of these drivers was their rescue, the light in the desert that would save them. Like the contradictions in a song, strangers were both a threat and a salvation.

Piper dragged along behind, the whupped pup he'd witnessed earlier that evening at The Maiden. Piper put on a plenty fierce face in daylight, but when things went catawampus, she was good for all of nothing.

They could call a taxi, he reckoned. Piper had her phone. He was willing to put up cash for a ride. He was just about to call out to her when he remembered where he'd left his backpack, his notebook, and every dollar he'd made. Sitting on the seat of Willard's motorcycle.

He walked faster, a bitter taste in the back of his throat. Carter's breath caught, his mouth filled with a sour, vinegary liquid. Before he recognized what was happening, he doubled over and threw up on the dusty shoulder of the road, inches from his Converses. He was broke. Again.

Piper's narrow figure stood frozen more than a hundred yards back. Carter was alone. Again.

Another round of vomit followed. He breathed hard, heaving. Bent at the waist, his hands on his knees, he became self-conscious in the flood of headlights as passing cars, trucks, and vans sped by. Music pumped from many of them, as though each vehicle was throwing its own party. Convertibles shot past, filled with twenty-somethings singing along to loud music. Carter felt another bout of vomit coming on and braced himself. His body rocked and pitched, heaving nothing but sharp, stank air. He wiped his face with the bottom of his T-shirt and squinted into the darkness. Far behind, Piper waited for him. He took off running toward her, one hand holding his sick stomach, his guitar weighing a ton on his back. When he reached her, she was crying. Piper wasn't so tough after all.

"It's too far," she said, sniffling. "Let's just hitch a ride or something." She tried on the sneer she'd worn when he first met her. "I'm not afraid."

Carter thought about the run-in he'd just had with Darren

Bartles at The Crusty Maiden. "Hitching's not so easy," Carter began, but he didn't have any fight left in him. He'd done the best he could. He'd thought he could get to his dad's on his own, but he was wrong and his mom was right. He belonged at home.

"I can't believe you talked me into this," she said, a tone in her voice sharp enough to imply the word *Crater* without even having to say it.

"I never made you—"

"Promise me you won't tell Mitch," she said, like it was a command, not a favor. She marched away from the road and plopped down in the dirt. "I can only imagine the earful he'd give me about making a mess this big."

"I won't tell him. But I'm willing to bet my last breath he'd come and help if we called."

"I know it," she said, irritated. "Even if he left Las Cruces this minute, he couldn't make it here 'til dawn anyway." Piper pulled her legs to her chest and wrapped her arms around them, shrinking herself to nothing but a rock. *Piedra,* Carter thought.

There wasn't much he could do. Just the one thing he'd promised he wouldn't.

Chapter Thirty-Nine

CARTER WALKED OUT TO THE EDGE OF THE FREEWAY and turned to face the oncoming traffic. He wasn't sure exactly how it was done, but he'd seen it in movies. He raised his right hand to shoulder level, his fist clear across the white line, edging toward the traffic. He pointed his thumb toward the stars and stared into the pairs of glowing white headlights.

Vehicles flew past him. The speed limit on that stretch of the I-10 was seventy miles per hour, but most shot past going eighty or more.

An older, tricked-out station wagon, painted school-bus yellow and lifted on thirty-five-inch tires, lagged behind the bulk of traffic. Carter watched it signal right to the slow lane. Jumping and flailing his long, lanky arms, he waved the driver over. There were only two guys in the front, with an empty backseat. He called Piper over as it slowed to a stop just ahead of them. Running to catch up, he leaned into the passenger side and chatted up the driver and his friend. Turned out, they were headed to Coachella, an annual music festival held every April right outside Indio. Considering how many passing cars were blasting music, Carter figured that's where most everyone was headed. The back of the station wagon was loaded down with boxes and crates of various glow sticks, glow jewelry, and glow-in-the-dark commemorative shirts. The guys were vendors, they said. They had a tent space reserved for the weekend, where they could sell gear and take turns checking out the various stages. Carter couldn't believe his luck.

Piper refused to get in the back of the car. "No way I'm getting into some beat-up banana car with people I've never laid eyes on in my life."

"Just how do you expect to make it to Indio? I'm trying to help us both here, Piper. We need a ride, you know? We're nowhere but nowhere." If he'd just ditched her that first night, used the plane ticket he'd bought before he left Las Cruces, he'd already be at his dad's in LA. Instead, he was babysitting a bitter woman in the middle of downtown Nowheresville, population two.

Dust crept up around his legs and gravel scattered across the highway. Carter stopped harping on her long enough to realize the station wagon had pulled away. He watched its taillights disappear down the highway.

"Now's when you decide to get picky? Perfect timing." Carter tightened his grip on his guitar and started walking backward, watching for another vehicle he might flag down. "Where was that high-and-mighty attitude when you chose a fine specimen of man like Willard?"

"I'm not going to discuss my love life with a little kid, *Crater.*" Piper stomped along the shoulder like she was giving it what-for.

Carter knew she was used to dishing up the sarcasm, not eating it. But he wasn't finished with her. "Yeah? Well, we're going to talk about it because who you decide to love, or stop loving, affects everybody close to you." He wanted Piper to be happy and any fool could see Willard was no good. But he wasn't talking about Willard; he was talking about his mother and he darn well knew it.

"Oh, I got that. Clear as a bell, little boy." Piper stuck out her arm, her thumb raised toward traffic. "Thanks to you, I'm trying not to love him. And look how that turned out for everybody."

She was yelling now. It was crazy, but Carter preferred it. He liked her fire. It showed her strength, the kind of determination it must have taken to establish her business and make a success of herself. Besides, he was through with taking care of everyone else's feelings. He could barely handle his own.

A large van approached with a familiar pattern of lights across the windshield's brow. Where'd he seen that before? It wasn't the one that stole Willard's motorcycle. Those guys were long gone. He could hear the van's rattle and sputter from half a mile up. It wasn't running well, like it'd been on the road a long while and was hurting for a rest. He knew the sound too well. His mother's vintage Chevy pickup had let her down plenty.

The van moved a little slower, then fell behind as several cars passed it. Carter watched the other vehicles, searching for a potential ride. That van wasn't going to make it another mile. Finally, it rolled out of traffic and onto the shoulder, only a stone's throw from Piper. Carter stopped in his tracks. He was sure mad, but not enough to let some random van pull up next to her two ticks before midnight.

The van's side-panel door swung open. Carter moved between it and Piper, calling to mind Mitch's instructions: eyes, groin, neck, and knees. From the corner of his eye, he spied Piper forming a fist in each hand. Two guys hopped out into the shadows. The driver's door opened, and out came a long, lean man in black jeans and a ripped black tee. He circled round the van with fluid, rhythmic movements.

Carter would've recognized him anywhere. It was Garrett from Poly Virus.

"Is that you, man?" Garrett flicked the switch on a flashlight, illuminating Carter and Piper.

"Does a one-legged duck swim in circles?" Grinning with relief, Carter reckoned the old Southern saying was as good as ID.

"What y'all doing out here?" Austin mocked his accent, offering his hand. Carter shook it, trying to keep up with the drummer's gang-style handshake.

"We were on our way to LA. We stopped to check out Joshua Tree National Park and some punk fool jacked our ride," Carter said.

"Dude, I thought you were just a kid or something," Garrett replied, shining the flashlight between Carter and Piper.

"He's fifteen," Piper said, still mad as a wet hen. "A freakishly overgrown child."

"And you're out here by yourself?" Garrett raised a questioning eyebrow at Piper. She mumbled something about delivering him to his daddy because she was done with babysitting.

"I'm the one doing the babysitting," he said, loud and clear. He'd had enough of her acting bigger than her britches. Carter walked over to the van, determined to hold his own. "Sounds like the van's giving you trouble." He gestured to Garrett to bring the light over to the hood. "I might be able to help."

"Hey, if you got the skills, who am I to argue? My phone's map says there isn't a garage for miles." Garrett used a glove to pop the hot lid and shone the light on the engine. "At about six, maybe seven hundred RPM, it makes a knocking noise," he told him, "like a bolt rattling around inside an aluminum case."

"Sounds like the heat shield for the catalytic converter," Carter said, checking the oil level. "What's the engine, a 5.3 liter?"

"Yeah, and it's mad nervous about getting to Indio," Garrett said, looking up and down the stretch of highway for a car repair shop that didn't exist. "There're tools in the back. Fix the van and you can be our guest at Coachella. What do you say, Oklahoma?"

Carter cracked a grin. He'd change the oil, plugs, and air

filter with his bare hands for a chance to go to the historic Coachella Valley Music and Arts Festival, a two-day concert featuring rock, hip hop, indie, and electronic dance music. "You have room for two?"

Chapter Forty

THE BOYS IN THE BAND DIDN'T KNOW WHAT
to make of Piper. She'd topped her black tank and skirt with
some kind of mesh minidress to go to The Crusty Maiden. The
outfit looked cool on stage, but Carter hadn't noticed Piper
wasn't half-bad to look at either. He was glad to help the band if
it meant he and Piper could catch a ride, but he needed to look
out for her, too. He introduced her as owner and head chef of
The Desert Willow in Tucson, and a fine singer to boot.

"You're the man, bro," Austin said, elbowing him in the ribs.

"C'mon, y'all, she's like my sister." Carter cast an apologetic
glance at Piper. She surprised him with half a smile. They were
kin of sorts, thanks to Mitch, Ledbetter, and the music they
shared.

Carter had become a string on his own guitar, an equal con-
tributor, as necessary as the other five. The strings were family,
just like they all were—Sandra, Eddie, Ledbetter, Mitch, Piper,
and Carter.

With Garrett holding the flashlight and Dex the bassist
handing tools as needed, Carter soon had the van purring again.
"Oklahoma, y'all saved our skins," the boys said, their attempts at
sounding Southern going over-twang. Even Piper found it in
her stony heart to punch him good-naturedly on his arm. "Nice
work, Carter," she said. "Don't know what I'd do without you."

They all piled in and headed west. Poly Virus's manager had
set the band up with a condo in Palm Desert, no more than an

hour's drive away. Piper piped up, telling the guys all about Carter covering "Shotgun Candle" and writing his own song. Carter was busy on Piper's phone.

He texted Kaia from a cramped corner in the back of the van, wedged between the drum kit and some mic stands.

Guess where I am?

There was no answer, so he opened his email and checked for new messages. He found a mess of notifications about his name being tagged in posted images on Kaia's social media timelines. He clicked through, landing on page after page featuring images of the letters he'd written her, uploads of the videos he'd sent, the line drawings he'd sketched, even his recipe, posted for anyone in the world to see. The one person he chose to spill his dern heart to was making a spectacle of him. Carter wished he could take it all back. The van lurched down the highway, and Carter's stomach see-sawed between embarrassment and anger. Why did she share my personal stuff, he wondered. *I trusted her.*

The truth was that keeping his promise to send her something every day had made him feel less alone, which was good because it seemed a lot of the people who mattered most were against him.

Carter couldn't tear his eyes away from the comments. A few kids had made some rude cracks about how he'd skipped school so many times they wouldn't have realized he was out of town. But to his surprise, Kaia didn't let anyone back home speak a bad word against him. She commented back with some good old-fashioned sass: *Is your butt jealous of the amount of crap that comes out of your mouth?* Carter had a laugh. It looked like she was getting more comfortable with living south of Jersey. Kaia had shared his dumb-fool letters as evidence to everyone back home that he wasn't the tough kid they thought he was. She was shining a light on his accomplishments, which came as a surprise because she'd pushed everyone away from the very day she arrived at Bob Bogle High School. Maybe that was her way of protecting herself as the new girl at school: shoot 'em down before they shoot you.

Piper's phone vibrated with an incoming text. Carter glanced at the screen.

Is that you, C?

Carter texted her back quickly.

Yup. And I'm in California with Poly Virus. Headed to Coachella

Kaia said she wished she'd run away with him. When he got home, she wanted him to promise he'd teach her how to make deep-fried yucca blossoms with hot sauce. Carter was more than obliged. He was glad she wanted to get back in the kitchen and he was even happier she wanted to cook with him. He scrolled back to the top to her latest post, the picture of his song, "Love Doesn't Walk Away," that he'd emailed her earlier that evening at The Crusty Maiden. Seeing it reminded him that Kaia hadn't walked away from him. Carter had been a friend to her, and she was proving to be a friend to him.

For a moment, the phone went still. There were no incoming texts, and Carter wondered if he should play it cool and not show how eager he was to hang with her. He put the phone down and pretended to be interested in the various amps lining the back of the van. A minute passed, and Piper's phone vibrated with another message. Kaia had sent an image of her just-completed independent research project, titled "American Southwestern Cuisine of Historic Route 66."

Carter about lost his stomach again. Checking the calendar on Piper's phone, he realized the independent research projects were due on April 30th, the day after next. He had to get a month's worth of schoolwork done in just over 24 hours.

He'd wanted to write about the various types of yucca he'd encountered. But after the motorcycle was stolen, the Joshua trees had creeped him out with their outstretched hands frozen in place, part zombie, part robber holding them at gunpoint. He had nothing to show for the last several weeks and the independent research project counted for everything. Without it, he'd fail ninth grade.

Carter brushed back his hair, clutching it in his fist. He imagined the fit his mom would pitch when she found out. He had no idea what his dad might say if or when he ever made it to the man's front door. "Hi, Dad. I'm repeating freshman year. Bet your new kids are smarter than me." He pictured Kaia, Caleb, and Landon starting sophomore year without him in the fall. He didn't like that image at all.

All he'd done was make one mistake after another. He'd known he had to write an IRP. Why hadn't he made his schoolwork a priority instead of running around the desert in Las Cruces, mixing mesquite flour at Piper's, or practicing guitar all hours? A minute passed, and then another and another. *I'm worn slap out*, he thought.

Carter couldn't help but shake his head. At the pancake house, he told Kaia he wanted to sell the guitar and be done with his past. That was ancient history now. He wanted to see his father again, know the man. Far as he could reckon, his mother had done them wrong. But she only wanted to protect him, and even though he was miles away, in truth he wanted to protect her too.

He rode in silence in the darkness of Poly Virus's van. Piper and the guys were singing along with the radio, laughing among themselves. Carter was glad she hadn't pulled her hard-as-rock act with them. She'd softened like desert air in the tight space, warm and substantial, the way he'd come to know her.

He looked over Kaia's timeline again at all the secrets he'd shared with her, the struggles he'd had with his earliest attempts to pluck the strings on his father's Martin. He'd come farther than he'd reckoned. On those pages, he'd recorded his journey, from the few songs he knew as a kid to a competent axman who knew the power of his own blues.

None of it would exist if she didn't care about his journey. He texted her:

Can't wait to read your IRP. I'll send you mine. Soon. I hope

Chapter Forty-One

WHEN THE BAND SETTLED INTO THE CONDO, Carter told Piper and the guys about the independent research project. Dex made a pot of coffee and ordered pizza. Garrett offered his tablet. He had a few moviemaking apps loaded and they were fairly straightforward.

The guys hit the sheets for the night. Their set was the next day and they wanted to rest up. They had no intentions of sleeping the rest of the weekend, so every wink counted.

Nighttime in Indio was warm as a summer night in Tulsa. Piper curled up on a chaise longue outside on the patio, a light blanket around her shoulders. "Get your homework done, baby bro," she said with a sly grin.

Carter sat at the patio table, his face illuminated by the tablet's glow. He created a folder with images of his letters, drawings, and videos pulled from Kaia's social media pages. As he clicked on each post, he scrolled further down the comments from his classmates. Turns out, he was building a grassroots fan base back home. Caleb and Landon had his back, chiming in with Kaia's support.

He worked through the night on a multimedia presentation, comprising every minute of his road trip, including highlights from his letters, images he found online of the places he'd been, a detailed map of his trip, clips of him playing music, the image Piper took of "Love Doesn't Walk Away," even his recipe for Carter Danforth's deep-fried mesquite yucca flowers with hot sauce. He threw in some facts about *yucca genera* of the American Southwest. His teachers would eat that up. The presentation just needed a title.

Carter saved his work and got up from the table. He crossed the parking lot of the condo complex and wandered out into the desert. Kicking at the raw, dry ground, so different from back home, he thought about how he'd run away from Albuquerque airport to get to his father. That wasn't what his trip was about anymore. His letters to Kaia had showed him what it meant and what he'd always remember. He saw how the kindness of strangers was founded on his own kindness toward others. It was like performing a song. The Creativity, Victory, Heart, and Discipline he gave of himself came back round a hundredfold.

When he made his way back to the patio table and sat down, Carter inserted a title sequence at the opening of his presentation. He called it *How I Learned to Play Guitar.*

Chapter Forty-Two

BRIGHT RAYS OF EARLY MORNING LIGHT woke him. Carter had sprawled out on a cushioned chaise longue on the patio and caught a few winks after saving the last draft of his presentation. It was good, decent enough, he supposed. All Carter needed was a C to pass.

Piper and the guys were still sleeping. The condo complex was silent, washed in golden light breaking through purple clouds. He had no clue what time it was in Indio or Tulsa, but he figured the best thing he could do was check in with his mother, let her know he was safe. At least he had his schoolwork done.

Carter found Piper's cell on a nightstand and took it for a walk around the complex. Keeping on the move fired up his courage. He took a deep breath, and before she had a chance to freak out again, he told his mom exactly where he was. He told her about his performance at The Crusty Maiden, about his duet with Piper, and about the bar fight with Darren and Willard. He told her about riding the motorcycle, how it got stolen, and even about the hitchhiking and Poly Virus. He was so hot on confession, he forgot to mention his independent research project.

Carter's mother listened. Her only responses were "Uh-huh" and "I see."

She didn't yell at him or freak out.

Carter pushed his hair back and squeezed his eyes shut. "You remember asking how I got Dad's guitar back from Tommy?"

"Of course, Cotton. It must have cost a fortune."

"You might say that." He sniffed. Dropping to a whisper, he finally confessed. "I used all the money you hid in your pickup to buy it, Mama. Just before the storms hit. I hated knowing the Martin was there, proof that Dad had once been in Tulsa too, and teaching me to play it. I wanted to destroy it and I didn't think you'd let me if I asked. I'm sorry I stole the money. I'm even sorrier for not telling you sooner." He waited for her to give him what he had coming. He expected she'd ground him for a full year. Maybe longer.

But she was quiet, just hearing him out.

At last, she said, "I don't want you to worry about the money."

Carter promised he'd pay her back every penny.

"No, sweet pea. It was all for you anyway. I was saving that money to buy the Martin back. I offered Tommy seven hundred fifty for it but he wanted another couple hundred."

Carter remembered her saying she was saving her money for something important. "You were the buyer Tommy had lined up?"

"Cotton, I always knew selling that guitar was a mistake. Once it was gone, your grades dropped, you started cutting classes, and even when I tried to keep you busy working on my old truck or in my workshop, you'd plumb lost your spark. I started putting away money to buy it back. After you disappeared, I got a call from Tommy saying he was having it signed and unless I made a more substantial offer, he'd find another buyer. I thought I'd never be able to get it back for you."

Her love, more than enough for two parents, filled the empty space where his prickly and troublesome secrets had taken up too much room. He should have trusted her. His mother made mistakes, just like he had, but she always stood by him.

"Son, I know I told you why I left Eddie, but I didn't tell you why I fell in love with him. I should have because you've got all the best parts of your father." Carter could hear her smile through her words. "He's a hard worker, and he picks up on the goodness in others. He's got compassion and he understands what makes people tick. That's why folks are drawn to him and his music. I'm afraid Tulsa was too small for a man looking to share his music with the world. Cotton, I'm the one who's sorry."

He held the phone, stunned. His mother wasn't mad at him; she was apologizing.

"I thought we'd be just fine on our own," Sandra continued, "and all this time I believed I was right. Now I see how much you need your father. Music is in your blood, too. You're his son."

Hearing her say that made his heart smile. He wanted her to be happy, too. He'd learned all too well what it meant to be alone. "Mama, I'm coming home soon, I really am. I just need to see Dad. I'm glad Lola May's helping you and all."

"We're helping each other. Lola invited us to live with her, Cotton." His mother's words were cut short with a cough. "And when the insurance money comes in, Lola says we should use it to build a music studio for you," she managed to add.

"For real, Mama?"

Carter's mother coughed for a full minute. Every time she tried to eke out one lonesome word, another round of coughs started up.

Lola May came on and got straight to yapping like nothing was amiss. "Here at the shelter, folks call your mama 'the Mother Teresa of Renovation,'" she said with the neighborly cheerfulness she used on her TV show. "Displaced families bring her salvaged wood and materials from what's left of their homes. Then Sandy and I create custom furnishings, so they'll have a piece of their past and something new to make a fresh start."

It reminded him a whole lot of his daddy's guitar. "You said Mama was doing a bit of carpentry last we spoke. Sounds like she's as good as new." Maybe her coughing spell was nothing.

"Getting stronger every day," Lola May assured him. "We've found new meaning in our work, Cotton. Every refinishing job we've ever done was only preparation for helping these people begin a new life."

"'*Garbage into glory*,' that's what Mama always said."

"She's tough as ever, believe me," Lola said, this time without her trademark confidence. "Cotton, you should know she picked up an infection at the shelter. But I'm keeping an eye on her."

Carter's first thought was to get her out of the dang shelter. He remembered Lola May had offered to put her up in a hotel and she wouldn't hear tell of it. Tough as ever. "She's always dishing out help. When's she going to learn to accept some herself?"

Lola and Carter agreed, there was no point expecting his mama might change.

"I reckon Mama's in good hands with you, Lola May. You're like family to us."

"I love you like my own, Cotton."

"I know it," Carter replied. He chewed his lip, realizing what she'd come to mean to him. "I love you, too."

♪♪♪

WHEN Carter got back to the condo, he padded inside and picked up the Martin, throwing the strap over his shoulder. It was his. A piece of his past that both his father and his mother wanted him to have. He didn't care that it was daybreak; he was in California and Poly Virus was playing Coachella that day. Plenty of reason to get the day rolling, and Carter knew the best way to do it. He broke into "Love Never Walks Away" like he'd given it a second life, a rush of happiness pumping through his veins. His song wasn't the blues. It was built for dancing, for rocking out, for tearing the walls down.

Chapter Forty-Three

"THAT'S THE ALARM CLOCK I'M TALKING ABOUT."
Garrett appeared at the door of one bedroom, rubbing at his
sleepy eyes in the bright early light. "What song is that, I don't
recognize it."

"I wrote it." Carter smiled.

"Oklahoma, you got it, man," he said, hooting and whooping
like he couldn't hold back the hum of energy building inside
him. "This is it, this is rock 'n roll." Garrett motioned for him to
keep going, unlatching his own guitar case and plugging in to a
small amp. Piper came in from the patio yawning, a smile breaking across her face. Soon Garrett had slipped into the melody,
joining Carter's rhythm by improvising his own harmony to
boost the song's power. It was early and they were too loud. By
the time the condo management pulled up in a golf cart to tell
them to knock it off, the entire band was jamming with a bad
case of bedhead and Piper had whipped up a giant breakfast for
everyone.

♪♪♪

CARTER had hoped he'd make it to Coachella one day. He'd
never imagined it'd be any time before he was old enough to
drive. His mother knew where he was, and gave her blessing to
let him help out Poly Virus as a roadie at the festival.

Whatever fantasies he may have cooked up were nothing

compared to what they pulled up to in the next hour. Several giant stages anchored the massive grass field, with smaller stages in between. A scattering of oversize carnival tents offered cool fans and shade from the blazing desert sun broiling overhead, over a hundred degrees by midday.

It was exciting to be there, to take it all in, become part of the energy. He couldn't help but recall how different it felt from when he played gigs with his Dad at festivals as a kid. Back then, he'd waited hours for his turn on stage, at the edge of the wave of happy families and couples rushing from one spectacle to another. That day, he was free to dive in.

Carter was surprised to find art installations and sculptures, pedicab drivers, and endless rows of vendor tents housing water slingers, band memorabilia, clothing, and henna tattoos, even farmers selling fresh fruit and vegetables. He kept his eye out for the glow-stick guys he'd met the night before, but it seemed every other tent sold something to light up the night. Carter felt his worries burn off in the hot sun. It was like a dream world, a musical city inhabited by thousands of crazed music fans, dancing, laughing, letting go. Girls went by wearing flower crowns, and many of the guys looked like famous rock performers. Carter soon realized some of them were. An all-day smile made its home on his face.

About an hour before Poly Virus went on, Carter and Piper met up with the band backstage. While it was the festival's seventh year, it was Poly Virus's first time there as paid performers. The boys in the band must have found a match because they were lit up like firecrackers, ready to blast. Carter rode the wave of their excitement, as thrilled for them as he was to bear witness to the chaos of the music all around him. Even Piper couldn't stop grinning. Waiting backstage for Poly Virus's turn to play, Garrett asked Piper to shoot some preshow footage on his tablet. She nodded, and Carter pulled the front man's tablet from his guitar case. He thanked Garrett for letting him make his multimedia presentation. When he first met the band back at the Shoretown Inn, he didn't have an inkling about the influence Poly Virus would make on his music, and on his confidence as a performer. The band was his Shotgun Candle, his rock when he didn't know which way the road would take him.

"Let's have a look at it, Oklahoma," Garrett said, opening a cold bottle of water.

Carter pressed Play. The band was impressed. Sure, Carter didn't have much experience with editing and he'd rushed to finish his IRP. But the movie's message was clear: he'd gotten plenty familiar with that Martin and grown a bunch doing it.

"You should hear him cover you guys," Piper teased. "If you're too nervous, I'm sure Carter here'll take your place on-stage in a heartbeat."

"Yeah? Maybe we could add a backup," Dex said. "Hey, the more the merrier, right?"

"Cool," Garrett agreed with a nod. "But you're going to need to plug in." Austin went through the band's equipment and chose an electric guitar for Carter. Once they had him fitted, the guys showed him the playlist and let him know when he could come on. Carter couldn't reckon if he was dumbstruck, awestruck, or starstruck. He tried to pull together some sort of thanks, but all that came out was a bent Southernism: "We're going to rock them so hard they'll see tomorrow today." Dex and Austin doubled over laughing and Garrett stuck his hand in the boy's hair, mussing it. Even big Nate cracked a grin behind that hornet's nest he called a beard.

The guys got the signal; it was time. Carter and Piper stood by while Garrett pulled Poly Virus together in a group huddle. They exchanged a couple of words, then Dex glanced over his shoulder. "C'mon already. What you waiting for?" Piper took Carter's hand in hers, and they stepped into the group, interlocking arms around one another's shoulders.

"This is the one," Garrett said, looking around the circle of his friends. "The big one. We came to rock and we're doing it, right here. We were called to make history. Today we're making Coachella history. There's no one I'd rather do it with than you."

Chapter Forty-Four

CARTER HUNG BACK AT THE EDGE OF THE STAGE, shielded from the random blasts of hot desert wind. It was late afternoon and he couldn't see the grass field for hundreds of yards, there were so many people. An LED thermometer near the main stage read 105 degrees. Most of the crowd had covered themselves with wet bandannas, sunglasses, and sun hats. Any other day, they might have stayed indoors to avoid the dust, the relentless sun, and the untamed wind. But this was Coachella. Today mattered. The music mattered to everyone present. It reminded Carter of a day not too long before, when the weather had failed to hold him back. He couldn't wait another day for his dad's guitar—no, his Martin. Now he knew music belonged to him. It belonged to everyone. It was why they were there, bucking some harsh weather like it was nothing. For the music.

Garrett introduced the band, then launched into an adrenaline-infused torrent of deliciously psychedelic lyrics.

Piper nudged Carter onstage, toward a mic set up away from the spotlight. He had his private corner of glory, living out the fantasy that this was his audience, that the favorite song of the playlist was his own. Carter played his best, like it was a do-over of his audition at The Little Yucca.

When Poly Virus finally launched into "Shotgun Candle," Carter found his confidence. He knew the song; he'd dedicated several hours of his practice to it. The band dove in, rocking it out. The crowd went crazy. It was a college radio station favorite. The wind seemed to love it, too. It howled across the faraway desert, blowing dust and hot air across the sunbaked masses.

Carter's guitar seemed louder. The heat made him realize he'd closed his eyes. When he opened them and looked around the stage, he realized Garrett had turned up his amp. He'd brought something to "Shotgun Candle"—maybe hot sauce, maybe the drawl of the Southwest—but Garrett sure seemed to like it. Carter played it through, giving every ounce of himself. Playing for the crowd was a mind trip, a dream in which he could see his father smiling up at him.

Wait, was that really his father? He scanned the faces in the front row. It must have been the heat. A fantasy had gotten into him and had its way.

At the end of "Shotgun Candle," Garrett grabbed the mic. He asked the audience to give a shout-out to Carter Danforth, and cheers rose from the crowd. Garrett put his arm around Carter and pulled him to the front of the stage. At six feet, he and Garrett were the same height. "You aren't gonna believe this, but Carter here is only fifteen years old." Wild hoots and whistles rose up. Carter couldn't get the image of his dad out of his mind. It was tripping him out because he looked older. In every dream he'd ever had about his daddy, he looked the same as he had six years before. "Carter's traveled all the way from Tulsa, Oklahoma, y'all!" Garrett hollered, tacking on an Okie accent. "He's here to share his newest song. And first, right?"

Carter just nodded, feeling as light-headed as the bubbles blowing from a machine invisible in the throng.

"You're going to love it," Garrett shouted with a grin. "I know I did."

Piper appeared at the front of the stage with Garrett's tablet. She was shooting video again, but this time Willard couldn't stop her. "Boys and girls," Garrett continued, "give it up for our buddy Carter Danforth, performing 'Love Doesn't Walk Away.'"

Chapter Forty-Five

GARRETT READIED HIS GUITAR FOR A REPEAT OF their early morning jam session. Carter stepped up to the mic. "Hey, y'all." The stage seemed to disappear from beneath his feet.

In the open air, the ginormous amps vibrated across the festival. In the distance, he saw thousands of camping tents dotting the grass to the horizon. To the farthest points on his left and right, huge stages loomed, larger than his. A thumping beat weighed the hot air around them, a heavy audio blanket wrapping the shoulders of every lost soul who'd found their way along the road to Indio. He dropped his hand, wrenching out the first chord. He'd never even played an electric version of his song. But that day, he was plugged into one of the nation's biggest amps. Even the best song can fall flat if it's performed without the right ingredients. Carter knew what the right ingredients were: Creativity, Victory, Heart, and Discipline. The melody blasted with massive power, a fresh, raw, electric stream giving it yet another new life, a new birth. Was that what it was all about? Being reborn, again and again, with every song, every mile, every new friend—and every loss? He remembered how old Ledbetter seemed to stop time every time he rocked the crowd, just long enough to pound out every regret, every bad decision, and all the pain of hurting the ones we loved and left behind.

Carter roared through the song, lifted sky high with the band's accompaniment. Kai's wicked drums beat in his chest, driving Carter's own rhythm into him—or out of him, he wasn't sure. The bassline held the melody afloat, even more than the drums. He tuned into its cadence, followed the pattern of the strings while belting out the lyrics. He'd been promoted to Garrett's mic and it commanded the loudest, clearest sound. The audience swayed to the beat, hands raised into the wind. The guitar, his instrument, was part of him, another limb, another brain, another heart. With pen to page, Carter could write his own songs, tell his own story. With the lungs in his chest, he could sing his message to the world.

The chorus he sang was about holding on to the past but living well in the present, just like his mother had taught him.

We need to take care of what we have,
See it in a new way.
We got two choices, follow or fight,
Love doesn't walk away.

There were all kinds of people at Coachella: teens, adults, girls, bros, even families. Carter was getting used to making eye contact with his audience, but there were thousands here, a sea of undulating bodies. He singled out the shining golden head of a little girl near the front row, maybe eight or nine years old, wearing noise-canceling headphones. She smiled up at him, cheeks painted with sparkles. She nudged a taller girl, likely her sister. The older blonde, maybe thirteen, ignored her. She stared at Carter, transfixed. A mix of suspicion and disbelief darkened her eyes, the same color as the sky. Carter locked his gaze with theirs, hoping the young kids in the audience might hear his music and know that nothing was impossible. Carter had dreamed he'd make it to out west to see his father again. Follow your dream and you get there, he reckoned, just maybe not the way you expect. After all, he was in California, playing his guitar.

And there was his father, right in front of him. But how did he know Carter would be there? It couldn't be a coincidence? If they hadn't lost the motorcycle, Carter would be in Santa Monica. He'd have ridden right past his father on the way.

A sweat broke out across Carter's brow. He played on, losing himself in his own music, leading the band note by note, chord by chord. He dared another glance. It couldn't be. Sure enough, the man he saw looked like a slightly older Eddie Danforth. He and the two girls wore lanyards with backstage credentials.

The sun bore down. Even with the oversize fans on either side of the stage, Carter thought he must be hallucinating from the heat. He closed his eyes, focusing on his own music, the immaculate sound of the band, and let the noise of the crowd fall away. He sang from his heart, pulling from the strength he'd built for himself over so many nights alone, far from the bed he'd never sleep in again back home. The music took on a shining, otherworldly quality, seeming to flow through his veins.

Goose bumps prickled his skin, even in the excessive heat. Carter floated, weightless, powering his song to its climactic end. Rather than quiet it, fading to nothing, Carter ramped it up.

The band drove on. Garrett's hand thrashed against his guitar, creating a gorgeous rising wave of sound that rocked the whole place. When they played together, the music seemed to weave inward, to seek harmony. Each brought a melody, a bassline, or a tone to strengthen and lift up the other, creating a sum greater than its parts. This was the song inside Carter. This was the song calling to each of them, filling the creases, voids, and empty crevices inside. Holes they thought had no bottom were filled.

At the end of the song, the crowd went crazy. Carter felt alive and alert, like he could outrun the Frisco train itself, from Tulsa clear to Kansas City. Anything was possible.

The show must go on, and Poly Virus was given a limited time onstage. Carter took one last bow. Piper set down the tablet and mouthed the word *awesome.*

As Poly Virus launched into the next track, Carter found himself searching the crowd. The man with the two little girls was chatting up the security guys watching over the backstage entrance, who seemed thrilled to be meeting Eddie Danforth in person. Security let them backstage, but Carter stayed close to the band, cheering on his new friends. He wouldn't let them down. Poly Virus had given him the best day of his life. Carter was suddenly worried what his father would have to say about him being all the way across the country on his own. Once again, it was confession time.

Chapter Forty-Six

AFTER THREE ENCORES, THE BAND WAS EXHAUSTED and drenched in sweat. They piled down from the stage into the private backstage area, all looking rode hard and put away wet. No matter; Piper fired up the tablet again and they shot video of their backstage celebration. The small space was packed with bodies. A few long-standing fans from Poly Virus's tour had scored backstage passes and everyone attacked a table of cold drinks and snacks.

Carter heard his own heartbeat in his ears. His throat burned parched and hot. "Dad?" he managed to say, edging nervously toward his father.

"Daddy gets us passes for everything," the girls both said at once, a blend of enthusiasm and arrogance. "The studios and record labels hook us up all the time." Eddie smiled, trying to hush them. Carter found himself face to face with his father. "Son, I'd like you to meet Scarlett," he placed his hand on the younger girl's shoulder, "and Aurora," indicating the older sister. Carter nodded to the girls politely, a warm flush of relief and pride creeping over him. His father called him "son" in front of his stepdaughters.

"You were incredible up there," he said, grinning red-faced at him, and opening and closing his arms like they couldn't decide whether to tackle him.

"You were so amazing!" Scarlett squealed, sweet as cherry pie. "I can't believe you're like, what, our half-brother? Step-brother? You're going to be a famous rock star, I know it!" She nudged her big sister Aurora, who held her arms folded tightly across her chest.

"You're not as bad as I thought," the older girl offered. Carter didn't know what to make of her until she smiled in a way that told him sass was her standard.

"Your mother called me this morning," Eddie said, shaking his head as though he still couldn't make sense of it. "She told me where you were. I asked if I could see you, just once," he said, opening his arms wider and then closing them again when Carter stood still as a parked car in the ruckus of noise and dancing and carrying on.

At last Carter floated toward him, stiff as old Ledbetter's back. Eddie enclosed his son in his arms. As his father squeezed Carter close, the scent of him, his hair and the skin of his neck, smacked Carter square in his memories, sending him tumbling back through time. This was his daddy.

His father released him, searching his face. Eddie looked him over, trying to take Carter in all at once. "Dang it, you're so big." Carter broke out in a grin, and Eddie put his hand on his son's shoulder, steadying himself as he looked in his boy's eyes. "Carter, she said you could stay with us for a while. If you want."

"Please, Carter?" Scarlett broke into whining. "It'd be so fun! We have a music studio at our house." Smiling down at her, he sure appreciated her enthusiasm.

Aurora shrugged. "I guess it'd be cool." Carter could tell she wasn't tagging along for any family reunion. Piper and Garrett called the girls over to help themselves to Poly Virus shirts, giving Carter and his father some time alone.

"Dad, check this out," Carter said, clicking the latches open on his guitar case. The Martin seemed humbled by the modern instruments all around it. Eddie picked it up and ran his hands along the familiar guitar, his gaze landing square on the inscription near the pickguard.

"I remember bringing this home when you were just a wee baby. It seemed forever before you were big enough to hold it yourself. You fought me through every cotton-picking lesson, always wanting to do things your way," he said, squinting into the past. Carter didn't like how similar his dad's memories were to his mother's. As he recalled, he loved playing the Martin. "I had a plan for you, but you had other ideas."

Carter stepped back from his father, blinking away spots flashing in his eyes. Maybe it was the heat. Or maybe his mom was right about his dad.

"I figured if I left this old beauty behind, it wouldn't hurt so bad," his father told him. "I didn't want it staring me down, reminding me of how I failed you." He laughed a sorry laugh at himself, as if sorrow and wishful thinking were one and the same. "But now I get it. You needed to make music your way, not mine."

"You gave me a love for music. You didn't fail, Dad."

"You're a natural born musician, took to that Martin like it was a third arm," he continued. "But I never gave you a chance to find your own sound." Eddie stared his son in the eye. "I promise you, not a day goes by when I don't think of you, son."

Before Carter could answer, Eddie set down the Martin and grabbed him in a bear hug, dragging him up off the ground and holding him tight. Carter's feet dangled in the air. He was pressed so hard against his father, he couldn't even return his embrace. His father held him there, long moments ticking by until Carter's toes came back to the ground, but still his dad held on. He realized his dad was crying into his hair, but Carter didn't mind.

"Back in Tulsa, at that run-down old house, those were some of the happiest days in my life," his father told him.

"Dad, we can't go back in time; we can only move forward," Carter said. He'd given up trying to bring back the past. He didn't want to go back to who he was before he left Tulsa. He couldn't ask his father to, either.

"I hope one day you'll be able to forgive me." Eddie broke from him, holding his son by both shoulders. "I'm never leaving you again."

"I just want you to be my dad," Carter said. "I reckon it's all I ever wanted."

"I am. And I will be," Eddie said. Carter dropped his gaze to the brown, trampled grass beneath them. The anger he'd felt toward his dad all those years had been longing, in truth. The Martin bound them together, and Carter understood finally why he couldn't stand the idea of it tucked away at Tommy's. It belonged in his family.

Eddie wiped at his eyes with the back of his hand. Aurora and Scarlett wandered back, checking in on their stepdad. Carter pulled them in and Eddie wrapped his arms around all three kids. Scarlett's pinky finger found Carter's and curled around it; Aurora did them all the favor of buttoning her lip. Carter had come to realize kin was more than another word for family; it was built on the love you gave — and accepted.

♪♪♪

OVER his dad's shoulder, Carter spotted Piper shooting more video footage. When he broke from the hug, she motioned him over. "You need this," she said. "It's part of your story."

"I'm not writing a story," he pointed out, "I'm trying to pass ninth grade." Piper sat him down right then and there and made him work. Eddie was setting up to take the kids home to Santa Monica before sunset. "After dark at Coachella is no place for kids," he said. Aurora went straight to back-sassing Eddie, arguing that other kids at her school were allowed to stay, and without having to drag around a parent, much less a baby sister. Carter wanted to stay and hang out, too, but he was plenty fine with being seen with Eddie.

He inserted the concert footage, and replayed the scenes Piper had shot of him and his father. There he was, his teenage, six-foot body off the ground in a bear hug. It was too much. "Add it," Piper commanded over his shoulder. He cut it to a two-second clip in black and white, replacing their conversation with the song performance, the words "Love Doesn't Walk Away" appearing over the top until the image and title faded away to a small line of text reading, "Special thanks to Kaia Liu, Mr. Ledbetter, Mitch Keller, Piper Piedra, and Poly Virus." The project was done. He saved it and emailed a copy to his homeroom teacher, and a copy to Kaia Liu, with the comment, "Smoother than a gravy sandwich." He sure hoped she'd like it.

"Ledbetter?" Eddie pointed to the screen, surprised. "You met Get the Led Out Ledbetter, the rock and blues legend? I didn't know he was still alive."

"Alive and well, I reckon." Carter laughed. "He gave me guitar lessons night and day at The Little Yucca." He reached for the Martin and held it in the right-hand position. "He restrung it for me, Dad. To play it my way. Hope you don't mind."

Eddie examined Ledbetter's handiwork like he'd unearthed a lost masterpiece. "I only wish I hadn't pushed you the way I did," he said. "You don't need a gimmick when you've got music in the veins."

Carter thought about the energy that drew an audience toward the stage during a performance. Music was meant to be shared, to connect strangers, to create a bond. He smiled at his father, a seasoned pro at pulling heartstrings. "Maybe not a gimmick, Dad, but there's something to be said for giving the audience a show."

It was time to get on the road. Piper grabbed his arm and pulled him in tight, hugging him. He remembered how she'd avoided Mitch's hug entirely and counted himself lucky for the quick embrace. "I'm heading home in a few days. The Desert Willow needs me. And it's time I told Willard to move on for good," she said. "Besides, I owe Mitch a visit."

"I wouldn't be here if it wasn't for you," he whispered in her ear. "Thanks for everything."

"Believe me, I owe *you*. Don't tell Mitch, but I always wanted a little brother." She squeezed his arm, then glanced back at Garrett, a flush warming her olive skin. "The band invited me to stay on for the rest of the festival."

"Cool," was all he could come up with. *Good-bye* didn't seem right. "Hey, watch out for these musician types. They might get you singing again," Carter teased her. He lingered on, wishing he had thanks enough for everything they'd been through. "If anyone gives you any trouble, just give 'em a taste of the butt-whupping you dropped on Willard."

"You got that right," she said with a laugh. Happy looked good on her. "Next time you're in Tucson, we'll rock The Maiden again."

Chapter Forty-Seven

CAMELLIA WAS WAITING WITH THE SUV AT A
hotel. A bigger and blonder version of her girls, Camellia's perfect white smile exactly matched the white crescent-moon tips
of her toenails in her sparkly flip-flops. She seemed hyper-
groomed, like a beauty-salon pit crew overhauled her from
bumper to taillights. At first Carter figured his mother would
dismiss Camellia for conjuring the same smoke-and-mirrors
fakery she accused Eddie of. But his mama found it in her heart
to focus on the best of Eddie, and he reckoned they both ought
to give Eddie's new wife the same benefit. Carter had his own
share of faults, but he sure hoped Camellia and the girls would
go easy on him, give him half a chance.

As they drove west toward Los Angeles, the girls filled several miles gushing over social media updates about the festival.
From behind the driver's seat, he saw Camellia considering him
in the rearview mirror. "I didn't know you were a musician like
Eddie. I'm sorry it's taken so long to meet you." She offered him
the kind of smile a talk-show host gives a guest with a hard-luck
story. "I guess we have a lot of catching up to do."

Carter nodded his understanding. Writing his song had
helped him sort out his feelings and put the past where it belonged. He needed to give Camellia room enough to do the same
in her own way. "I reckon we do, ma'am." Carter met her gaze in
the mirror, holding it for a beat.

A light pink rose to her cheeks. "You sound just like Eddie

when we met," she said, reaching over to the passenger seat and placing her hand lightly on her husband's shoulder.

Eddie laughed, squeezing her hand in his. Carter liked seeing his father so happy. It couldn't have been easy when his mama told Eddie to go follow his dream alone. "You can take the man out of Oklahoma, but you can't take Oklahoma out of the man," Eddie said, Tulsa coloring his words. "Hey, Carter," Eddie turned to look at him, "we've got studio time on Monday to record the jingle for Ma Joad's pancake house. The chain is paying big bucks. You think you're ready, son?"

Carter was thankful his father wanted him to perform the duet. But his mother was right. They could make it on their own. His dad had made a success of himself, and Carter aimed to do the same. "I was thinking maybe Mr. Ledbetter would be a better match for a duet with you. It'd be great to see him again, give him a proper thanks for everything he did for me."

"They'd go crazy if I brought in a legend of his caliber," Eddie said, with a whistle. "You think he'd do it?"

"Couldn't hurt to ask." Carter grinned. He hoped Ledbetter would agree. Performing in a national ad would provide his friend a small income for years.

Aurora and Scarlett had plenty of questions about what Eddie was like back in Tulsa, before he became a pop star. They teased him about his cornball ballads, but Carter could tell they were proud of him. Eddie knew how to pull heartstrings with his music, but he'd found his way into their hearts, too. It seemed Tulsa was a foreign country to them, and they wanted to know all about Carter's hometown. As the miles wore on, the conversation turned around to life in Southern California. The girls insisted Carter get a VIP tour of all their favorite places. Eddie leaned over and whispered in Camellia's ear, and before long, Carter found himself on Santa Monica Pier.

Eddie pulled out his phone and snapped Carter's photo next to a sign on the Santa Monica Pier marking the end of the legendary highway: "Santa Monica Route 66, End of the Trail." After Darren Bartles took him south, away from the 40, Carter'd given up on 66 altogether, but it still brought him home, just as he'd reckoned it would. Little Scarlett hammed it up for the camera, fishing a rainbow pen with a unicorn design from her bag and asking for his autograph. Carter scrawled his name awkwardly on her Coachella ticket, while Eddie snapped some photos, laughing. Then Scarlett took a few pictures of Eddie and Carter until Aurora shoved her little sister out of the way and took over, complaining that "Scarlett's composition was all wrong." Carter didn't mind their squabbling; it reminded him of the kind of sass Piper or his mama might dish out. Camellia busted it up, dragging the girls in the direction of tacos and cold drinks. Before disappearing into the crowd, she leaned in close and whispered to Carter, "He's missed you." He couldn't help but hope they'd all become as familiar as sitting on a porch at sundown.

They texted a few pictures to Sandra, and she straight up called Eddie right back. He put her on speaker phone, and they had their first family conversation in years. His mom and dad were on speaking terms and, to Carter, that was enough.

"Eddie, I hope you don't mind my asking for your help," she said, "just until the insurance company fixes the roof on Lola's house."

"Carter can stay as long as you need. He's my son, and I want you to know you can count on me. We can work together, Sandra. I'm sorry I didn't tell you that six years ago."

"I didn't give you the chance," she said. Laboring to say more than a few words at a go, she managed to congratulate Carter on his video. Back home, radio and news stations were blasting clips of the teenage runaway from Tulsa performing at Coachella. Kaia Liu had posted it to her social media channels. When kids from Bob Bogle High School saw how he'd turned his own garbage into glory, they'd hit Share on his independent research project. It soon warmed the hearts of thousands in Tulsa, and caught the attention of Poly Virus's fans. "I spent so much time worrying about lining your nest, I forgot to let you fly," she said. "I'm proud of you, Cotton."

Carter ran to the end of the pier, the farthest west he could go. Below, the salty ocean lapped the posts of the pier. A new song rose among the waves. Still holding Scarlett's rainbow pen, Carter wrote the lyrics bubbling up within him into the palm of his hand. His father caught up with him, and wrapped his arm around Carter's shoulder, pulling him toward the Ferris wheel glowing neon in the setting sky.

THE END

ACKNOWLEDGMENTS

It may surprise readers to learn that I grew up in Canada. My father was passionate about stories and songs from early radio, and the dawn of American folk and country music. Dad used to play his old records—Johnny Cash, Loretta Lynn, and Hank Williams—on a scratchy record player, loud enough to hear the music over the band-saw and lathe in his woodworking shop. He always cracked up over funny Southern idioms, *even when they didn't amount to a hill of beans*, and often laced them into polite Canadian conversation. He kept dusty used books in his office that told the tales of the people who lived in the time of the Depression, before he was born. My dad could fix anything in our house. To this day, he restores historical vehicles, painting burled wood-grain dashboards and custom-fabricating tools and parts no longer available. If he doesn't have the right tools for a job, he makes them with his own hands. My heartfelt thanks go to him.

I'd also like to share my gratitude for dear friends who tirelessly and tenderly supported me through the long process of bringing this book to you. They include Lisa Manterfield, Margaret Nevinski, Lesley Holmes, and Mark Sarvas, editors Jason Sitzes and Lorin Oberweger, Oklahoma native Patrick Weems, and publisher Brooke Warner. Special thanks to Rebecca Lown for hand-drawing the cover. In the habit of playing acoustic guitar and making his own sketches, Carter would appreciate its "unplugged" quality.

From the time our children were newborn, my wonderful husband Joseph and I have loved reading stories with our sons. It is a special treat to share this book with my family. They are my true loves, now and always.

ABOUT THE AUTHOR

Rayne Lacko believes music, language, and art connect us, and she explores those themes in her novels, *Listen To Me* and *A Song for the Road*, and in the guided journal *Dream Up Now*, an interactive exploration of emotions for teens. She now resides on a lush, forested island in the Pacific Northwest, where she sits on the board of trustees at a performing arts organization. She cohosts a library youth writing workshop and an annual filled-to-capacity writing camp, and she established Teen Story Slam, a twice-annual spoken word event for teens. Rayne is married with two children (a pianist and a drummer), and she and her family share their home with a noisy cat and their canine best friend.

Photo credit Susan Doupé

Connect with Rayne

Website: www.RayneLacko.com

Instagram: @RayneLacko

SELECTED TITLES FROM SPARKPRESS

SparkPress is an independent boutique publisher delivering high-quality, entertaining, and engaging content that enhances readers' lives, with a special focus on female-driven work. www.gosparkpress.com

The House Children: A Novel, Heidi Daniele. $16.95, 978-1-943006-94-6. A young girl raised in an Irish industrial school accidentally learns that the woman she spends an annual summer holiday with is her birth mother.

The Leaving Year: A Novel, Pam McGaffin. $16.95, 978-1-943006-81-6. As the Summer of Love comes to an end, 15-year-old Ida Petrovich waits for a father who never comes home. While commercial fishing in Alaska, he is lost at sea, but with no body and no wreckage, Ida and her mother are forced to accept a "presumed" death that tests their already strained relationship. While still in shock over the loss of her father, Ida overhears an adult conversation that shatters everything she thought she knew about him. This prompts her to set out on a search for the truth that takes her from her Washington State hometown to Southeast Alaska.

The Frontman: A Novel, Ron Bahar. $16.95, 978-1-943006-44-1. During his senior year of high school, Ron Bahar—a Nebraskan son of Israeli immigrants—falls for Amy Andrews, a non-Jewish girl, and struggles to make a career choice between his two other passions: medicine and music.

The Forbidden Temptation of Baseball, Dori Jones Yang. $12.95, 978-1-943006-32-8. Twelve-year-old Leon is among a group of 120 boys sent to New England in the 1870s by the Emperor of China as part of a Chinese educational mission. Once there, he falls in love with baseball, even though he's expressly forbidden to play. The boy's host father, who's recently lost his own son in an accident, sees and cultivates Leon's interest, bringing joy back into his own life and teaching Leon more about America through its favorite sport than any rule-bound educational mission could possibly hope to achieve.